INFLATING A DOG
THE STORY OF ELLA'S LUNCH LAUNCH

Also by Eric Kraft

Herb 'n' Lorna

Reservations Recommended

Little Follies

Where Do You Stop?

What a Piece of Work I Am

At Home with the Glynns

Leaving Small's Hotel

INFLATING A DOG

THE STORY OF ELLA'S LUNCH LAUNCH

ERIC KRAFT

Picador USA
New York

Picador® is a U.S. registered trademark and is used by St. Martin's Press under license from Pan Books Limited.

www.picadorusa.com

Author's note: A portion of Chapter 46, "A Dead Dog, Beached (Afflatus, Part 4)," is based in part on information in "Colonoscopy," Publication No. 98-4331 of the National Institutes of Health, published in June 1998 and posted as an e-text on the World Wide Web 7 July 1998 by the National Digestive Diseases Information Clearinghouse (NDDIC). This e-text is not copyrighted, and the NDDIC encourages the free dissemination of the information it contains. However, the NDDIC probably never anticipated that anyone would adapt the information with so free a hand as I have used. The adaptation is, of course, my own, and the NDDIC cannot be held responsible for any inaccuracies that I may have introduced. The tone and style of the adaptation are also my own, and the NDDIC cannot be blamed for those either.

ISBN 0-312-28804-2

First Edition: July 2002

10 9 8 7 6 5 4 3 2 1

For Mad

Bien sé lo que son tentaciones del demonio, y que una de las mayores es ponerle a un hombre en el entendimiento que puede componer e imprimir un libro con que gane tanta fama como dineros, y tantos dineros cuanta fama, y para confirmación de esto quiero que en tu buen donaire y gracia le cuentes este cuento.

Había en Sevilla un loco que dio en el más gracioso disparate y tema que dio loco en el mundo. Y fue que hizo un cañuto de caña puntiagudo en el fin, y, en cogiendo algún perro en la calle, o en cualquiera otra parte, con el un pie le cogía el suyo, y el otro le alzaba con la mano, y como mejor podía le acomodaba el cañuto en la parte que, soplándole, le ponía redondo como una pelota, y, en teniéndolo de esta suerte, le daba dos palmaditas en la barriga y le soltaba, diciendo a los circunstantes, que siempre eran muchos: "¿Pensarán vuestras mercedes ahora que es poco trabajo hinchar un perro?"

"¿Pensará vuestra merced ahora que es poco trabajo hacer un libro?"

Miguel de Cervantes
The Ingenious Gentleman Don Quixote de la Mancha,
Part Two, Prologue, "To the Reader"

I know what temptations the devil has to offer, one of the greatest of which consists in putting it into a [boy's] head that he can [help his mother make her dreams come true] and thereby [win the affection of the girl for whom he yearns, or, to put it more accurately if less delicately, win sexual favors from the girl for whom he lusts]; in confirmation of which I would have you, in your own witty and charming manner, tell him this tale.

There was in Seville a certain madman whose madness assumed one of the drollest forms that ever was seen in this world. Taking a hollow reed sharpened at one end, he would catch a dog in the street or somewhere else; and, holding one of the animal's legs with his foot and raising the other with his hand, he would fix his reed as best he could in a certain part, after which he would blow the dog up, round as a ball. When he had it in this condition he would give it a couple of slaps on the belly and let it go, remarking to the bystanders, of whom there were always plenty, "Do your Worships think, then, that it is so easy a thing to inflate a dog?"

So you might ask, "Does your Grace think that it is so easy a thing to [make a mother's dreams come true]?"

(translated by Samuel Putnam, adapted by Peter Leroy)

I know well what the temptations of the devil are, and that one of the greatest is putting it into a [boy's] head that he can [keep his mother's sinking boat afloat] by which he will [win the affection of the girl for whom he yearns, and so forth]; and to prove it I will beg of you, in your own sprightly, pleasant way, to tell him this story.

There was a madman in Seville who took to one of the drollest absurdities and vagaries that ever madman in the world gave way to. It was this: he made a tube of reed sharp at one end, and catching a dog in the street, or wherever it might be, he with his foot held one of its legs fast, and with his hand lifted up the other, and as best he could fixed the tube where, by blowing, he made the dog as round as a ball; then holding it in this position, he gave it a couple of slaps on the belly, and let it go, saying to the bystanders (and there were always plenty of them): "Do your worships think, now, that it is an easy thing to blow up a dog?"

Does your worship think now, that it is an easy thing to [keep a sinking boat afloat]?

(translated by John Ormsby, adapted by Peter Leroy)

INFLATING A DOG
THE STORY OF ELLA'S LUNCH LAUNCH

Preface
The Story of Ella's Lunch Launch

WHEN PEOPLE ASK what my mother was like, I tell them the story of her lunch launch, because in that story so many of her best attributes show to good advantage—particularly her enthusiasm—and also because the lunch launch—Ella's Lunch Launch—was a success, her only successful entrepreneurial venture, coming after a long string of failures, of which I will mention here only Ella's TV Colorizer, Ella's Cards for Forgotten Holidays, Ella's High-Heel-Low-Heel Convertible Shoes, Ella's Peanut Butter on a Stick, and the final failure, Ella's Lacy Licks, an enterprise that was for a while known as Ella's Ribbons of Dee-Lite.

Throughout my childhood and adolescence my mother dreamed of going into business for herself. This desire first began to manifest itself when I was very young, too young to understand that there was a motive for her yearning beyond wanting to make some money, but by the time I was thirteen or so I did understand. I understood that she wanted recognition more than she wanted money. She wanted to make people—in particular, my father—see that she could accomplish something, build a business from nothing and become a woman who was defined by a business rather than a woman who was defined by a husband who ran a garage, a son who salivated at the sight of a girl in a tight skirt, and a suburban tract house with a partially finished attic. She wanted to make the world—or at least my father—think of her as Ella Piper Leroy, hairdresser, for example, rather than Ella Piper Leroy, housewife.

My mother had many schemes for businesses and many dreams about their success, and many of her schemes and dreams got as far as the dinner table. While my father and I ate, she would smoke and talk, nervously, laying out a plan for her audience of two, full of enthusiasm, until, in most cases, a moment came when her face fell, and she finished her proposal with her eyes down, as if the scheme were there on the tablecloth in front of her, falling apart before her eyes, shattering like the fragile ribbon candy that, at Christmastime, she liked to put out in dishes decorated with images of evergreen trees.

Sometimes, though, a scheme survived the dinner-table test. Some survived because they were the sturdy, boring sort of undertaking that my mother never would have enjoyed pursuing, like a window-washing service, and others because she put them back together out of the broken bits and held them together with the force of her determination, as she did with her plan to make ribbon candy, package it, and ship it far and wide as Ella's Ribbons of Dee-lite.

I think it was obvious to all of us, even to her, that ribbon candy must be made in a factory by machines especially designed to extrude sugar syrup in a continuous ribbon, fold it back upon itself uniformly, and snip it off in lengths that fit into boxes. I know it was obvious to me, because I was a watcher of industrial documentary films, which were in those days purveyed to youngsters via television on Saturday mornings, as entertainment. I knew, to name the first examples that come to mind, how Coffee-Toffee soda bottles were molded, filled, and packaged; how the glass for the bottles was made; how the caps for the

bottles were cut from sheets of metal and printed and fluted and lined with a thin disk of cork; and how Coffee-Toffee soda itself was made, though the films stopped short of initiating me and the other early risers into the mysteries of the secret process that gave the soda its inimitable flavor; and I knew that all of these processes required intricate machines with precision parts that were polished to gleaming brightness and operated with uncannily accurate timing in a handsome industrial dance.

Looking at her, smiling, tossing out ideas for a name for her ribbon candy, I felt the weight of her inevitable disappointment. I was certain that she was going to find out that she couldn't make ribbon candy, but she certainly wasn't going to find it out from me. Because I understood very well from personal experience the heavy emptiness that filled one's heart when the words "you can't" were spoken, I rejected after only the briefest consideration the thought that I might tell my mother that she was up against something that she probably could not accomplish without the aid of intricate machines. I would not play the dark angel of defeat. She wasn't going to hear a discouraging word from my father, either. He had given up trying to dissuade her from her schemes because he couldn't stand the aftermath. He had learned to let her fail rather than telling her that she would fail because the gloom that settled over the house when she merely failed on her own was a lighter and briefer gloom than the gloom that followed his telling her that she couldn't do what she yearned to do, and so instead of saying "You can't make ribbon candy," he just shrugged and said, "Why not give it a try?"

TRY SHE DID. I came home from school one afternoon to find the kitchen glazed with sugar. Threads of crystallized sugar crackled when I pushed the back door open, and they webbed the room, running along the walls, across the countertops and the stove and the sink, across the faces of the white metal cabinets. My mother had spun a sugar cocoon like one of the sugar eggs that were sold at Easter.

(These eggs were molded in two halves, a top and a bottom, the joint cemented and concealed by a decorative squiggle of colored sugar paste, but before the halves were joined a tiny scene was constructed inside, made of images printed on stiff paper, cut and mounted with candy syrup that held them in place to make a diorama, sacred or profane, the buyer's choice. I don't know how all that was done; if there was an early-morning documentary on the process, I missed it.)

My mother seemed not to be aware that I was in the kitchen. She was drizzling hot syrup from a can in which she had punched tiny holes, waving the can over a strip of aluminum foil that she had rolled out onto the floor, making intricately layered swirls and squiggles along the foil. When the sugar crystallized, she would have an edible action painting.

While I watched, something came over her, something that I might, at the time, have called sudden inspiration—or a fit.

(Now, I think I would call it the untrammeled expression of her true self and her aspirations for that self, a girl who lived within my mother and still expected that someday she would actually become the woman she hoped she would become.)

She began swinging the can beyond the limits of the foil so that the swirls of syrup looped onto the floor. This seemed like an inspired idea to me. The completed candy, when trimmed around the edge of the foil, would seem to have no edge but the edge that had been imposed on it by the knife, would seem to have been cut from a candy composition without limits. I liked the artifice of it, and I admired her style. Her swings grew wider and wider, though, and began to go far beyond the foil. As she swung the can in wider arcs, she began to swing herself, to dance with the can, swinging and swaying with it.

I was smiling. I realized that my mother was doing something a little mad, and, judging from the spun sugar around the room, had been doing something mad for a while, but I thought it was, as my friends and I, my group, my little local tribe, said at that time, "inflated." In fact, if I had had to define what we meant by "inflated," I could have done worse than to describe a suburban housewife flinging sugar syrup around her kitchen, turning it into a sugar egg with a little window in the door through which an interested observer could have witnessed the curious diorama of a suburban housewife flinging strands of sugar around her kitchen while her teenage son, bemused but proud, looked on and thought her inflated, blown up like a madman's dog. It was, for us, a term of praise.

She whirled herself around, and the can swung in my direction. I said, a little tentatively, in awe of her advanced degree of inflation, "Hi, Mom."

She stopped swinging the can, and the syrup ran in a dozen streams straight down onto the floor. She noticed me for the first time since I'd cracked my way into the kitchen. I was amazed—and a little hurt—to think that she could have been unaware of me for so long, that she had been too wrapped up in what she was doing to pay attention to me.

The expression "wrapped up in something" was common at the time, a time when I and many of the people I knew, perhaps most of the people I knew, still expected that we would be able to shape the future to our liking, long before we had begun to think of ourselves as sailing sinking ships, a time when we were often lost in dreams of our individual futures (mine, for example, were full of complaisant girls who competed for my company, and my father's were, I think, awash in beer). Recalling my mother now, involved in her sugar work to the exclusion of everything else, I really understand what we meant by being "wrapped up in something." I had seen it in her expression. It was the expression of a person who has slipped out of context and into something more comfortable: full attention to a single idea. The eyes of such a person seem unfocused, because it is the mind's eye that's doing the seeing. My mother's occupation had become her insulation, like a coat that she might have wrapped around her on a winter's day and pulled tight at the neck to warm the self that was wrapped within, to protect it from the inhospitable conditions that lay without, to protect her ambitious inner self from the icy reception that she received outside her wrap.

"Oh! Peter!" she said. "I didn't notice you there. I guess I got all wrapped up in what I was doing. I just—" She looked around the room, beaming. "I've been so busy here," she said, "making candy. Not ribbon candy—that didn't turn out too well. Lace candy—Lacy Licks, that's what I'm going to call it. Ella's Lacy Licks. See it all?"

She swung the can to indicate everything that she had accomplished, and the syrup followed, but when she turned toward me again, her expression had changed. The smile was gone. She stopped turning and stood there looking at me for a moment, as if she thought that I might want to say something to her, and when it became clear that I had nothing to say, she said, "I've made a mess," and let the can slip from her hand.

MY FATHER WOULD BE HOME in two or three hours. I think that I felt the pressure of that deadline more than my mother did, because she knew that his attitude toward her would be little changed by the fact that his kitchen was inside a sugar egg. Both my mother and I had made messes before, but mine still made my father angry, while he had stopped being angry about my mother's messes long ago. He had a much more effective way of showing his annoyance with her now: disdain. I could predict what he would do when he came home. He would give the kitchen the once-over, deliver his opinion with a dismissive snort, refrain from saying "I told you so," crack the sugar lace around the refrigerator door, open it, get a can of beer, and retire to the living room to watch television. My mother would drop another notch in her own estimation.

Disdain, contempt, dismissal—they all hurt much more than a display of anger. I'm excluding violence from this calculation. I never saw my father strike my mother, and I honestly think he never did, but he battered her by belittling her, and I had reached an age when I knew how she felt because I felt battered when he belittled me. I was also at an age when I wanted to fight back. I was growing, and all my juices were flowing, and I had developed a competitive tongue. I'd begun to give back as good as I got, and I had begun to turn back on him the same abusive trio he turned on my mother and me: disdain, contempt, dismissal.

"We've got to get this cleaned up," I said to her, almost in a whisper, as if he might be somewhere nearby, listening.

"I'll do it," she said, dispirited. She looked around the room, and I could see what she felt from the way her shoulders drooped, and I winced at the thought of the load of contempt my father would be bringing home in a couple of hours.

"We'll both do it," I said, and then, as if we were in a movie, one of the Western movies I watched at the Babbington Theater, in a one-room cabin on the plains, where a pioneer woman was going into labor, I added, "We're going to need lots of hot water!"

We fell into a frenzy of cleaning. We worked without pausing, and we worked without talking. Now and then we exchanged a glance. I think each of us was checking to see whether the other was tiring. Each time our glances met, we grinned and winked. We had become conspirators, and we were enjoying ourselves.

The closer six o'clock drew, the likelier it became that my father would pull into the driveway, and the thought that he would surprise us still at our work was beginning to send us into a panic. My mother stopped working for a moment, stood up, and said to me, tentatively, "I've got an idea."

"Great," I said. "We need an idea. What is it?"

She told me, and it struck me as such a good idea that we put it into effect immediately. We carried my father's favorite chair out onto the front lawn. We carried the table that stood beside it out there, too, and placed it beside the chair. We carried the television set out and put it in place in front of the chair. I ran the long extension cord that he used for his electric drill through a cellar window and plugged the set into it. We carried a few more pieces of furniture out, and two small rugs, and by the time he came driving up, the effect was quite convincing. I know that it was, because when my father got out of the car and walked across the lawn, he said, "Spring cleaning?"

"Right!" said my mother. "Peter's helping me, but we didn't get started until he got home from school, so we're not quite finished. You don't mind sitting out here, do you? It's a nice night."

I came out the front door with six cans of beer in a bucket full of ice and set the bucket on the lawn beside my father's chair. I handed him an opener. He sat in the chair and opened a can. I turned the television on.

"We won't be much longer," said my mother, and she and I went back inside to finish our work.

At the door, I paused for a moment and stole a look at him. He was ˉitting there in his chair in precisely the attitude he assumed every night when the chair was in its accustomed place in our living room, watching television as he always did, but his chair was not in its accustomed place, and neither was he, and that alteration of the ordinary arrangement of things had a wonderful consequence: he looked ridiculous.

Just then, Mr. Morton came by, walking his chickens as he did every evening. Raising chickens in the back yard was at that time and in that part of Babbington a popular hobby among adult males, and Mr. Morton had a flock of champion birds. When he reached the end of our front walk, he stood there and worked his jaw without speaking. My father squirmed in his chair. I like to think that he was experiencing the unsettling feeling that he looked ridiculous in the eyes of the chicken champion of Babbington Heights.

Finally, Mr. Morton spoke. "Sitting out on the lawn, Bert?" he asked.

My father snapped his head in Mr. Morton's direction and said, "Spring cleaning."

"Uh-huh," said Mr. Morton. He looked up at me for a moment. I shrugged and rotated my forefinger beside my head. Mr. Morton nodded, gave a shake to the leashes on his chickens, and he and his little flock went on their way.

AFTER THE CANDY-MAKING FAILURE, my mother tried nothing else; she didn't even talk about trying anything else. She had been defeated. She was finished. One day when I came home from school, she was sitting at the dining room table, looking straight ahead, weeping. There was something so bleak and hopeless about the way she was just sitting there, with no obvious provocation for her weeping, no sad letter in front

of her, no bandage on her finger, that I stopped inside the door, dumbstruck, immobilized, unable to go to her and ask her what was wrong, certainly unable to offer her any comfort, unable even to tiptoe through the
kitchen and into the living room and leave her in private.

Grieving, I have decided since then, was what she was doing, grieving
for the loss of someone who had never existed: that Ella Piper Leroy
whom she had hoped to become, a woman whose potential existence had
depended on the possibility of success, on hope.

If hope is like a warm breeze that lifts and lofts and carries us on when
we hardly have the will to carry on otherwise (and it is), then the candy-
making failure had let my mother down, deflated her. She sank under the
weight of her failure. She had lost hope, and having lost hope she had lost
someone she had hoped to know someday, someone she had hoped would
make her proud, as a mother hopes that a child will make her proud: she
had lost Ella Piper Leroy, tycoon, child of her own ambition.

When I saw her crying at the dining room table, she was, I think, grieving over the death of that hoped-for self. In her own mind's eye, she could
no longer imagine a future for herself that was different from and better
than the present in which she found herself, so she had no future at all,
and that was the end of her.

I didn't recognize that at the time. I was too full of myself. I was embarrassed by the sight of her, weeping there. I suppose that she was embarrassed too, because she made a stab at pulling herself together, forced
a smile in my direction, and shrugged. I returned her false smile with one
of my own and went upstairs and into my own cares and my own hopes
and my own ambitions for my own little self.

MANY YEARS LATER, I had attained some small success. I was about
thirty-four. I had taken over the authorship of a series of books for boys—
the Larry Peters adventure series—and I was being paid fairly well for the
tales I was churning out. With some of the spoils I bought a classic car, a
powerful Kramler V-12, gleaming white, redolent inside of rich leather
and leaking brake fluid. My parents had retired to a small house near but
not on a small lake in a small town nowhere in New Hampshire. When
Albertine and I and the boys arrived in the Kramler, my mother was delighted by the sight of it.

A few days after we had returned home, a gift from my mother arrived in the mail: a pair of driving gloves. The gift card read, "To my son with a very special car." She had read the Kramler correctly; she understood what it had been designed and built to say, and she understood why I had bought it: to say that I was a success, and she thought of me as a successful person—which, I think, for her meant someone who had succeeded in defining himself. At the time I thought it ridiculous that she assumed that I had defined myself as the driver of a powerful Kramler, that she thought I was someone who might want to define himself in that way, but, more than that, I felt sorry for her because I saw from her gift to me that she would have liked to have been someone who had earned herself a powerful Kramler. Mark my words: I didn't say that she would have liked to own a Kramler; I said that she would have liked to have been someone who had earned herself a Kramler. She would have liked to have made herself into such a person. She would have liked to have made herself into *someone,* someone she thought of as someone.

BEFORE SHE DIED, I visited my mother in an intensive-care ward. She was fettered by wires and tubes, bloated with accumulated fluids, barely able to speak. She was dying of lung cancer brought on by regret, by the tens of thousands of cigarettes she had smoked while she sat in the dark, sipping mediocre wine and mourning the loss of her hope, mourning the spunky self who had chased so many harmless follies, the young and ambitious Ella Piper Leroy who had died years before.

If things had gone as they ought to have gone, we should have been able to talk about her success. There should have been *one* business that finally succeeded, and we should have been able to reminisce about the crazy things that had happened while she was running it. We should have had some laughs. She should have been able to sigh and smile and shake her head in wonder at all that she had done, and she should have been able to say, "It was quite a ride."

Instead, she had almost nothing to say, and I had almost nothing to say to her—unless I talked about myself. I retreated into that, but when I realized what I was doing I caught myself and we fell again into silence.

I held her hand, and when the silence between us became embarrassing, I squeezed it and said that I would see her again the next day. I didn't. She died in the night, as Ella Piper Leroy, housewife.

MUST IT BE? Must it be as it was when the way it was was wrong? No. Not while I'm around. Time has made me see that I might have helped her. Maybe all she needed was a sidekick. All the cowboys I lionized as a little boy had sidekicks, descendants of Sancho Panza who carried the luggage of comic relief. I should have learned from them the lesson that even the boldest of us needs a little help from a friend, needs somebody on his side, even if it's a bumbling simpleton who lards the earth when he walks. I could have been that comical sidekick, and if I had been, who's to say that with me taking pratfalls by her side she might not have made a success of something?

That's why, when people ask me about my mother, I don't tell them about Ella's Lacy Licks or any of her other failures; I tell them about Ella's Lunch Launch. I tell them how she bought a clam boat that was slowly sinking from the day she stepped aboard it; how, together, we repainted it in tropical colors, fitted it out with a rudimentary kitchen, rigged a canopy over the deck and flew pennants from a dozen poles; how we plied the bay selling chowder and sandwiches to vacationers and baymen; and how I kept the boat afloat all summer without ever letting her know that it was sinking. I tell them about the mishaps and merriment; I tell them how my mother became known (not far and wide, but near and narrow, which was enough) as "Ella, who runs Ella's Lunch Launch"; and I tell them how the lunch launch, in the fall, when I was back in school and unable to keep it pumped dry, sank.

At the end of the story, my mother and I stand on a bulkhead at the edge of Bolotomy Bay looking down at the sunken boat, reminiscing about the crazy things that happened while she ran it, with me at her side as first mate, sous chef, busboy, and sidekick. When we have run out of stories, my mother puts her arm across my shoulders and gives me a squeeze. She sighs and smiles, shakes her head and says, "It was quite a ride," and I agree.

Peter Leroy
New York City
December 24, 2000

1
On Being a Bastard

BASTARDY has been good to me. I don't actually know that I am a bastard, but I've tried legitimacy and I've tried bastardy, and, on the whole, bastardy has been more rewarding.

For one thing, bastardy gave me the inspiration for the first doo-wop song I wrote, although, because it was a subtle piece of work for a kid my age, no one but I noticed that it was about bastardy. It began like this:

Woh-oh, woh-oh-oh-ohhh,
There's a space between
What you say and what you mean.

And it went on like that for quite a few lines before ending like this:

Woh-oh, woh-oh-oh-ohhh,
There's a space between
Who I am and who you say I am.
Woh-oh, woh-oh-oh-ohhh,
That's where the shadows fall.
Woh-oh, woh-oh-oh-ohhh,
And where the shadows fall,
Anything can happen
Anything at all.
Woh-oh, woh-oh-oh-ohhh,
Bah doobie doo wah.

I sang it to Patti Fiorenza one afternoon when I was walking her home from school. Patti was not the sort of girl who blushed easily, but I thought I saw the color rise in her cheeks as I sang, and I interpreted the cause of her coloring as embarrassment, arising from her recognition of the theme, a controversial one at that time.

"What do you think?" I asked.

"I think, um, I think there's too much 'woh-oh, woh-oh-oh-ohhh,'" she said.

"Really?" I said. I didn't want to argue with her, though I disagreed with her. In the entire song "woh-oh, woh-oh-oh-ohhh" accounted for only fifteen lines out of forty, not too many at all.

"Yeah," she said, "and—" She seemed reluctant to go on, and this time I was certain I saw her blush.

"That's okay," I said. I touched her hand. "You don't have to say anything else."

"It's just that—I—I really think I should tell you that—you really can't sing, you know?"

The adorable little thing. The song apparently embarrassed her so much that she couldn't even bring herself to admit that it embarrassed her.

"Well," I said, seizing the opportunity that she had given me, "in that case, why don't you sing it? Why don't you sing it with the Love Notes?"

Eventually she did, after some rewriting that cut six "woh-oh, woh-oh-oh-ohhh" lines, and it became popular enough at high school dances that soon most of Babbington knew—in a subtle, almost subconscious way—that I considered myself a bastard.

Hasn't every boy everywhere at some time wondered whether he might be the child of some man other than his declared father? I think so. At some time or other, I think, every one of us suspects either that the beer-swilling Yahoo sitting in the living room watching television, the one who claims the perquisites of fatherhood, he who must be obeyed, must be a fraud, a usurper who has ousted our real father from the nest, or that the poor sap drowning his sorrows with beer and old jokes must have been defrauded, must be a cuckold, and that our real father, a dashing figure, a rogue, a restless profligate, is out somewhere roaming the world making conquests and siring our siblings.

I certainly wondered whether that might not be the case in my case.

Some nights, many nights, I would slip from bed, creep partway down the stairs, and sit silently there, where I had a view down along the length of the living room, and I would spend some time observing Bert Leroy in the flickering television light, looking for some sign that would convince me one way or the other, and though I never saw anything that constituted incontestable proof, just the sight of him sitting there slack-jawed and gaping was enough to send me back to bed shaking my head and asking myself, "How on earth could I be the son of that fool?"

We have only a couple of options if we want to alter our beliefs about our paternity. We can decide that we were adopted, or we can decide that we are bastards. I favored bastardy because it brought with it an illicit, romantic, and passionate history, a history far more attractive and desirable than adoption could have provided, with its official procedures and forms in triplicate. Choosing bastardy also seemed like a nice thing to do for my mother; not only did it improve my paternity but also her love life, inserting into her past a wonderful night when, with someone handsome and clever, she conceived me. Cue the moonlight, please. Woh-oh, woh-oh-oh-ohhh.

I began testing Bert, the man who claimed to be my father, by calling him "Dad," with a pair of oral quotation marks that called into question his right to the title. He ordinarily called me Peter, but after a couple of weeks of "Dad" he began calling me "Son," and I decided to think that he was confirming what I suspected. To my surprise, my relationship with him began to improve. I felt sorry for the guy, I guess.

2
Dudley Beaker, a Hypothetical Father

ANY FATHER WOULD DO, any one but the one I supposedly had. I chose Dudley Beaker; by that I mean that, one afternoon late in June when I returned home from school full of thoughts of Patti Fiorenza and found my mother sitting at the dining room table alone, weeping, I chose to believe that my mother had chosen Dudley Beaker. "Why is she crying?" I asked myself.

I crept up to my room and tried putting two and two together. Deaths make people cry. How about the death of Dudley Beaker? He had been interred in the Babbington municipal cemetery without benefit of clergy just two weeks earlier. Dudley's death and my mother's weeping were sequentially appropriate—his death having preceded her weeping—and sufficiently proximate to suggest a relationship of cause and effect. (A little logic is a dangerous thing.)

Not many other people would have been weeping for Dudley. He had in his final years become embittered and snappish. He told anyone who would listen that he had wasted his life and had produced "not one single thing of value in the time allotted to me," and insisted that his grave be marked with only the simplest and cheapest of headstones, bearing the epitaph *de nihilo nihil.* Even Eliza Foote, who had married him, hadn't wept at his funeral, but my mother had, and now she was downstairs sitting alone with her thoughts or her memories, and she was weeping again, which surely proved something.

In the interest of objectivity, I should say that there might have been another explanation for my mother's weeping: she had a few days earlier failed at an attempt to make ribbon candy on a commercial scale, working in the kitchen of our suburban house. That failure didn't seem to me to be a sufficient cause for weeping, but, while I was recalling her attempt to make the ribbon candy and assessing it as a possible cause of her weeping, I remembered that I had observed something that lent support for the theory that Dudley Beaker was my actual father, because for a brief time while she was involved in the effort to make ribbon candy she had seemed to become someone different from the woman I knew, knew as "my mother." I think I had seen some remnant of the girl she had been, someone easier in her attitudes toward life and toward herself, someone who nursed expectations of a better future, who allowed herself to hope. Most of the time, there was a deadness in my mother's eyes, the blankness that comes with the expectation that nothing will make today different from yesterday or tomorrow different from today, but while she was working on the ribbon candy she had a twinkle in her eye, like the twinkle in the eye of a girl in love.

I began looking for that girl in old family photographs. I was immediately struck by how often Dudley appeared in those photographs. The fact that he had lived next door didn't seem a sufficient explanation for his presence at so many of the Piper family occasions. I began examining the images of Dudley with as much interest as I examined those of the girl who was to become my mother.

To be able to imagine Dudley as my father, I had first to imagine that my mother found him sexually attractive. This wasn't easy. I tried to see Dudley as my mother might have seen him, but it proved impossible. I stared at the Dudley Beaker I found in those creased photographs slipping their moorings in an old album, barely held in place by black corner anchors coming loose as the glue aged and dried, decaying into gripless dust, and I found a youngish man, not a bad-looking man, who was usually wearing a tweed jacket or a cardigan sweater and nearly always puffing a pipe, but I couldn't see him as my mother might have seen him, couldn't feel for him what she might have felt for him.

Instead, I began to be able to feel what he might have felt for her. I began to discover a private Dudley Beaker, a man who wore a mask of aloof sophistication to hide the ardor he felt for the dark-haired bobbysoxer who lived next door, a man who sat at home alone most evenings, wishing, wishing, wishing that the girl next door would come tripping gaily over to his house to ask for help with her homework. He must have wondered why she didn't find him more attractive than high school boys, or at least more interesting, since they hadn't his advantages of tweed suits and a college education.

I also discovered in those photographs an attractive young woman whom I had never met. (Imagine here the embarrassment of a boy of thirteen who has never thought of his mother in any but maternal terms, discovering that she was once an attractive young woman, and discovering that finding her attractive meant that she had joined the group of girls he found attractive, the group that included Patti Fiorenza.)

Had the twinkle that twinkles in the eye of a girl in love been in my mother's eyes when Dudley Beaker was around? I couldn't be sure. Had there been a twinkle in Dudley's eyes when my mother was around? Yes. I saw it in those old photographs, and I seemed to remember it from personal observation, and that twinkle made Dudley a likely father.

3
Martinis with the Merry Widow

A COUPLE OF WEEKS LATER, about a month after Dudley's death, his wife, Eliza, telephoned me and said that she would like to see me. She had, she said, a proposal that she would like me to consider.

A proposal? A proposition? I was on my bicycle in a minute. Riding southward toward the five-way light that marked a point in the boundary between the old, genteel Babbington, and the new, vulgar Babbington where I lived, I speculated about the proposal Eliza intended to make. I was, I remind you, a thirteen-year-old boy (more precisely, nearly thirteen and two-thirds) just finishing the ninth grade, since I had skipped the third, so I fervently hoped that the proposal would have something to do with sex. It seemed not impossible to me that Eliza might want me to provide her with a sexual outlet now that Dudley was gone. She would propose a sophisticated and civilized arrangement. I would assure her that I would be more than happy to comply, that I would gladly provide her with any sexual services that she cared to teach me to provide.

How old was Eliza then? Let me see: she was considerably younger than Dudley and, of course, considerably older than I. It would be a good guess to say that she was thirty-two or thirty-three, just about my mother's age.

She interviewed me in the living room. It was, as I recall, early afternoon. She was wearing something cream colored, silk, possibly thin enough for me to make out the outlines of her underwear, but I can't be certain about that, because I find that when I bring the women of my past to mind, their clothing has become far finer and sheerer in memory than it ever was in fact, and I can see lovely bits of them now that I know I never saw then.

She was drinking a martini. I'm sure of that.

"Do you want anything?" she asked.

At thirteen? I wanted everything.

"Um, no," I said, as I'd been taught to say when offered anything I wanted. "No thanks."

"Some lemonade or something?"

"Well—do you have Coffee-Toffee?"

"Coffee-Toffee?"

"It's soda, a kind of soda."

"No, I don't have that. I'm sorry."

"That's okay," I said. "I'll have whatever you're having."

She raised her eyebrows, gave a little laugh, and got up. She took a cocktail glass from a cabinet, and she filled it from a shaker on a sideboard where there were several cut-glass decanters and equipment for the making of drinks.

"This will be mostly water," she said, "but you can tell your friends that you spent the afternoon drinking martinis with a merry widow."

I tried it. It seemed strong to me. "Mmm, delicious," I said.

"Let me explain what I have in mind," she said.

"Okay," I said, trying not to seem too eager.

She sighed and lit a cigarette.

"I'm going abroad for a few weeks."

"Huh?"

"Abroad," she repeated, shaking the match out, dropping it into an ashtray, removing the cigarette from her mouth, exhaling. "Overseas. To Europe."

"Oh." This was a surprise. Europe. She wanted me to join her for an extended stay in Europe. Of course. She understood that I had always been attracted to her, and she had developed an attraction for me, but Babbington was no place to carry on a liaison with a boy considerably less than half her age. On the other hand, from what I'd heard Europe was just the place. This would be a great opportunity for me. I would learn a lot from Europe and from Eliza. I would be richer for the experience. I would have stories to tell when I returned. I would stand out from all the

Babbington boys who had never traveled through Europe with Eliza. Patti would notice my European patina, my worldly air, savvy and cynical demeanor, my *je ne sais quoi*. It would be wonderful.

"I'm going away so that I don't have to endure all this sympathy."

"I understand," I said. I didn't. I hadn't noticed that she had had to endure much sympathy.

"Or maybe I'm just going away to be away for a while. What do you think?"

"I don't know."

"Neither do I." She knocked the ash from her cigarette. She used her cigarette much as Dudley had used his pipe, using the business of smoking to create a rhythm for the things she said. After a moment had passed in the business of smoking, she said, "Peter, I want to offer you a job."

"What is it?" I asked. Translator seemed a possibility, since I had started taking French. I didn't have much of a vocabulary yet; I'd have to get to work.

"I'd like you to take care of this house for a while," she said. I felt a great disappointment, as you might expect. *Arrivederci, Roma.* So long to Germany. Farewell to France.

"Are you interested?"

"I'm not sure," I said, honestly. It wasn't nearly as attractive an offer as traveling through Europe, kissing and cuddling our way across the Continent in first-class railway compartments.

"Well, let's discuss the duties and responsibilities and the remuneration, and then we'll see whether you're interested."

I liked "remuneration." It sounded much classier than "pay," and it sounded like more money.

"Uh-huh," I said, and at that point I think that I had already decided to take the job. I think I had decided that I would take any job that involved remuneration, whatever the responsibilities might be.

"Peter," she said, "what's happened to you?"

"Happened to me?"

"You don't seem to have anything to say. You've become awkward and hesitant, as if you were dull-witted, but I know you're not a dull boy. You—ahhhh—I see."

"See what?"

"You've reached the awkward age, haven't you?"

"I guess so," I said. It was true. I often seemed to get in my own way, and I mean that both literally, since I sometimes tripped over my own feet as if some prankster had tied my shoes together, and figuratively, since my thoughts sometimes tripped over one another and tied my tongue.

"Well," she said with a knowing smile, "it doesn't last forever." She got up, keeping her glass, and said, "Come on—let's walk through the house and I'll show you what I want you to do."

"I'll try not to break anything," I said.

"Good," she said, and she tousled my hair.

My duties as she outlined them wouldn't be many. I would have to check the house daily, water some plants, dust and vacuum regularly, run the water and flush the toilet so that rust wouldn't accumulate in the pipes, fix or have fixed anything that broke, keep the windows open a bit so that the place wouldn't get musty, but close them if rain was predicted, then open them again when the skies cleared, and keep the lawn mowed and the weeds down. She would remunerate me handsomely; since yesterday's pay scales seem quaint today, and today's are likely to seem quaint tomorrow, I'll put my remuneration in terms of purchasing power: the amount that she was willing to pay me each week would be equivalent to the price of dinner for two with drinks, tax, and tip at a modest restaurant in Manhattan. Not bad for a kid of thirteen. With that much money coming in each week, I could take Patti out on dates, if I could persuade her to go on dates with me.

"The key to the back door is under the mat," she said. She paused and looked me over. Then she decided to add something.

"You can snoop around. I know that you're *going* to snoop around, so I'll tell you that you can snoop around, but don't *break* anything, and please put everything back just as you found it."

"Okay."

"And don't do anything that will ruin my reputation, okay?"

"Like what?" I asked.

"You know—no parties, no seducing teenage girls, no plying them with drink, no playing the bachelor playboy just because you have the run of the house."

"Oh."

"Or if you do, no getting caught at it."

She winked at me, and I winked back.

"Okay," I said. Parties; there was an idea. Seducing teenage girls; there was an even better idea. Bachelor playboy. Not getting caught. These were all good ideas.

"And if people should ask—not that I think they will, but if they should—tell them that I had to get away for a while because I couldn't endure all the sympathy."

"Okay." The most attractive idea of all was the thought that with the run of the house and license to snoop I could look for evidence of Dudley's role in my conception.

4
A Lot to Learn

AS SOON AS ELIZA HAD LEFT for Europe, I visited the house on my own. I told my parents that, as a diligent lad who took his duties seriously and meant to go about them in an organized way, I intended to get right down to work and would be spending most of Saturday looking the place over, making an inventory of what was required, listing the jobs that would have to be performed, and making a schedule on a calendar that I had been given when I visited the showroom of Babbington Studebaker. I thought I gave a fine performance.

"Stay out of trouble," said my father, but that didn't necessarily mean that he had seen through my act; he said it all the time. There wasn't any reason to think that he knew that what I really intended to do was snoop around.

At the back door to Dudley's house, I lifted the mat and found the key. I picked it up. I held it in my hand. It was heavy.

(Of course it was heavy, freighted as it was with allegorical import. In the fairy tale version of this story, a beautiful and worldly woman gives to an adolescent boy the secret of the location of a hidden key that will unlock a door that leads into a house—make that a castle—within which are hidden treasures physical, metaphorical, and sexual, like rubies, gold, knowledge, power, and women of all ages. He uncovers the key and takes it into his possession. He fits the key into the lock. He pauses for a moment to give a thought to the step he is about to take. We return to my story at that point.)

I held in my hand the key that would—could, might—unlock the mystery of my paternity. I paused, since I had begun thinking of myself as a character in an allegorical tale, and reflected on the step I was about to take.

"This door," I murmured aloud, acting the lead in my own drama, "opens onto a new phase of my life."

I opened the door. I stepped inside.

I was in the kitchen. It seemed not very different from any other kitchen, and not at all like the start of a new phase of my life.

I walked the length of the hall that ran down the center of the house and looked through the glass set into the panels beside the front door. I imagined Dudley waiting for my mother to come up the walk and ring the bell, and I decided that if I were he I would not be waiting there at the door, nervously watching out the window. If I were awaiting a visit from the girl next door, I would be elsewhere, in the kitchen, perhaps, fixing a snack, or in the living room, sitting in front of the fire, reading a book, sipping a drink, scarcely aware that the time had come when the girl was expected, certainly not annoyed that the girl was late.

The living room was just off the entry hall, to my right as I stood facing the front door. In front of the fireplace, two chairs faced each other. I had often sat in one of those, with Dudley in the other, and listened while he lectured. His lectures were usually instigated by my mother, who would send me to Dudley if I asked a question that she couldn't answer— or didn't want to answer. I would pedal on down to Dudley's house, usually in the evening. He and Eliza would greet me, and we would all chat about nothing for a while. Dudley would have a drink, and Eliza might, too. She would make me cocoa if the weather was cold, lemonade if the weather was warm, and then after a while she would excuse herself, close the pocket door between the living room and dining room, leave through the door to the hall, and close that behind her, and I would be alone with Dudley. There had been a time when I had enjoyed those sessions, when I welcomed the information and advice Dudley gave me, but I had come to enjoy them less and less as I had come to think that I knew more and more. I no longer wanted to know what he thought I ought to do; I wanted to decide for myself. I had become impatient with his counsel. I fidgeted while he spoke, and I rarely did as he advised me to do. I hadn't want him as a mentor, and he had decided that he didn't want me as a pupil.

"You're becoming stubborn, willful, and headstrong," he had told me at our last session. "I have the clear impression—and clearly it is the impression you want me to have—that you think our talks are no longer of any use to you. You think that I have nothing to teach you. Correct?"

"I think that I can think for myself," I had said.

"And I think that you have a lot to learn."

"That may be," I had said, "but the lot that I have to learn is—" I had stopped because I didn't know what to say. If there had been something clever somewhere in my mind that I could have stuck onto the end of my sentence, I hadn't been able to find it.

"Yes?" Dudley had asked, with a hint of a smirk and a raised eyebrow.

Nothing. I had gotten up out of my chair and left the room. I hadn't allowed myself to run, though I had wanted to run. I closed the door behind me, and I stood in the front hall for a moment, trying to recover my self-esteem. Eliza had put her head around the corner of the door to the kitchen and looked down the length of the hall at me.

"Peter?" she had said.

"I've got a lot to learn," I had said, and I had let myself out the front door and into the night.

5
The Cynical Detective

IF I STILL HAD A LOT TO LEARN, and I did, I felt that I'd come to the right place. In Dudley's own house I ought to be able to find out what I wanted to know, and Eliza had given me permission to poke and pry.

I sat for a while in the chair that I had sat in so many times before, and when I remembered Dudley's saying that I had a lot to learn, I said, "That may be, but the lot that I have to learn is not the lot that you can teach me." It wasn't clever, and it didn't seem quite grammatical, but at least I'd found my tongue.

I tried taking Dudley's place and addressing the other chair as he would have if I had been sitting in it. I let my eyelids droop and allowed my mouth to twist itself into something that was not quite a sneer and could be mistaken for an indulgent smile. *He supposes that he has become clever,* I thought, *and what he would probably describe as cynical, and apparently I am to be the object of this newfound cleverness and soi-disant cynicism. Well, we shall see who wins that contest, but at least he shall know what a cynic is.*

"The Cynics," I told the empty chair, as Dudley had once told me, "are widely misunderstood. Originally, they were a sect of Greek philosophers, flourishing some twenty-three-hundred years ago, who advocated the doctrines that virtue is the only good, that the essence of virtue is self-control, and that surrender to any external influence is beneath human dignity. In our time, as you have doubtless noticed, greed is considered the only good, people have no self-control nor wish to exercise any self-control, and the mass of them happily surrender to any external influence provided that it saves them the effort of thinking for themselves."

"I wish you'd let *me* think for myself," muttered the impertinent boy in the opposite chair.

"*Plus ça change,*" I went on as Dudley had, ignoring the impertinence. "Even in their day the Cynics were disparaged. Their foremost member, Diogenes, was slandered by Seneca, who claimed that he lived in a tub. The mob nicknamed him 'Dog,' which gives us a rather vivid idea of what people thought of him. Revere him, Peter, and wear the label 'cynic' proudly, for it is derived from that nasty nickname, *kyon* in Greek, and today it designates those of us who point the finger at human vanity and pride, who recognize that selfishness is the motivation for every human action, who scoff at claims of disinterest or altruism or love, who ask, always, '*Cui bono?*' In other words, what the world calls a cynic, a dog, I— and, I hope, you, my boy—would call a reasonable human being."

When Dudley had finished, he began the business of emptying and cleaning his pipe, and he said to me, "I trust you will remember that." I resolved to forget it as soon as possible, but despite the passage of time I hadn't managed to forget it, and sitting in Dudley's chair had brought it back to me so completely that if I had had someone sitting opposite me I could have delivered the lecture on the Cynics just as Dudley had delivered it to me, word for word. I resolved to try delivering it some evening, if I could find an acolyte, a young novice to sit in the chair opposite me, someone to educate and belittle. I might even try smoking one of Dudley's pipes. In the befuddled logic of adolescence, becoming more like Dudley seemed somehow to be a way of getting the better of him.

I didn't stay long in the living room. There wasn't much there that seemed likely to provide the answers I was seeking, nor did I find what I was after anywhere else in the house that night. Over the course of the next couple of weeks, I visited the house daily, as Eliza had asked me to do, and sometimes I visited twice a day, to find what I could find, to learn what I could learn. I investigated every inch of it. I came to know everything that was in every dresser and cabinet and bedside table. I knew the title of every book on every bookshelf, and I flipped through many of them. I knew everything that was in the desk in Dudley's study. I tried on Dudley's life as if it were a suit of clothes. I sat in his chair in the living room, drinking his Scotch, reading his diary. I read his mail, the letters he had saved and the copies of letters that he had sent. I sat at his desk, and I took notes on a pad that I found there, writing with Dudley's pen. I used his toilet and bathed in his tub, where I read the little volume on Diogenes from which he had taken the text of his lecture on the Cynics. I slept in his bed, on the side that the contents of the bedside table told me was his, beside the side that Eliza would have occupied.

Did I come to understand what it had been like to be Dudley Beaker? Somewhat, I think. Did I find any evidence that he was my father? Yes. What I found wouldn't have convinced anyone; it didn't even convince me, but it did suggest that further investigation was called for. This is what I found: some photographs of my mother in an album in the bottom drawer of Dudley's desk. There was nothing sexually suggestive about these photographs, but there was in his having kept an album exclusively devoted to photographs of my mother something strongly suggestive of his having played the essential role in my paternity, it seemed to me. Dudley had been an amateur of photography, and he was always volunteering to take photographs at family gatherings. Apparently, he had kept copies for himself of the pictures in which my mother appeared. I would say that the photographs showed my mother from about thirteen to twenty-four, her age when she gave birth to me. In the last photographs of her that he had pasted into the album, she was pregnant. At that point, he had stopped adding pictures to the album. It contained no pictures of me.

6
One Handy Package

THERE WAS AT THAT TIME a vogue for combining everything one might want in a particular area of interest or endeavor into "one handy package," and the cult of miniaturization had already begun. Devotees of the backyard barbecue, for example, instead of buying separate tongs, fork, spatula, and similar implements could instead buy the Hand-e-Que, which combined tongs, fork, spatula, spoon, skewer, and salt and pepper shakers in one handy package. In the supermarket (actually, at that time, the grocery store) one could buy Box o' Supper, a box that held a bag of macaroni, a can of cheese sauce, a can of peas, a can of brown bread, a small package of cookies, a couple of paper napkins, and a short stack of antacid tablets. The intrepid traveler could buy an Aeronautomobile, a vehicle with folding wings and a "leakproof" hull that could navigate the skies, the seas, and the highways. In cynics, Diogenes would have been everything one could have wanted in one handy package. In sexpots, it would have been Patti Fiorenza.

I was, at that time, obsessed with Patti. She was a year older than I, which meant that she was fourteen. She had many admirable qualities. I might mention her pretty face, her quick mind, her sparkling personality, her winning smile, or the cooing voice in which she sang backup for the Bay Tones, the Four Plays, the Half Shafts, the Glide Tones, and the Love Notes.

I see from a quick skim of the preceding paragraph that I neglected to mention that Patti possessed, to a degree unmatched in the experience of

Babbingtonians until that time, a quality that was then called "sex appeal." She had an amazing little body, tiny but breathtaking. That tiny body was bursting with the promise of sexual gratification. From the long view of fifty-six, I see that Patti was the walking, talking embodiment of a hoary old fantasy, the child-woman, sexually a woman, but in so many other ways still a child, but what I remember from that time was the impression I had that under the right conditions I could pick her up and put her in my pocket, hide her in a shoe box under my bed and take her out and play with her under the covers at night. (I was, at that time, I ask you to recall, and enter as a plea in my defense, an adolescent boy.)

I do not have the talent to do justice to Patti's body here. Any description I attempted would, in the estimation of a couple of hundred of the aging men and women who once were boys and girls with me at Babbington High, fall laughably short of the mark.

The best I can do is try to make you understand the effect that Patti had on us. Imagine a day in the spring, that first warm and brilliant day that takes everyone by surprise. Let's say that, after school, Patti decides to take a walk downtown to get a milk shake. Every Babbingtonian she passes pauses to watch her go by, and in her wake they sigh, and they spend the rest of the day in wishful thinking. She sits at the counter in the malt shop and drinks a chocolate shake.

Old Eben Flood, just a week shy of eighty-six, finds that he has developed an almost uncontrollable urge to lick the chocolate from Patti's lower lip, and to keep himself from licking her he begins whistling "The Happy Wanderer." He knows that he looks like an old fool, but he doesn't dare stop.

Mrs. Dorothy Inskip, a respectable matron, president of the Ladies' Village Improvement Society, finds that she can't stop staring at the beautiful buttocks of this girl so pertly perched on a counter stool. To prevent herself from giving in to a desire to touch what she admires, she rushes from the shop; outside, she collides with Harrison Barker, the president of the First National Bank of Babbington, an old flame, a flame that hasn't flickered since she was Patti's age, but a flame rekindled on the spot, a flame that will bring to the seven quiet and wrinkled years that Harry and Dotty still have ahead of them a warmth greater and more perdurable than either of them could possibly have imagined when first that flame was lit.

When Patti pays the soda jerk, young Frederick Lawson Stillwell, his hand shakes, and his lips move in a silent prayer that he manage somehow not to surrender to the vast catalogue of impure thoughts inspired by the salacious way she chews her gum, that he not be led into temptation by the wanton way her little hips swing, and that he not be made to turn from the straight path and follow her out the door and wherever on earth she might choose to lead him. By dropping to his knees as soon as she's out the door he manages to keep himself from following her, but he discovers in another minute to his horror that he's praying that she'll come back, so to purge himself of this devilish perversion he whips out the pocket-size discipline he carries to keep impure thoughts at bay and spends a few satisfying moments mortifying his flagitious flesh. Years later, when he has finally given up trying to fight the fire that burns within him, he will found the Little Church of Perpetual Passion at the southernmost end of Bolotomy Road, in a building that was once a clamdigger's shack, and on "Flagellation Fridays," his disciples will join him in exploring the erotic potential of the lash, flailing at themselves and one another.

Patti, meanwhile, has left the shop and stands in the sunlight at the corner of Bolotomy and Main. It's such a nice day! Who wants to be indoors? Instead of heading directly for home as she had intended, she spends the rest of the afternoon strolling willy-nilly, wherever fancy takes her, here and there, all over our little town. By nightfall, the town can scarcely think of anything but her. We are all drunk on Patti Fiorenza. Some of us are leaning against our porch posts, smoking, yearning for her, others lying in our bedrooms, sweating, with Patti on our minds and our hands between our legs.

As the night comes on, all Babbington falls into one great orgy of desire for her. All over town, we pet and paw one another, or toy with ourselves, while visions of Patti dance in our heads. We take our pleasure from her, and in our collective fantasy we enjoy her every which way that night, every one of us who saw her walk by, the men and the women, the old and the young, the fit and the feeble, all of us pushing and pulling and thrusting and slipping and sliding our way toward a rippling wave of pleasure that shudders through us all, trembles from one end of town to the other, a shudder strong enough for Patti to feel it at home, in her bed, where she lies alone, and mistakes the tremor of our pleasure for her own, for she has succumbed to her own sweet charms. She soughs, and stretches, and sleeps, and dreams. So, at last, do we, and we dream of her, every sort of sexual pleasure in one handy package, oooh-oooh-oooh, oooh-oooh-oooh, sha-boo-bee-doo-wahhh.

7

A Bubble Bursts

NATURE had assigned Patti a sexy part, and she played it. She dressed the part. She looked the part. She cultivated a knowing wink and a provocative pout. Soon she had a reputation. People assumed that she was the sexual adventurer she seemed to be, and many claimed to have explored the territory with her. Since I was both a cynic and a dreamer, I told myself that the claims I heard were certainly exaggerated and probably untrue, and I managed to convince myself that, in all likelihood, Patti was a virgin—a very sexy virgin, to be sure, but still a virgin—and I tried to hold on to that conviction, but it wasn't easy, given the sheer number of claims to the contrary. Some I could easily dismiss, because the claimants were no likelier sexual partners for Patti than I was myself, but others were more convincing, none more so than the claim I heard Nicky Furman make one afternoon when I was sitting in the school auditorium during a study hall.

Patti had just come into the room, late. I watched her walk down the aisle, watched her hand a note, an excuse for her tardiness, to Mr. Cantrell, an English teacher who affected bright silk squares in the handkerchief pockets of his threadbare jackets, watched her stand, shifting her weight from one foot to the other, canting her hips while her note was read, watched her idly look around the room to see who among the assembled scholars might interest her, and blushed when she spotted me and winked.

Two louts were sitting in front of me. One was known as Greasy; I don't remember his last name. The other was Nicky Furman. A low groan came from Greasy. "Oh, man," he muttered, "I would really like to get into Patti's little snatch."

"Mm," said Nicky.

"I mean," said Greasy, superfluously and boorishly, "I would love to fuck her."

I was shocked to hear this, because *fuck* was rarely used in those days. It had not yet become what it is now, a limp bit of oral punctuation that lies in a sentence like a slug, flaccid from overuse, as impotent as a comma. It had power then. It was outrageous. I was outraged that Greasy should employ it to name what he wanted to do to Patti. I would have liked to give him a piece of my mind, but I didn't because I had seen the damage he could do to boys my size.

In the privacy of my own mind, I told myself that what Greasy wanted was not at all what I wanted. I wanted romance, love, a love taller than the tallest mountain, oo-oo-oo, deeper than the deepest sea, oo-oo-ee, a love that would never die, a passion for the ages. I wanted to know the magic of all her charms, under the moonlight, one summer night, which meant, I can tell you, because I was there, pretty much the same thing as wanting to fuck her, but in a loving and beautiful way, oo-oo-oo, oo-oo-ee, ohhhh yeah.

"Yeah," said Nicky. "She's a great lay."

What? How did he know?

"You fucked her?" asked Greasy.

"Yeah," said Nicky, as if it were not a particularly interesting thing to have done. "She's a great lay, a terrific piece of ass."

He was slandering the piece of ass I loved! I didn't want to believe him. He hadn't—Patti would never have—he couldn't—this was just—

"Bullshit," said Greasy. I was beginning to feel a kinship with him.

"If you say so," said Nicky. He let a moment pass. He snorted. "I'll tell you something funny, but you got to promise not to tell anybody."

"What?"

"Promise."

"Okay."

"I had a rubber that I swiped from my father's bedside table, because I didn't want to get her in trouble, you know?"

"Yeah."

"Well, I never used a rubber before—"

Uh-oh. This was not good. It put him in a bad light. It was not the sort of detail he would include unless he was being really honest.

"—so I open the package and I take the thing out and it's a little flat round thing. I don't know what the hell to do with it. So I start fiddling around with it, trying to figure out which end is up, and she says, 'What's taking you so long?' And I say, 'I don't usually use this brand. I'm not familiar with it.' And then I see that it's all rolled up, so I figure I gotta unroll it, which I do. So I've got this long rubber bag that I'm trying to get onto my pecker, and it ain't easy, let me tell you that. When I finally get it on, there's a big bubble in the front, like a balloon, and when I stick it into her, it goes 'pop.'"

"No shit."

"I told my uncle what happened, and he cracked up. I thought he was gonna bust a gut. And then he tells me you're supposed to put the thing onto your prick and roll it down. You don't unroll it first."

"Oh, sure," said Greasy. "You didn't know that?"

"No," said Nicky. "I didn't know that. I already told you."

Silence. Then Greasy, convinced now, asked, "How did you get her to let you do it?"

"Just asked," said Nicky.

Just asked? That couldn't be. It couldn't be that easy, couldn't *have been* that easy.

"What did you say, exactly?" asked Greasy. I bent over my notebook.

"I said, 'You want to get into the back seat?'"

Damn. You had to have a car. Wouldn't you know.

"Yeah?" asked Greasy. He waited a moment and then prompted Nicky with, "And?"

"And what? We got into the back seat."

"You didn't say anything else?"

"No. I said, 'You want to get into the back seat?' That's all. She knew what I meant. Everybody knows what the back seat is for."

"Yeah," said Greasy, and he laughed a laugh that sounded very much like the sound that would be made by the outrushing air if one inflated a dog till it was as round as a ball, then gave it a couple of slaps on the belly, and let it go.

8

You've Got to Ask for What You Want

I TOLD MYSELF that if I couldn't get what I wanted from Patti, I would have to learn to be content with what she was willing to give me, which was friendship. She didn't consider me a candidate for boyfriend, but she did consider me a friend, and as her friend I often got to walk her home after school. We walked, and we talked, but we didn't touch. On nice days, we sometimes took a very long way home, strolling all the way downtown, where we stopped at the malt shop at the corner of Bolotomy and Main.

This shop was called Malt's; I think that whoever originally opened it intended to call it Malts, so that people wouldn't mistake it for the shop around the corner called Shoe Repair, but the signmaker's rascally sidekick, that old demon apostrophe, crept in, and as a result many a Babbingtonian believed that the shop was originally owned by the eponymous Malt, who had concocted the drink that bore his name, a personage of whom all Babbington ought to be mighty proud. Malt's was an institution of long standing, but its time had passed. Old people went there, and parents brought children there, but no one from Babbington High went there. That's why Patti and I began frequenting it. We went to Malt's because we wouldn't be seen by our classmates. Neither of us said that, but I think it was true. I wanted her to myself, and I think that she wanted me to herself, as a friend. That's all, just a friend. Damn it.

I suppose it was because Patti and I were friends and because Malt's offered the security of relative solitude that I brought up the question of my bastardy on one of our afternoons there. I didn't do it to try to seduce her. Honest.

"This is really inflated, our coming here," I said.

"Yeah," she said.

"My mother used to come here."

"Did she?"

"Uh-huh. Everybody used to come here, all the high-school kids. That's what she says." I looked around. The shop was still, hushed, and almost empty except for us and the leering soda jerk. "You know," I said, "back then, bringing a girl to Malt's was a date."

"It was?"

"Under the right circumstances, at the right time of day."

"Your mother told you that?"

"Mm," I said, distractedly. I was wondering how often my mother had come to Malt's and who had brought her there.

"Is something bothering you?" Patti asked.

"Yes," I said. "Something."

"What?"

"Something—personal."

She touched my arm and said, "Tell me."

Clasping, but not actually wringing, my hands, I said, "I've started wondering whether my mother—"

"What?" Patti asked after I had allowed a moment to pass in silence. "Is she sick?"

"No. Nothing like that. I—I've begun to wonder what my mother— and boys—men—"

"Oh," she said. "I know what you mean. It's a real shock, isn't it?"

"A shock?" Did she know something?

"When you first think about your mother that way. It's a shock, right?"

She tilted her head and raised her eyebrows. I would have agreed with anything she said.

"It sure is," I said. "It's a shock."

She giggled and shook her head in wonder and said, "Just think about the things that you want to do with me—"

"What?" I said. "What things? I—"

She leaned toward me and gave me both the knowing wink and the provocative pout. The soda jerk dropped a glass.

"Just think about the things you want to do with me," she repeated.

"Uh-huh," I said, doing precisely as she asked.

"Now think about the possibility that your mother was sitting right here where I'm sitting, and some boy was sitting right where you're sitting, and that boy wanted to do with your mother what you want to do with me— "

"Huh," I said, exhaling as if I'd been punched.

"—and maybe he did."

This was a way of considering my mother's past that I hadn't previously tried, but now that Patti had introduced it into my thoughts, I found that I could easily imagine how Dudley Beaker had felt about my mother. All I had to do was look at Patti and I knew with unsettling vividness. But what about my mother? What had she felt for Dudley? An idea came to me so suddenly that I announced its arrival as if I'd won a prize.

"I've got an idea!"

"Good for you," she said. "What is it?"

"I'm going to take a trip into the past."

"You've got a time machine?"

"No," I said, modestly, as if it were possible that I might have built a time machine (and for a moment, I wondered whether I could). "This will be an imaginary trip, like a play. I want to look around and see what I can find out about whether my mother—if she might have had—that is, if my father—might not be my father."

"Oh, so that's what this is all about."

"I want you to come with me—and play the part of my mother."

"Your *mother*? And what part are you going to play?"

"Dudley Beaker, who might be my father."

"You are a little pervert, you know that?"

For a moment, I wasn't sure how to take the remark, but she pouted the provocative pout, so I took it as assent. "So you'll do it?" I said.

"Sure," she said, winking the knowing wink. "We're friends. Anything you want, just ask."

9
An Aside (Afflatus, Part 1)

THE IDEA that I reported on the preceding page came to me not on that sunny afternoon in Babbington but on a nasty night in Newark, Delaware, a night when rain was falling in sheets and a blustery wind made umbrellas useless. In a back corner of a bookstore there, I had, earlier, read some passages from my "modified memoirs" and was now delivering a response to a question on the subject of inspiration.

"What we call inspiration is really just chance," I was saying, trotting along on one of my favorite hobbyhorses, "the chance conjunction of events and the random association of memories and ideas," but I could see that their minds were wandering, worries about the weather leading them anxiously into the night, to their cars, and out along their several wet ways home.

I glanced at Albertine, who was sitting in the audience, and gave her the wink that we know means, "On the whole, I'd rather be in Paris."

There, in Montparnasse on a windy, rain-soaked afternoon at the midpoint of a week-long symposium on the very large contribution that even the smallest details, *tous les petits,* make to the texture of reconstructed time, I sat listening to the participants in a panel discussion called *"De Doo-Wop à Hip-Hop: la musique qu'on apprends dans l'ascenseur de la mémoire,"* but I was elsewhere. I was in the auditorium of Babbington High School, cupping Patti Fiorenza's tight little buttocks in my trembling hands.

A moment earlier I had been standing outside the auditorium, looking through the oval window set into one of the doors. After a period of indecision, I pushed the door open, quickly, so that no one would notice, trotted down the aisle, and sidled up to Patti, who was waiting while dapper Mr. Cantrell examined a note excusing her tardiness. (The note was a forgery; Patti had been in the girls' room, smoking, gossiping, and fussing with her hair. Mr. Cantrell was not fooled.)

In an aisle seat to my right, my younger self sat, sighing, and in front of him sat Nicky and Greasy, sniggering.

I stretched my hand out toward Patti and touched the tips of my fingers to her bottom, the smooth satin of her skirt, *ooh-ooooh, baby, baby.* I held my breath and waited to see whether she could feel my touch across the years. She looked around the room, idly, spotted my younger self sitting there, and winked at him. She didn't see me at all. I could palpate the past, and the past could not feel my fingers.

I ran my hand around her hip and over her belly and up across her breasts, and chills ran up and down my spine, *uh-woh-oh, ohhh, yeah.* I slipped the tips of my fingers down into her pink angora sweater, to the edge of her bra, and down along the curve of her small perfect breast, and I told myself that if I could just touch the nipple of this breast I would be satisfied, *ah-eye would be satisfahh-eyed,* and that was what I did, but I wasn't satisfied, and in another moment I was on my knees, running my hands up Patti's legs, reaching up the inside of her little thigh, smooth, silky, and so very, very fine, *wohhh-ohhhh, so fine,* and then Mr. Cantrell cleared his throat and I jumped as if I'd been discovered, stood up and straightened my clothes, and took a couple of steps backward. "You and I know what this is," he said, barely audibly, holding the note like a used handkerchief, "but we'll pretend that we don't." Patti pouted, and Cantrell said, "Just take a seat and get to work."

I walked up the aisle toward the door. Before I left, I turned and looked back. Patti was heading toward the row where my younger self sat. She was going to sit beside him, and he was going to spend the rest of study hall trying to find a way to tell her that he wanted to go to bed with her without having her laugh, poke him in the ribs, and say, "Oh, Peter, you're such a kidder," but it was Albertine who poked me in the ribs, and although I was in the audience at the symposium in Paris I jumped as I had when Mr. Cantrell cleared his throat.

"What?" I said.

"Clap your hands," she said, and I did.

The panelists called for questions, and Albertine gave me a wink that we know means "I'd rather be in bed."

We gathered our things, slipped out of the hall, put our raincoats on, and pushed our way out the door and into the evening, where the bluster nearly blew us back inside.

"Talk about wind!" she said, putting her arm through mine. It was not yet dark; the wind was strong, but the temperature was mild and the rain was light.

We were walking through the Jardin du Luxembourg when we noticed that people were hurrying past us, as if they were fleeing something.

"I guess there must have been a call for volunteers to sit through the next panel," Albertine said, but when we turned to see what was propelling the crowd, we saw a whirlwind, a miniature tornado, moving through the park along the path that we had taken, as if it were pursuing us.

"In here," said Albertine, and she pulled me into a little cabin, like a phone booth but without a phone. In another moment, the whirlwind began shaking the chestnut trees around us, and nuts thundered onto the roof. Albertine laughed at the oddness of it and hugged herself against me, and I wanted to make love to her right then, right there, to open her raincoat, lift her skirt, and have her while the crowd rushed past, but I didn't tell her what I wanted, because most of the people rushing past paused long enough to look into the cabin to see if they might find shelter there, and because I have never been good at asking for what I want and because I knew that part of my desire for Albertine was desire for Patti.

When the twister had gone by, we put our heads out of the little cabin and looked around, and when we were sure the coast was clear we started on our way back to the Hotel du Quai Voltaire, chattering like nervous kids on a date.

About halfway there, I suddenly stopped and confessed. "I wanted to make love to you back there, in the little cabin, like strangers thrown together by chance and chestnuts."

"Peter!" she said, giving me a little swat, "you've got to ask for what you want! Do you want to go back?"

"No," I said. "I guess not. We'd have to get all the rest of the people back and we'd have to get Aeolus to replay the attack of the tornado or find someone to throw nuts on the roof and—"

I meant to tell her about Patti, honest, but she didn't give me a chance. She all but dragged me the rest of the way to the hotel. In the little lift she threw herself at me, jumped up and wrapped her legs around me, and when we got to our room she pushed me to the bed and onto my back and straddled me, and at that moment, through some chance conjunction of events and random association of memories, the idea came to me.

Sign posted in a little cabin in the Jardin du Luxembourg, Paris

10
Testing the Hypothesis, Part 1

SO IT WAS THAT, a few nights later, I waited for Patti in front of Dudley Beaker's house on No Bridge Road. I saw her turn the corner, walking through the circle of streetlamp light. She had dressed in the style of my mother's high-school days, with saddle shoes, bobby socks, a flippy skirt, and a sweater over a white blouse.

"How did you do this?" I asked her when she was beside me, indicating with a sweep of my hand the head-to-toe verisimilitude she had achieved.

"Research and rummaging," she said. "The attics of Babbington are full of relics."

She turned and looked at the house. "So this is the place," she said. "Does anybody live here now?"

"Eliza," I said. "Eliza Foote."

"Who's that?"

"I guess you'd say she was Dudley's girlfriend," I said, and in a whisper I added, "I don't think they ever got married."

"This Dudley was quite a guy."

"You mean because of Eliza?"

"Eliza . . . your mother . . . were there others?"

"I don't know."

"I'll bet he was filling the idle hours of women all over town."

"Do you think so?"

"I just said it, didn't I?"

"Yes," I said, "you did."

"Where's Eliza now? The house looks dark."

"She's abroad—"

"I'll bet she is."

"No. Overseas. In Europe. 'Abroad.' That's the way she put it. She said, 'I'm going abroad for a few weeks so that I don't have to endure all this sympathy.'"

I took the key from my pocket and started toward the door.

Patti put her hand on my arm and said, "Uh-uh. Let's do this right. You go in. Get into the mood. See if you can find any of Dudley's clothes to put on. Get into the part. I'm going to walk around the block, and then when I come back and knock at the door it's going to be a winter night about thirteen years ago, and you're going to be Dudley and I'm going to be—what's your mother's name?"

"Ella."

"I'm going to be Ella."

I LET MYSELF IN and went directly to Dudley's bedroom. I rummaged through his closet and chose a jacket. I put it on and went downstairs and sat in his chair in front of the fireplace and waited. Time passed, more time than I had expected to have to wait, and I began to wonder what had happened to Patti. I went to the front door and looked out through the window beside it. Patti was at the curb, playing the coquette, flirting with a couple of guys in a car. I couldn't hear what they were saying, but from the way Patti leaned against the car and wiggled her bottom as she spoke, I could guess. I drew a deep breath. I felt jealous. I wished that she would send the boys on their way and come into the house to see me. She looked so adorable in her flippy skirt, with her smooth calves showing above her bobby socks and saddle shoes. I wished that there might be some reason for her to come to see me rather than going off in that car. "Come here," I whispered. "Please come here. Make some excuse and come here." She hugged herself and made the gesture of an exaggerated shiver, and then she flung her arm backward in my direction, and I had the thought that she might be indicating that she was coming to see me. I felt pleased and a little surprised. I had really come to expect her to go off in that car.

When the car went off without her and she turned and opened the gate and started up the walk, I felt the loneliness begin to lift from me. I felt thrilled, nervous, eager. If I had been Dudley Beaker, I would have felt rejuvenated.

I RETURNED TO MY CHAIR, and when Patti rang the bell I got up as if I hadn't been expecting her, went to the door, and opened it. She was standing there, smiling and hugging a notebook to her breast.

"Ella!" I said.

"Hi, Dud. I wondered if you could help me with my homework."

"Well," I said, packing tobacco into my pipe and trying to hide a tremor of desire, "it has been quite a long time since I did any homework, but of course I'll help you. Come in."

"Thanks," she said.

"What homework do you have to do?" I asked when I had closed the door behind her.

"I—" She shrugged and pouted, and there formed in my mind the thrilling thought that it wasn't homework that had brought her to see me, that she now had to make up some sort of homework to hide the truth.

"Do you—um—have to—ah—write an essay?" I asked, patting the pockets of my jacket in search of matches.

"Yep," she said, rocking on the balls of her feet. "That's it. Gotta write an essay."

"Well!" I said. "An essay. I think I can help you with that."

Impulsively, she reached out and grasped my hands, which held pipe and matches.

"I knew you could," she said, and I thought that I could see in her eyes the sort of starry-eyed admiration that young girls so often feel for men of accomplishment.

"I'm flattered that you came to me," I said. "I do know quite a bit about writing essays, what with my having gone to college and all, and also my work in advertising, of course, where I do quite a bit of writing, as you might expect."

"Do you have anything to drink?" she asked.

"To drink?" I asked, taken aback by such a question so abruptly posed by such a slip of a girl.

"I'm a little nervous," she said. I could understand that; I was, of a sudden, feeling a little nervous myself.

"I have—I have a liquor cabinet." I led her to the dining room. "It's right there." I pointed toward it.

"Solid, Jackson!" she said when she opened the cabinet and saw the booze. "Make us a couple of sidecars, okay, Dud?"

"Sidecars?"

She got girlish and playful. "I've never had one," she said, "but I know they're really popular now. I read that they were the most popular drink of 1944."

"Do you know how to make one?" I asked.

"Of course not!" she said, giggling as if she ought to be shocked by the suggestion. "They don't teach us that at Babbington High!"

"Heh-heh-heh," I chuckled urbanely. "Of course they don't, you sweet young thing. I was just wondering how much experience you've had with—sidecars—and that sort of thing."

"Oh, not much. There's always a boy with a flask at parties or dances—you know." She winked in a way that I thought suggested more experience with these boys and their flasks than I might have wished her to have had.

"Ah! I see. Yes, I suppose so. A sidecar. Hm. You know, I make my own version of a sidecar. Will that be all right?"

"Oh, sure."

I made some sort of drink, and she helped, after a fashion, a delightful fashion, stretching to reach glasses on a high shelf, squatting to look into a low cabinet for a shot glass and such, and in the stretching and squatting she found many occasions to display her charms, or at least some of them, including her calves, and even her thighs, when her skirt somehow got caught on a cabinet knob as I was helping her down from a precarious perch.

Her search for the cocktail equipment and supplies required a great deal of pleasant assistance on my part. At times she leaned upon me as an aid to balance, and at other times I was required to grasp her around the waist and lift her to a height where she could see into an upper cabinet. All of this would have been unalloyed pleasure had my conscience not insisted on reminding me that I should not be finding it quite so great a pleasure as I did to have the girl next door here in my house, almost, at times, in my arms.

We took the drinks to the living room. I thought that we would sit in the chairs in front of the fireplace, the obvious and customary place to sit when entertaining a single visitor, but she settled onto the sofa and patted the cushion beside her.

"Come and sit here, Dud," she said. "It's more relaxing."

Relaxing I suppose it may have been for her, but it was awkward for me. Her proximity, the drink that I ought not to have given her, the essay that I would have to help her write—these things made me increasingly uneasy. Relaxing I did not find it. Exciting, yes, agitating, stimulating, arousing; certainly not relaxing.

She actually drank the concoction that I had made. I didn't care for it much, but I sipped at it in my worldly way, humoring this sweet girl who was pretending to a sophistication that she hadn't earned—surely hadn't earned.

"Drink up, Dud," she said. She put her hand on mine and guided the glass to my lips, and I did as she advised, draining the drink.

Swallowing the last of hers, she leaned against me and said, "Don't tell my mom," breathing the request into my face.

"I won't," I said, and as soon as I had said it I was aware that I had crossed a line into a conspiracy that, in my position as friend of the family, trusted adviser, and grown man, I ought never even to have approached. In a moral sense, I was already lost, but to be truthful I must admit to you that I was more concerned about my physical situation: I was in an extreme state of desire. I will try to avoid descending into vulgarity in this account of that night, but in order for you to appreciate fully how I felt with her leaning against me like that, I must tell you that I was as upright and rigid as an oak, or perhaps an ash—one of those sturdy trees that produces the fine hardwoods so prized in cabinetry—and I didn't want the obvious evidence of my desire to frighten or disgust the girl, certainly not to send her running into the night, screaming accusations.

Swallowing hard and buttoning my jacket over my manhood, I said, "Why don't we go up to my study and see what we can do about that essay?"

"Okay," she said. "Let's go."

IN DUDLEY'S STUDY, I seemed to return to myself. I think it was the memory of the hours I had spent there being tutored by him. The subordination I had always felt during those sessions, the inadequacy I'd felt, returned when I entered the room.

"So this is your study!" she said.

"Yeah," I said. "I mean, yes."

She walked around the room, swinging her little hips, poking at things here and there, then stopped at the window and looked out into the darkness.

"That house next door—" she began.

"Your house," I said.

She giggled. "Oh, of course. Of course it's my house. That sidecar went right to my head."

She leaned forward, toward the window—her skirt riding up so that I could see a bit of the backs of her legs above her knees—peered into the darkness, and said, "That window right across the way, what room is that?"

I went to her side and in a friendly, possibly protective way, put my arm around her waist as I leaned in a manner similar to hers to peer into the dark.

"That," I said, my breath catching, "is your bedroom."

She turned away from the window, toward me, and as she turned I relished (and committed to lifelong memory) the brushing caress of her hair, her breasts. Her eyes were teasing.

"Why, Dud," she said. "What exactly do you study up here in your study?"

"Beauty," I said, surprising myself.

"Meaning me?"

"There are nights when I sit here with the lights out just hoping that you will come up to your room."

"Wouldn't you rather I came here to yours?"

"That is more than I have ever allowed myself to hope. You see, hope is sustainable only when its object seems attainable."

"Is that an aphorism?"

"I think it is, and I just made it up, just now."

"And just now, here I am, attainable."

She was looking into my eyes. I was looking into hers. We were breathing deeply, excitedly, our mouths nearly touching, inhaling each other's breath, and then she kissed me, and it was thrilling, but after a single kiss, she drew away from me and looked out the window again, and, as Patti, not Ella, said, "Before we go any further with this, I'd like to meet your mother."

11

An Aside on the Sidecar

ONE AFTERNOON during my work on the preceding chapter, I was cursing my ignorance of the sidecar while Albertine was clipping something from the *Times.* She stopped her work and said, "What's bothering you now?"

"Oh, nothing," I claimed.

"You were muttering under your breath," she pointed out. "What is it?"

"Ahhh, it's this damned sidecar problem," I confessed. "Because I didn't know how to make a sidecar, the drink that Patti and I concocted in 'Testing the Hypothesis, Part 1' bore no resemblance to a sidecar, so I'm not able to use the sidecar in the manner of tea and madeleines to aid me in netting my flitting memories, and the thought keeps nagging at me that if I *had* known how to make a sidecar, and had made actual sidecars that night, I would be able to sip one now and then during my reconstruction of the story of my mother's lunch launch, and the occasional sipping of a sidecar might make my reconstruction more vivid, so I was cursing my ignorance."

"I don't think I can help you there," she said. She extended toward me a coupon that she had clipped. It could be exchanged at a shoe store for two passes to a preview of Luis Villanueva's six-hour one-man show *Me Llamo Sancho,* an evocation of the personal history, adventures, experiences, and observations of Sancho Panza, famous sidekick. "Want to go?" she asked.

"Sure," I said, heading for my workroom.

"By the way," she added, as if it were an unimportant afterthought, "what *is* a sidecar?"

"It's—well—it's a cocktail—"

She raised an eyebrow.

"Damn it!" I said. "I *still* don't know what a sidecar really is!"

"If you don't know how to make a sidecar," she said, in the measured, patient tone probably employed by saints, "how do you know that what you made for Patti *wasn't* a sidecar?"

"I don't," I admitted.

"Come on," she said, opening the hall closet and reaching for her coat. "We're going to go to this shoe store, and then I'll take you somewhere where you can learn all about sidecars."

A couple of hours later, we stopped at a bar called the Silver Hound. "Let's try this," she said. "It looks interesting, a little out of the ordinary."

The bar was dark, and it was empty except for the bartender—a tall red-haired woman with tattoos who was wearing a tight black top and a very short gray skirt—and a pale fellow playing a video game.

The pale fellow called out, "Fuck! I fucked the game! I don't believe it! I fucked the game!" He smacked himself on the forehead, leaned across the bar, accepted a long consolation kiss from the bartender, said, "I gotta go," and left.

The bartender moseyed on down to our end of the bar and asked, "What would you like?" The long consolation kiss came to my mind, but Albertine must have read it, because she shot me a glance that we both know means, "Don't you dare."

I asked, "Can you make a sidecar?"

"Sure," she said, and she shook up a couple right before our eyes (two parts cognac, one part Cointreau, and one part fresh lemon juice, shaken with ice and poured into chilled cocktail glasses). She said as she poured them, "It's happy hour, so you can have another round if you want."

I took a sip. Albertine watched.

"Are you awash in memories?" she asked.

"No," I said. "I guess the drink I made that night really wasn't anything like a sidecar."

"Disappointed?"

"No, not really. At least I know—"

I was distracted by the bartender, who, bored without a barful of barflies, had entered a photo booth at the back of the bar, the kind of booth equipped with a camera that produces a strip of black-and-white pictures.

She hadn't closed the curtain fully, and through the narrow opening I could see her making faces, as people are inspired to do inside those booths, while three flashes went off. Then, just before the fourth and final flash, she stood up and lifted her skirt.

I turned toward Albertine to see what her reaction to this photographic flashing was, but she hadn't seemed to notice it.

"Maybe you should try to reconstruct the drink you did make," she suggested.

Had I actually seen what I thought I saw in the photo booth, or was it just the effect of a sidecar on a guy with a vivid imagination?

"Yeah," I said. "Maybe."

The bartender emerged from the booth, skirt in place, and waited until the strip of pictures dropped from a slot on the side and landed in a hemispherical metal cup. She plucked the strip from the cup, began waving it in the air to dry it, and sashayed back behind the bar. She stuck the strip of pictures into the frame of a mirror there, where, I noticed now, there were others, strips of grinning faces, patrons mugging for the camera after they'd pickled themselves sufficiently to become inspired to mug for a camera and discovered that, thanks to the foresight or experience of the proprietors of the Silver Hound, there was in the back of the room a camera for which to mug.

"Want another round?" she asked.

"Yes," I said, and when she had shaken the drinks and began pouring them I added, "and I'd like to see those pictures."

She pulled the strip from the mirror and held it out for us to see. "The last one's a little naughty," she said, girlishly, as if she might start giggling.

Albertine and I bent over the strip and examined it closely. The first three pictures were like the others stuck around the mirror, but the last little image showed her from waist to mid-thigh, naked. It was a black-and-white picture, of course, but the tone of the grayness of her pubic hair allows me to report with certainty that it matched the red of the hair on her head.

"Yes, it is a little naughty," I said, "but on the whole quite nice." The three of us chuckled amiably.

OUTSIDE, on the way to the theater, with a brace of sidecars in her, Albertine said, "Well, as I predicted, the Silver Hound *was* interesting, and it was a *little* out of the ordinary, and what *I* learned about sidecars was that if you *had* known how to make a sidecar that night with Patti, then the ones you had tonight might or might not have brought the memory back to you, but I will bet you two more pairs of shoes that the *next* time you drink one, you will be transported in memory to the Silver Hound, and you will see in your mind's eye that tiny snapshot of the redheaded bartender's nether parts."

I HAVEN'T TESTED that hypothesis yet, because, to tell you the truth, I found the sidecar too sweet and fruity for my taste, but I'm sure she's right.

12

Not That Kind of Boy (or Girl)

I NEVER ASKED Patti to allow me to walk her home; it was always she who asked me. She would say, "Hey, Peter, come on and walk me home," and sometimes she would add, "My mother loves it when you walk me home."

The shortest way to Patti's house, the route we most often took, began with a walk south along Purlieu Street, where we had an audience of our schoolmates, walking with us or passing us in cars and buses. Many of them had something to say as they went by, and much of what they said was meant to be insulting, but it wasn't insulting enough to make me want to abandon the walks, because it was also thrilling. After all, I was walking with the most desirable little package in Babbington High, and everyone noticed.

When we passed Stillman's delicatessen, we would stop and look at our reflection in the window. Patti would smooth her clothes and hair, and she would usually straighten me up a little, too. When she had me looking the way she wanted me, she would give me a little pat and say, "There. You look nice."

Just beyond the delicatessen, we would slip through a gap in a board fence and slip out of the public eye. We followed a winding path through a scruffy wooded lot, where the ground was uneven, and from time to time I would assist Patti with a touch or an offered hand, which she would accept. When we left the wooded lot, we would walk along the edges of the back yards of three houses occupied by old women with nothing better to do than watch us walk by and cluck their disapproval. Then we would approach Patti's house from the rear, but we would always go around it and enter from the front, because Patti's mother thought it was common to let guests in through the back door.

Patti's mother was always glad to see me, and once, after I had left and was walking around the side of the house on my way home, I heard her exclaim, "What a nice boy he is! Just the kind of boy a mother wants her daughter to bring home."

On my way from Patti's to my house that afternoon, walking back along the path through the wooded lot, I tried to read its litter as an archeologist would, looking at the beer cans and cigarette packages and condom wrappers for some sign that would tell me whether this was a place where Patti's charms had been bestowed, had been enjoyed. I couldn't tell. When I reached Stillman's, I looked at myself reflected in the window, in my corduroy pants and checked shirt, and I thought that I might as well be wearing a sign that said Nice Harmless Little Boy.

By the time I reached home I was thoroughly depressed. I didn't want to be that kind of boy, and I comforted myself by telling myself that really, deep down, in the secret recesses of my heart, I wasn't that kind of boy at all.

ON THE DAY WHEN Patti walked *me* home for the first time, we didn't pass Stillman's deli, since I lived in the opposite direction, but we did pass the Babbington Heights Florist Shop, and we stopped there to look at ourselves in the window. I was stunned by what I saw. There was something about seeing us standing there side by side and being on the way home, to my house, to introduce Patti to my mother, that made me think I could see Patti as my mother would see her. My jaw dropped; my eyes popped. I looked her up and down, and I looked her up and down again.

"What's with these looks you're giving me?" she asked my reflection.

I couldn't tell her that I feared that everything about her that appealed to me was going to scare the living daylights out of my mother, so I said, "It's—I'm just—"

"Yeah?"

"I think my mother—look—I—"

"You think I look like your mother?"

"No! I—"

"You don't want me to meet your mother, do you?"

"What? What makes you think—"

"You don't want your mother to meet me."

She looked down at the sidewalk. Her feet, in sexy little black boots that came to her ankles, were pressed together, side by side. She held her arms straight down with her fists clenched. Her brow was furrowed, and she was pouting.

"I know what they say about me," she said. She turned toward me, and there was a tear in her eye. "You know what they say about me, don't you? 'She's not the kind of girl you'd take home to meet your mother,' that's what they say." She raised her head high and stuck out her chin. "But I'm not that kind of girl," she claimed. "I'm not the kind of girl you wouldn't take home to meet your mother."

She turned back toward the florist's window. So did I. We both inspected her reflection.

"Am I?" she asked softly.

"No," I said, although she might as well have been wearing a sign that said SLUT. "Come on." I took her hand, and we held hands all the way to my house, and all that way I was hoping that my mother might not be at home when we got there and hoping that what I hoped didn't show.

13

The Nut and the Slut, Together at Last

WHEN WE REACHED MY HOUSE, I headed for the back door, as I always did when I came home from school. I went up the back steps to the tiny stoop and turned to find that Patti was standing at the foot of the steps looking hurt.

"What's the matter?" I asked.

"Do you want me to use the back door?"

"No!" I said, realizing how matters looked to her. "Of course not. I'm going to go in this way and open the front door for you. Okay?"

"Okay," she said, and with a smile she bounced off toward the front of the house.

I let myself into the kitchen and discovered my mother sitting at the dining room table where I had seen her weeping not many days before. This was not a good sign. She was bent over some papers on the table; I couldn't tell what she was doing, but I didn't like the implications of her posture; it suggested sorrow and despair. I decided to tell Patti that we were going to have to put the meeting off, and I was making my way through the kitchen toward the front door—well, sneaking through the kitchen toward the front door—when my mother looked up and called out to me in a voice full of hope and joy, "Peter! You're finally home! Come here! I've had a wonderful idea!"

"I—uh—brought somebody with me—from school," I said, extending my hand vaguely in the direction of the front door.

"Really? Who is it?"

"It's a girl named Patti."

"Patti?" said my mother, trying the name out to see whether it belonged to anyone she knew. "Patti," she repeated, trying it again, and this time her eyes widened and her eyebrows shot up. "Patti *Fiorenza*?" she asked.

"Um, yes," I said, not entirely surprised that my mother should know who Patti was. Why shouldn't her fame, her reputation, have reached my mother, after all, if all the other people in Babbington knew her, or knew about her, or thought they did?

"Wow," she said. "Where is she?"

"Waiting at the front door."

"Well, don't leave her standing there, Peter. She'll think we're talking about her."

"We are talking about her."

"Go let her in!"

I went to the front door and opened it. Patti was waiting there, looking wary.

"You were talking about me, weren't you?" she said, frowning.

"No—we—my mother had one of her ideas—and—I should tell you about these ideas—I mean I should warn you—"

"Do you think I should go home?" she asked.

"No," I said. "Of course not, but—"

From over my shoulder came my mother's voice, calling out "Patti Fiorenza!" as if she'd been wanting to meet Patti for a very long time. "Come in! Come in!" I stepped aside, and Patti stepped across the threshold. My mother was holding both hands out toward her, and Patti grasped them. With a hand on Patti's shoulder, my mother led her through the kitchen to the dining room. I followed. "Sit down!" my mother said. Patti sat, and I sat, too.

My mother looked Patti over—stared at her, really, looking for clues, I thought. "I've heard so much about you!" she said, with something like awe in her voice.

"It's not true," said Patti. "Honest."

"It couldn't be," said my mother. She paused as if she'd startled herself, considered what she'd said, and added, "Not all of it, anyway."

I wondered what she meant by that. What had she heard about Patti, and which parts of what she'd heard did she not believe?

"Everybody thinks I'm a slut," said Patti, "but—"

"And everybody thinks I'm a nut," said my mother, "*but*—"

They burst out laughing, like schoolgirls who fall into a fit of giggling over an invisible something like a puff of wind.

"I think it was the candy that did it," said my mother, with the short sharp nod of one who has come to a firm opinion after giving a matter some thought. "The lace candy. That convinced them. Ella's nuts. Nutty as a fruitcake."

"My mom bought some," said Patti.

"I remember that," said my mother.

"For me, it was that famous blow job," said Patti with a frown and a shake of her head. "Dennis Jarvis! He was the one. He told half the town that I gave him a blow job in the woods behind Stillman's delicatessen."

"But you didn't?" asked my mother.

"Only in his dreams," said Patti, and she and my mother burst out laughing again.

This conversation was making me very uncomfortable. Patti Fiorenza was sitting at my dining room table chewing her gum, winking and pouting, and chatting with my mother about a blow job; my mother was waving her cigarette in the air as she spoke, pushing her hair askew, and giggling like a girl. Did they really have to do such a good job of playing the slut and the nut? And how on earth could my mother possibly know what a blow job was?

To change the subject, I picked up one of the papers from the table and asked, "What's this?"

They looked at me, and then at each other, and fell against each other, shrieking with laughter, astonished to discover that I was still there.

14
An Aside on Blow

THE ENGLISH LANGUAGE is a distributive language, one that conveys meaning partly through the distribution of discrete words within a sentence, as distinguished from synthetic languages, such as Latin, in which the forms of the words themselves contribute more to the grammatical component of meaning than does their placement within a sentence. Because English is also a singularly acquisitive language, its lexical corpus contains many words borrowed from other languages, including the synthetic ones (borrowed in the way that a neighbor "borrows" your hedge clippers and returns them, if ever, only years later, after they have been nicked, battered, bent, and otherwise neighborized almost beyond recognition). As a result, modern English has many pairs of nearly synonymous words with one member that is homegrown or, to use a borrowed word, native, and the other borrowed from a synthetic language.

Among these adoptive siblings are many pairs in which an Anglo-Saxon verb composed of a base word and a separable particle is matched with a Latinate verb composed of a root form and an inseparable affix. The affix may be a prefix, such as *in-*, or a suffix, such as *-ize*. The particle is a small word, such as *up* or *off*, that resembles a preposition but does not function as a preposition in a sentence. Like the sidecar on a motorcycle, the affix is bound to the Latin root to which it is attached and cannot stand on its own. The English base-and-particle combination, sometimes called a phrasal verb, is more flexible. Within a sentence the particle may be separated from the base by other words; the particle functions not like a sidecar but like a sidekick, an associate of secondary de-

gree, a squire who ordinarily rides beside his knight but can, if required to
do so, move a few words away without falling down.

Consider *inflate,* which came into English from Latin, arriving in in-
flected form, with the prefix *in-* an integral part of it. The older English
equivalent, closer to Anglo-Saxon, is the phrasal verb *blow up,* which en-
dures, of course. Notice that the particle *up* is a separable element:

> That odd little man actually inflated a dog. I tell you he blew it up,
> right before my very eyes!

We would not say "blew up it," because we recognize that *up* is a part of
the verb, the equivalent of a suffix, not a preposition; *up* has no object of
its own, but *blew up* does have an object, *it.* The object stands in the sentence like a tree in a path, but since the root and particle are separable,
they move to either side and pass it by.

So we arrive at *fellatio.* The Anglo-Saxon equivalent is *blow job.* The
corresponding verbs are *fellate* and *blow,* the former a back-formation
from *fellatio* and the latter the surviving base word of a phrasal verb, *blow
off,* soldiering on without its particle. Neither appeared in print until relatively recently. Hugh Rawson, in *Wicked Words: A Treasury of Curses,
Insults, Put-Downs, and Other Formerly Unprintable Terms from Anglo-
Saxon Times to the Present,* cites as the earliest reference to their use a
1939 glossary of prostitutes' and criminals' argots in which the phrasal
verb *blow (someone) off* is defined as "to hold intercourse through the
mouth." It seems reasonable to assume that *blow* in this sense was established in the vernacular long before it appeared in print, and that *blow job*
came into oral use soon after *blow* did, but Rawson found no citation for it
until the 1975 *Dictionary of American Slang*—with one exception.

The exception was an entry in the 1953 *Thesaurus of American Slang.*
There *blow job* was defined as "jet plane," a definition illustrated by a
passage from the July 26, 1945, issue of the *San Francisco Examiner*: "A
P-59 jet-propelled Airacomet, affectionately called the 'blow job' by flyers, will make several flights . . . in 1946."

Dawson characterizes this definition as "then-current, now-archaic."
Oh, sure. I would be willing to bet that it was a joke. Picture this: One
night, we come upon a flock of flyers sitting in a bar getting confidential

over a few beers, trying to find the words to tell one another how they feel when they open the throttle on that P-59, and one of them, franker or drunker than the others, says something like, "I can't describe it, but I swear it's as good as a blow job." The rest of them crack up, laughing like high school boys in a locker room, over a joke that they can't share with anyone who hasn't experienced both a blow job and the thrust of a jet at full throttle. In time, the usage spreads among those in the know. When the flyers use their private expression in the presence of an inquiring reporter from the *Examiner* and see that he *doesn't get it,* that he jots it down, all earnestness and incomprehension, they snort and snigger (and the reporter, hearing them snort and snigger, scribbles "affectionately" on his pad), and a day or two later, when they see *blow job* appear in print, they fall against one another, roaring with the laughter that we use for something a little naughty.

I sympathize with the naive reporter from the *Examiner,* because when I first heard *blow* used in its sexual sense my own inexperience led me to misinterpret it. I recall hearing, in a whispered exchange in a locker room, "she blew me." Something in the attitude of the whisperers, some sniggering or a glance around to see if anyone was listening, was enough to make me realize that the reference was to a sex act, and some contextual clue that I no longer remember made me understand that it was oral-genital sex, but how it was performed I did not know. In my ignorance I came to imagine that "she blew me" was the equivalent of "she blew me up." I supposed that when, someday, I got blown, a girl would put my penis to her mouth like the neck of a balloon and inflate it. My penis was, I well knew, an erectile organ; apparently, on the evidence of this overheard remark, it was inflatable, too, though mine had never yet been blown up. Perhaps, when that girl, whoever she might turn out to be, had inflated it as far as she dared, she would release it, and the air—her breath—would be expelled in a great exhalation, a rushing sough of pleasure, like the hot gas blown out the back of a P-59.

15
Afflatus, Part 2

INT. THE LEROY FAMILY DINING ROOM. DAY. ELLA PIPER LEROY,
her son, PETER LEROY, and his sexy schoolmate PATTI
FIORENZA are seated at the dining table. Ella and Patti
have been laughing like schoolgirls. Now they clear their
throats, giggle a bit, and try to pull themselves together.

> PETER
>
> (repeating himself,
> indicating some papers on
> the table)

What's this?

Ella sweeps the papers from the table onto her lap so that
Peter and Patti can't see them.

> ELLA
>
> (coyly)

These are part of my idea, but I
don't want you to see them just
yet because I want to tell you
all about the rest of it first.
The boat can wait.

> PETER
>
> (raising an eyebrow)

The boat?

> ELLA

The boat, yes. I'll get to it.

>   Oh, I've had such a wonderful
>   idea, and I want to tell you all
>   about it, but I don't know quite
>   where to start. Let me see . . .

Absently, thinking about where to start her story, she gets
up and goes to the kitchen.

>   ELLA (CONT'D.)
>   I was sitting in the dining room,
>   just daydreaming . . .

She opens the refrigerator and takes a platter from it. On
the platter are sandwiches in many colors -- some made of
pink bread with green filling, others of blue bread with
orange filling, and so on. The colors are pale, like
pastels, not vivid.

>   ELLA (CONT'D.)
>   (dreamily)
>   . . . thinking about how nice it
>   would be to give a party -- a
>   really smart party, with
>   interesting people, a cocktail
>   party -- and somehow I got the
>   idea of making tiny sandwiches on
>   colored bread.

She brings the platter to the dining room table.

>   ELLA (CONT'D.)
>   (indicating the platter of
>   sandwiches)
>   Have one.

Peter and Patti lean over the platter to inspect the
sandwiches. They exchange a look. Then each takes a
sandwich and takes a bite from it.

>   ELLA (CONT'D.)
>   (her eyes widening)
>   The idea just came to me . . .

>   DISSOLVE TO:

Magazine advertisement for Tintoretto's Tasteful Tints food
coloring. The headline is "You Can Color More Than Eggs,

You Know!" spoken by a comical cartoon chicken. The copy
reads "They come in three tasteful colors, but you can't
taste them at all!" The artwork shows a box holding vials
of red, yellow, and green food coloring, and, in the
foreground, a platter of muffins, cookies, and sliced bread
in various colors. To one side, a domestic scene is
depicted: a trim housewife, dressed for a cocktail party,
holds a platter of pastel treats of some unidentifiable
kind, offering them to a smiling man in a suit who may be
her husband. On the floor behind them are two children, a
boy and a girl, giggling behind their hands at a cat they
have tinted pink. The tag line is "There's a rainbow in
every box! Be creative!"

> ELLA (CONT'D., V.O.)
>
> . . . wherever ideas come from.
> Out of the air, I guess.

CUT TO:

THE DINING ROOM. Ella picks up a sandwich and inspects it
critically.

> ELLA (CONT'D.)
>
> I didn't have any little bread
> pans, so I used muffin tins.

> PATTI
>
> (impressed)
>
> Very creative.

> ELLA
>
> (peeling the sandwich
> apart)
>
> And the filling . . . do you know
> what it is?

> PATTI
>
> (considering)
>
> Well, they all look different.

> PETER
>
> (with his mouth full)
>
> But they all <u>taste</u> like cream
> cheese.

DISSOLVE TO:

Magazine advertisement for Bland & White Brand Cream
Cheese. Headline: "Nature's Most Flexible Food." Copy: "You
can spread it, squeeze it, mix it, shape it, even tint it!"
The artwork shows a rectangular red-and-white box of Bland
& White Brand Cream Cheese, and, below it, a row of small
drawings of chefs using it. The first is spreading it on
toast, the second squeezing it from a pastry tube onto a
cracker, the third pouring chopped chives into a bowl of
it, the fourth rolling little balls of it in chopped nuts,
and the fifth pouring red food coloring into a bowl of it.
The tag line is: "It's bland. It's white. It's putty in
your hands! Be creative!"

> ELLA (V.O.)
>
> They <u>are</u> all cream cheese! I
> colored it with Tasteful Tints!
>
> PATTI (V.O.)
>
> What a great idea!

CUT TO:

THE DINING ROOM.

> ELLA
>
> (shrugging, beaming)
>
> I don't know where I get these
> ideas. They just come to me.
>
> PATTI
>
> (awed)
>
> It's amazing.
>
> ELLA
>
> (puzzled at first)
>
> Isn't it? But just wait till you
> hear what happened next! I was
> sitting here sampling the little
> sandwiches and daydreaming of
> myself at that cocktail party --
>
> PATTI
>
> What were you wearing?

                    ELLA
          A white satin dress.
                    PATTI
          Slinky?
                    ELLA
          Mmm.
                    PATTI
          That's very smart.
                    ELLA
          I was sipping champagne and
          holding a long cigarette holder
          and after a while I realized an
          amazing thing.
                    PATTI
               (all ears)
          What?
                    ELLA
          I was on a ship.

                                        DISSOLVE TO:
          A series of what look like clips from romantic movies of
          the 1930s and 1940s, set on ocean liners.
                    ELLA (CONT'D., V.O.)
               (dreamily)
          In my daydream, I was on a ship.
          A MAN in a dinner jacket pours champagne for a woman in a
          long, slinky white satin dress who is nibbling daintily at
          a little sandwich; the woman is Ella, but we don't see the
          man's face.
                    ELLA (CONT'D., V.O.)
          An ocean liner.

                                        DISSOLVE TO:
          Ella and the unidentifiable man lean on a railing and watch
          the rippling moonlight on the waves; now and then they take
          bites from little sandwiches.

ELLA (CONT'D., V.O.)

There were women in white satin
gowns. And men in tuxedos.

DISSOLVE TO:

Ella and the unidentifiable man whirl effortlessly around a
dance floor; a waiter approaches them with a silver platter
of little sandwiches.

ELLA (CONT'D., V.O.)

And romance.

DISSOLVE TO:

Ella and the unidentifiable man kiss, silhouetted against
an impossibly large full moon.

ELLA (CONT'D., V.O.)

And little sandwiches.

DISSOLVE TO:

The unidentifiable man produces a little sandwich and feeds
a bite to Ella, who in turn produces a little sandwich and
feeds a bite to him.

ELLA (CONT'D., V.O.)

(still dreamily)

And for a while I imagined that I
was on a ship like that . . .

(now matter-of-factly)

. . . then you came home,
Peter . . .

The film stutters as if something has gone wrong with
Ella's mental projector. It freezes on one frame, and the
projector lamp begins to melt a hole in it.

CUT TO:

THE DINING ROOM.

ELLA (CONT'D.)

. . . and I snapped out of it.

Patti gives Peter a disapproving look, as if he had
deliberately turned his mother's dreams to dust. Peter
shrugs his shoulders and returns a look that says "Gee
whiz, Patti, it wasn't my fault."

                    ELLA (CONT' D.)

               (brightly)

          But it doesn' t matter, because I
          know how to make the dream come
          true.

                    PATTI

               (hopefully)

          You do?

Instead of responding, Ella simply smiles, her eyes
twinkling, and produces the papers with a flourish. She
spreads them out on the table. They are drawings of a boat
and sketches for advertisements, and one advertisement is
nearly complete. It is clearly inspired by art deco
advertising for transatlantic steamship lines. The headline
is "Ella' s Elegant Excursions."

                    PATTI

               (dreamily running her
               finger over the words)

          Ella' s Elegant Excursions.

                    ELLA

          So, my idea is that maybe you
          can' t go on an ocean voyage, but
          we can take you on a <u>bay</u> voyage
          . . .

                    PETER

               (warily)

          "We"?

                    PATTI

               (impatiently)

          Shush.

                    ELLA

          . . . and you can have champagne
          and moonlight and dancing and
          romance . . . and little
          sandwiches.

She has finished. A silence falls over them. Patti sighs,

lost in Ella's romantic dream. Peter looks doubtful. Ella
looks from one to the other. At last she speaks:

>   ELLA
>
>   (tentatively)
>
>   Well, what do you think?
>
>   PATTI
>
>   (in the deferential,
>   awestruck manner of a
>   sidekick)
>
>   I think that is really inflated,
>   blown up big and round.
>
>   ELLA (puzzled)
>
>   Inflated?
>
>   PATTI
>
>   (as one who knows)
>
>   It means it's good. Very good.
>
>   ELLA
>
>   (hopefully)
>
>   Peter?
>
>   PETER
>
>   (a pause, and then, to
>   please her)
>
>   Blown up like a blimp. Lighter
>   than air.
>
>   ELLA
>
>   (delighted)
>
>   Isn't it just amazing the way so
>   many things come together to make
>   an idea?
>
>   PATTI
>
>   It's more than amazing. It's a
>   gas!

16
To-Do, Undone

FOR A MOMENT THERE, while we were sitting at the dining room table, right after my mother turned to me to find out what I thought of the plan, in that moment when I paused before telling her that I thought that her idea was blown up like a blimp, lighter than air, we were, the three of us, at a point somewhere on the metaphorical bay voyage of our lives from which we might follow either of two courses, leading toward alternative versions of the next few months of our collective future. I had understood what my mother had meant by "Peter?" though the terms in which I had understood what she had meant would not have been the terms in which she would have expressed herself, since they were technical terms, shibboleths of teenage Babbington that she neither knew nor understood. In those terms, she had meant, "Peter, are you going to join me and my delectable new sidekick Patti in an attempt to inflate the particular dog I have chosen to inflate, or are you going to stick a pin in the poor pup before we even get started, so that our dream dog will lie limp and ugly at our feet like a deflated gas bag, brought to earth before it ever had a chance to rise and float?"

Knowing what she meant by "Peter?" what should I have done? I might have . . .

- prepared a profit-and-loss analysis for the enterprise;
- calculated the investment that would be required to get it under way;
- stopped looking over at Patti to see what she wanted me to do;

- conducted a telephone survey to find out how many Babbingtonians were out there longing for moonlight cruises to East
  Hargrove and back;
- held a taste test to find out whether people enjoyed eating little
  pastel cream cheese sandwiches;
- stood up suddenly and enacted a scene in which I played the
  part of my mother trying to explain this project to my father, a
  performance that, had I had the nerve to embark on it, would
  almost certainly have put the kibosh on the whole thing then
  and there;
- sought the advice of knowledgeable experts, such as business-
  men, heads of steamship lines, restaurateurs, tuxedo-rental
  agents, and food colorists;
- avoided visualizing the business as if it were a movie, a romantic comedy in which I played the male lead, saved all hands
  when heavy weather hit, sang quite well, and got the girl;
- avoided trying to convince myself that the sandwiches were
  pretty tasty;
- found out how much champagne cost;
- avoided picturing myself feeding little sandwiches to Patti;
- avoided picturing Patti in a slinky white satin dress, illuminated
  by the pale light of a summer moon, woo-hoo, woo-hoo-hoo;
- looked at the entire undertaking from my father's point of
  view, considering whether it was likely to succeed as a way of
  making money and not just as a way of making my mother's
  dream come true;
- estimated the cash flow;
- calculated the return on investment;
- listed potential investors;
- prepared a good story for the investors, a story that would
  blind them to all the venture's obvious faults, a narrative of
  possibility that would convince them that they had better than
  a snowball's chance in hell of seeing a return on their investment, in real money;
- visited those potential investors and taken a shot at pulling the

wool over their eyes to see if it could be done, to see if we
could do it;

- persuaded my mother to at least consider alternatives to pastel
cream cheese on pastel bread;
- not allowed myself to give in to the desire to do whatever it
took to see that my mother got what she wanted from Ella's
Elegant Excursions, got whatever she needed to make her the
captain of her fate, got this chance to chart her own course, to
become Elegant Ella;
- avoided picturing Patti in tiny shorts and a halter top, polishing
the brass and cooing over the masterly way I manned the
wheel;
- based my decision on hard facts, cold hard facts;
- found out how much we would have to spend on a boat;
- run ads in the *Babbington Reporter* to find out how many
excursionists we were likely to attract before spending a dime
on anything else;
- found out what we were going to have to pay in fees for
licenses or permits;
- found out which town officials would require bribes and how
much they would want;
- investigated our competition in the business of meeting
Babbingtonians' perceived need for romance in their lives;
- poured hot wax into my ears to muffle the siren call of my
mother's dream and steered a cautious course;
- not been so darned eager to please my mother's delectable new
sidekick.

I suppose I should have done all of that, but my mother's hope was
infectious, and Patti and I had caught it from her. It was so pleasant an
illness that the three of us just sat there for a while, grinning. Then we
pulled ourselves together and went out to buy a boat.

17
Persuading Captain Mac

CAPTAIN MACOMANGUS'S classified ad in the *Babbington Reporter* said

> Unfortunate circumstances force me to sell the most beautiful boat presently afloat. Captain Macomangus, Bay Way, Babbington.

Bay Way was a stub of a street that ran from Bolotomy Road to a canal that led to the bay. There was only one house there, a tiny white one that had to be Captain Macomangus's. A low white picket fence surrounded a front yard no bigger than my bedroom at home. Rambling roses grew along the fence.

My mother brought the car to a stop in front of the house, but she left the motor running. I was sitting in the back seat, and Patti was riding in the front passenger's seat, the sidekick's seat. A fine drizzle had begun to drift lazily down from the gray sky, and a chill was in the air.

"It's like a doll's house," said my mother.

"Yes," said Patti, exhaling the word, pressing her nose to the window like a girl in front of a toy store. Her breath condensed as a circle of dew.

"Do you think he's home?" my mother asked.

"I don't know," I said, "but I'll find out."

I walked to the front gate, which came no higher than my knees. I swung the gate open, and in two strides reached the front door. A length of string extended from a hole beside the door, and I pulled it. I heard a

tiny tinkling sound from inside, as if I'd rung a bell made of glass. I waited for someone to come to the door, but no one did. I rang twice more,
and when no one answered the third ring, I returned to the car.

"I guess he's not home," I said.

"He's looking out the window," Patti whispered. "I saw him. He looks
kind of frightened. Maybe he thinks we're burglars."

I looked over my shoulder and caught a glimpse of a man watching
from behind a raised curtain. Then the curtain fell and he withdrew.

"Come with me," I said to Patti and my mother. "Maybe he'll feel better if he can see all of us, instead of having you in the car." Together, we
went to the door, and this time I knocked.

"Hello!" I called. "Anybody home?"

The door opened a couple of inches, and a short man with a worried
look peered out at us.

"I guess you didn't hear the bell," I said.

"I heard it," said the man, "but I thought you might go away."

"Go away?"

"Most of 'em go away, if I just wait 'em out."

"Who?"

"People who come about my *Arcinella.*"

"Who's *Arcinella?*"

"My boat."

"But your boat is for sale, isn't it?"

"Maybe," he said. "Maybe not."

"Aren't you Captain Macomag—" I tried, consulting the advertisement in the *Reporter.*

"Yep, that's me," he said. "Cap'n Mac."

"Did you place this ad for the boat?"

"Yep."

"Well, then we'd like to see it," I said. "My mother and I and—" I saw
an opportunity to give myself a harmless thrill, so I took it. "—my girlfriend."

"Don't get carried away," muttered Patti.

"Sorry," said Captain Mac, eyes downcast.

"You mean we can't see the boat?" I asked.

"I just don't want a lot of strangers poking around my *Arcinella.*"

"There are only three of us," I said, "and we'll be really careful."

"I—I just don't think I want to sell her to you," he said.

"What's wrong with us?" I asked, hurt.

"Nothing's wrong with you," he said gently, "It's just that, well, maybe I don't want to sell my *Arcinella* at all."

"But you advertised it—her," I said.

"I did, but I don't see as how that obligates me to sell her. I've had a change of heart."

"At least let us see *Arcinella*," I said, "after we drove all the way down here."

"Maybe some other time," he said.

He began closing the door, but I put my foot in the opening, as door-to-door salesmen were said to do under similar circumstances. I turned away from Captain Mac and gave Patti and my mother a wink. "Can't we at least come inside so that the ladies won't have to stand in the rain?" I asked the captain.

"Oh, my goodness!" he said, apparently quite embarrassed to realize that he had forgotten his manners in his anxiety over the fate of *Arcinella*. "Of course you can come in. Get in out of the rain and dry off and I'll make you some tea."

So Captain Mac took us in. He fussed over us. He made tea for us. He told us stories about *Arcinella*, stories about himself, stories about bygone days in old Babbington, and legends of life on the bay. He told us, several times, that he considered *Arcinella* the most beautiful boat afloat, and his eyes grew misty when he told us that his age and failing health meant that he really did have to sell her, and finally, after nearly an hour, he allowed us to persuade him to let us have a look at her. By then, we had persuaded ourselves that *Arcinella* had to be ours.

18

Oo, Oo, Oo, What a Little Moonlight Can Do

IF YOU'RE TAKING NOTES, jot this down: never buy a boat while you are under the beguiling influence of moonlight. Captain Mac kept us in his tiny house, telling us stories and delaying the moment when he finally gave in to our pleas to see *Arcinella* until the clouds had begun to part picturesquely and moonlight shone on the narrow path that led from the end of Bay Way through some cattail rushes to the canal. The path was so narrow that we could walk it only in single file. Captain Mac stood to one side and suggested that my mother should go first, followed by Patti, followed by me, with himself last. As a result, my mother saw the moonlit boat first, alone, and became a victim of the phenomenon known as love at first sight. Patti might have been less susceptible to the phenomenon if she hadn't found my mother already beguiled, and I might have been able to play the part of the rational and dispassionate cynic if I hadn't arrived to find the two women I most wanted to please cooing and mooning and all but swooning over *Arcinella,* a luminous vision floating on the silver water, her wet deck glistening.

Only after the moonlight and *Arcinella*'s graceful lines had done their work did Captain Mac join us and ask, unnecessarily, "Isn't she a beauty?"

"She is," we breathed.

"Of course, beauty is only skin deep," he said. We clucked and frowned as if he'd insulted our *Arcinella.* "I suppose you'll want to take a look at her innards, poke her and prod her, give her a good going over." He made it sound obscene.

"Oh, I don't know," said my mother, gently.

"That's what the other people said they were planning to do, give her a good going over."

"Other people?" asked my mother.

"The people who looked at her before you."

"You didn't mention anybody—"

"They'll be back first thing tomorrow—bringing somebody who really knows boats—"

"Oh," said my mother, and then, brightening, she announced, incredibly, "Peter knows boats."

"Does he, now?" said Captain Mac.

"Some," I said, exaggerating.

"Well, then, I expect you'll want to get into her," he said, with a be-my-guest gesture that, it occurs to me now when I recall it, might have been ironic and patronizing.

"Right," I said.

I stepped aboard, made my way gingerly along the deck to the cabin, fumbled with the latch, and crouched to crawl through the opening that led below, into the dark. I found myself on a narrow planked way laid over the ribs of the hull. The air down there was dank, and it smelled of dead clams, sea water, motor oil, and gasoline. I couldn't see much, but that didn't really matter, since I had no idea what to look for. I spent some time running my hands over *Arcinella*'s engine and wiggling its wires and belts. Then I began inching forward, picking up whatever I found and putting it back down, making as much noise as I could to show that I was on the job. I'm certain that Patti and my mother wouldn't have considered *Arcinella*'s innards beautiful, but I could tell that the space below decks would be a fine place for a boy to go to work.

When I came to a porthole, I looked through it and saw Patti and my mother standing on the bulkhead, side by side, gazing at the boat and talking in low tones. They had their heads together, and from the blissful looks they wore I could tell that they were praising *Arcinella*'s attributes and dreaming. In the moonlight, it was easy to join their dream, to sign on as lad of all work—cabin boy, waiter, busboy, it didn't matter—and it was easy to imagine the lazy hours the lad would pass in the company of Elegant Ella's sexy sidekick, who would probably, in her role as hostess, wear a very revealing low-cut satin gown. Even Captain Mac looked good in the moonlight, puffing on a corncob pipe, squinting with the gruff but kindly look of a simple, honest old salt. I could give all of these people what they wanted with a single word, even a wordless gesture, a thumbs-up, a nod of the head, even the right kind of smile.

I'd been below long enough. I pushed the hatch upward and rose from the hold. My mother and Patti laughed and applauded.

"Very dramatic, Peter," said my mother.

No one said anything while I made my way back onto the bulkhead. Then, with a nervous grin, my mother asked, "Well?"

I glanced at her. I glanced at Patti. Why not? How much could possibly be wrong with the boat, after all? If she had served Captain Mac so well for so long, standing up to the demands of clamming, she should find life easy with us. I smiled and nodded, and they threw their arms around me and hugged me as if I had just given *Arcinella* to them as a gift. In a blissful blur, I watched my mother write a check to Captain Mac, who wished us luck and left. For a while we stood there smiling in triumph, but then, with a start, my mother said, "I haven't made dinner."

We got into the car and started for home. Somewhere along the way, clouds drifted in again and hid the moon, and we began to have our doubts.

19

Morphology and Aesthetics of Clam Boats

A BOAT FOR HARVESTING CLAMS from the bays and basins of
coastal waters must have a hull with a shallow draft; a deck that is flat and
unobstructed; a cabin; and a hold. Those are the essentials (and they also
apply to boats for harvesting scallops or oysters).

The expanse of unobstructed deck should extend entirely around the
boat so that the clamdigger can work from every side, manipulating the
tongs or rake on the bottom to dislodge and raise the clams. There can be
no railing of the type that would prevent passengers from falling overboard or against which romantics could lean when murmuring sweet
nothings and watching the moonlight play on the rippling water, since
such a railing would impede the digger's action, but there should be a low
rail, just a strip of wood running around the perimeter of the deck to prevent the harvested clams from slipping off the deck and into the water.

The cabin should be small. It must provide protection from the ele-
ments, but it must not be comfortable, for if it is comfortable, the digger
who has retreated to it for shelter from the heat of the summer sun or the
stinging bite of winter's icy blasts may be unwilling to leave it and return
to the work, which is tiring and tiresome; or, having in his cozy cabin a
place to think, he may conclude that he's a lonely mite in a world that
cares not one whit what becomes of him and fall into inconsolable despair, making him emotionally incapable of returning to the work or, finding the cabin such a comfy place to relax, he may invite women aboard,
and they will probably distract him from the work; and this is a boat that
is made for work.

There should be a hold, where the clams can be put out of the summer sun so that they don't get steamed before they reach the table. The hold isn't strictly required, though; the captain of a very small clam boat (who is captain and crew in one handy package), having no hold, is likely to keep the clams cool by throwing buckets of bay water over them now and then.

The simplest way to provide the essentials of a clam boat is to build a scow, a rectangular flat-bottomed boat with sloping ends. (See Figures 1 and 2 on page 82.) Add a shack as a cabin, and you've got a clam boat. It's not hard to build such a boat, nor is it expensive. A person can build one of these clam boats in his back yard, and many have. You could. It does the job, and it's cheap, but it's a graceless thing. Even if the builder gives the various rectangles the classic proportions of the golden section, the result is still a stack of boxes.

There is no need for a clam boat to be beautiful, yet some are. If you had visited Babbington when I was a boy, you would have seen some clam boats different from those boxy utilitarian scows, a curvaceous bunch of boats, curvy not because someone thought that curves would make them beautiful or sexy, but because they had originally been designed to sail. *Arcinella* was one of these. (See Figures 3 and 4 on page 83.)

If a clam boat can be said to be beautiful, *Arcinella* was a beauty, though she was no longer young. She had a past, which we knew, or thought we knew, from Captain Mac. Long ago, she had been under sail, a working boat, carrying goods from one town on Bolotomy Bay to another, but when sail gave way to power, and shipping by water gave way to shipping overland, *Arcinella* was abandoned, a casualty of progress. She spent the war years in a shallow backwater of the Bolotomy River, anonymously settling into the muck, and when Captain Mac's father found her she was well on her way to becoming a rotting hulk. He bought her for next to nothing and transformed her from sail to power, from shipping to clamming. He pulled her from the water, and in Leech's Boat Yard he removed her mast and rigging, cut her keel down and rebuilt her bottom to give her a very shallow draft so that she could float in the shoals of the bay's clam flats without scraping her hull. He installed a six-cylinder engine from a 1946 Studebaker Champion, driving her prop through the first and reverse gears of the car's transmission. According to Captain Mac, his father had undertaken the project with the intention of

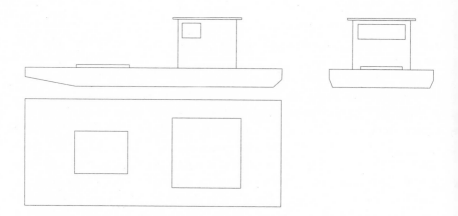

FIG. 1. My sketch of a basic clam boat, a scow.

FIG. 2. The scow is such a simple and obvious design for a clam boat that it is nearly universal; this picture of an oyster boat, which Albertine snapped last year in a settlement of shellfisherfolk along the inner edge of the Bassin d'Arcachon on the Atlantic coast of France, could have been taken in Babbington when I was a boy, except that the clam boats of Babbington were gray and the oyster boats of Arcachon were as colorful as my mother's little pastel sandwiches.

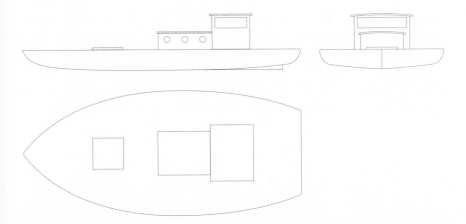

FIG. 3. My sketch of *Arcinella,* from memory.

FIG. 4. A clam boat with some of *Arcinella*'s attributes, photographed near Babbington. (The devices on a rack above the cabin are tongs for harvesting clams from the bay.)

selling *Arcinella,* but when he looked her over and saw what he had wrought, he was struck by the beauty of her, seduced by the beauty of her. Stripped down, without her mast and rigging, the lines of her hull and the gentle curve of her gunwales showed to better advantage than ever before. She was sturdy and stable, broad in the beam, solid but graceful, a beauty. The Galatea effect kicked in. He kept her.

20
Inflated by Beauty

MY DIFFICULTIES with the meanings of *blow* were compounded by a local Babbingtonian teenage slang term derived from it, *blow up,* which meant "amaze and delight" with a touch of "impress." Something that blew one up came unexpectedly, brought pleasure, and affected one strongly enough to make one expect that it would leave a lasting memory.

Variations emerged, as you would expect. *Inflate* became a more elegant, learned, and formal synonym; so, while one might say of the doo-wop tune "Trickle, Trickle" by the Videos, "that blows me up," one might say of the duettino "Viens, Mallika," in act one of Delibes's *Lakmé,* "it inflates me," as I did upon being asked by Dudley Beaker what I thought of it, following his playing a recording of it, to which he had required me to pay close attention.

"What do you mean by that?" he demanded.

"I mean I liked it," I said. I also meant, of course, that I was surprised and delighted to find that I liked it, in part because I had not expected to, but I wasn't going to add that.

"What a curious locution," he said, because he was not a teenage Babbingtonian.

Naturally, we came to use *inflating* and *inflationary* to describe the things that blew us up, with such elegant variations as *exhibiting inflationary tendencies* and *exerting inflationary pressure.* We used *gas* for the ineffable something that inflationary things filled us with, or, sometimes, *hot air,* which put a positive twist on an expression that our parents used disparagingly. To emphasize the action of an inflationary thing, we called it a *pump* or a *gasser,* or, sometimes, whispered, with the speaker sniggering at his own bit of wit, a *blow job.*

People who made a calculated effort to inflate others we called *blow-hards*; people who were particularly susceptible to inflation were *inflatable* or *easily inflated*; those who were incapable of feeling wonder and delight were called *uninflatable,* of course, and those who were not incapable of being inflated but succumbed only under conditions of extreme inflationary pressure, we called *dogs,* from the old tale about the madman of Seville, well known among the boys and girls of Babbington, which purports to show how hard it is to inflate a dog.

When we suspected people of faking or exaggerating a response, we said that they were *pumping themselves up.* People who tried too hard, particularly those who wanted to make very sure that everyone saw how blown up they could get in the inflationary presence of art or nature, we called *blimps* or *gas bags.* Those who deliberately chose not to be easily moved, who set their threshold high and scoffed at the indiscriminate enthusiasms of gas bags, we called *cynics,* after Diogenes, the dog of Athens, who famously did not inflate easily. Of people who so desired the sensation of inflation that they sought it and aided the inflator in their own blowing-up, we said that they *sucked* or *inhaled*; and of those who brought inflation on themselves we said that they *blew themselves up* or *masturflated*; those who made a cult of it we called *inflationists,* on the analogy of *sensualist* and *sentimentalist.* We also called such people *blowfish* or *puffer fish,* after a type of fish common in the waters of Bolotomy Bay that when threatened gulps air to make itself appear larger and more formidable and, I suppose, harder to swallow.

In fairness to the blowfish, I have to admit that I was almost one of them; I felt wonderful while being blown up or while in an inflated state. Just imagine how that dog in Seville must have felt when the madman inflated it: enlarged; a grander, bigger, better being than it ordinarily was; full, and so in a sense satisfied, but full of lightness, in a state of aerostatic buoyancy, light and lightheaded, paradoxically both bigger and lighter, rising above the common pack of uninflated dogs, even above the artful madman who inspired this buoyancy; elated, elevated. The dog must have enjoyed it. I know I did, so much so that I actively sought inflation. I became a sucker.

Beauty was my pump of choice, the ultimate blow job. It filled me with helium and nitrous oxide, lifting gas and laughing gas, lifted me out of time for a while, and filled me with joy. So I sought beauty. I relished it; it blew me up; I was, as the song says, a fool for it. I sought it in art and music and sunsets and moonlight. Some people said that the capacity for being amazed and delighted by beauty resided in "the soul," so I supposed that I had begun to develop a very fine soul, and I seemed to feel it swelling in my chest when under the influence of beauty.

However, at some point toward the end of my adolescence I became embarrassed by my affection for beauty and by my tendency to become so quickly and fully inflated in the presence of it. I felt that I was in danger of becoming an aesthete, one of those people who is inflated by his own marvelous susceptibility to inflation, one, ultimately, who inflates himself, a blowfish.

So I trained myself to play the cynic in the presence of beauty. I sneered at it and at the swooning blimps who rhapsodized about it and at the inflationary works that pumped them full of it. If I had a soul, it seemed to me to be a liability. Applying the wisdom behind the slang of *blow up*, I concluded that the soul must be an inflatable bladder full of hot air, something I neither needed nor wanted.

Secretly, though, the truth about me at that time was that I feared beauty. All beauty, whether it was natural and accidental or artificial and deliberate, seemed threatening to me, because beautiful things had the power to rob me of my reason, making me susceptible to romance and guile. I was a fool for beauty, and anyone who knew it could use it against me. I could imagine a wily blowhard observing me, taking the measure of me, and sidling up to me, some moonlit night, with a whispered, "Pssst—hey, buddy."

"Yeah?"

"Wanna buy a dog?"

"A dog?"

"Sure. Take a look."

"It's—it's dead."

"You bet it is. It's a dead dog."

"And it's all—bloated."

"Inflated."

"Inflated?"

"Yeah. I blew it up. Not an easy thing to do."

"I'm sure."

"But now, you see, you can play this dog like bagpipes."

"You can?"

"Yep. Squeeze him right and old Shep will fart Mozart."

"Really?"

"As sure as the moon's up there shinin' down on Bolotomy Bay."

"How much?"

And however much he might be asking for the inflated carcass of old Shep, I'd probably pay it, because for all that I tried to play the cynic, deep down, where the irrational decisions are made, I was a helpless gas bag for beauty.

21
Porky Darling

WE DROVE ALONG in silence for a while, and I thought I knew what my mother was thinking, what she was worrying about. When she spoke, I knew that I was right. "Your father is going to be in quite a state," she said. She spoke in the direction of the windshield, without turning her head, and her grip on the steering wheel was hard enough to turn her knuckles white.

"We could get him some clamburgers for dinner," I said. Clamburgers were a favorite of my father's.

"Oh, Peter, that's a good idea," she said, and Patti rewarded me with a smile.

"Kap'n Klam is just back that way," I said. The clamburgers at Kap'n Klam were the best in town. "We can call home from there and tell him that we're on our way home—with clamburgers."

"If you like, Ella," said Patti, "I could come home with you, and help you break the news to him." When had she started calling my mother Ella? "I could call home from Kap'n Klam, too, and tell them that I'm having dinner with you." She paused, then added, "If you want me to."

"Sure we do," I said.

"Of course we do," said my mother. "We've got to stick together."

"All for one and one for all," said Patti.

"Sink or swim," said I, and regretted it.

To turn around and head toward Kap'n Klam, my mother made a right into a driveway. Then she backed out onto the street again into the path of an oncoming car. The driver swerved into the wrong lane and rushed on, sounding his horn and shouting something that wasn't entirely intelligible but included ". . . you crazy?"

"Probably," muttered my mother. She took a deep breath, put the car in gear, and drove on without disturbing any other drivers.

When we swung the screen door open and entered Kap'n Klam, Porky White called out, "Hello, hello, hello! Welcome to the home of happy diners!" Porky and I were friends and business associates, despite the difference in our ages. We had met when I was in elementary school. In those days, Porky drove a school bus and I was a regular passenger on it. Later, when he opened his first clam stand, I was an investor, the first investor, in fact. He and my mother knew each other from high school.

"Ella!" he said. "It's great to see you. How's that lucky son-of-a-gun Bert?"

My mother burst into tears.

"Hey, hey," said Porky, rushing to us and gathering my mother in his arms. "Don't do that. It's bad for business. This is supposed to be a place where people have a good time."

"Oh, Porky," said my mother, striking her forehead with her fist, "I've done a terrible thing! A terrible thing!"

"Come on, Ella," said Porky. "Chin up. How bad could it be? What did you do?"

"Oh, Porky," she said. She looked at him and said, "Oh, Porky," again, and then she lowered her eyes and shook her head from side to side and wouldn't say any more.

"Ella," said Porky, gently. "Tell me."

"Ohhhh," she wailed, "I bought a clam boat!"

"Huh!" said Porky. This was evidently not what he had expected to hear. "A clam boat." He knit his brows. He turned aside. He opened two beers and two bottles of Coffee-Toffee. He handed the bottles around and clinked his bottle against my mother's. He shook his head a couple of times. "You bought a clam boat," he said. "Why did you do that?"

My mother just shook her head and brought her hand to her mouth, as if her reasons were too horrible to tell. Patti put her arm across my mother's shoulders and said to Porky, "We're going to take people on excursions. On the bay. In the moonlight. Elegant excursions. Ella's Elegant Excursions. With champagne. Champagne and moonlight."

"It's going to be so elegant, Porky," said my mother, sniffling. "Wait'll you see." She managed a smile through her tears.

"So why are you crying?" asked Porky.

"Because I wrote a check for the boat," she said, "and—" She stopped. She looked at us, and we were all embarrassed to see how much it pained her to have to say what she had to say. We looked away, at the floor, or the counter.

"You don't have the money to cover the check," said Porky, quietly.

"I don't have the money to cover the check," said my mother, even more quietly.

"Well," said Porky, "I know all about that. That's how I got started here. Didn't have a dime and didn't have the intestinal fortitude to ask the old man for a nickel. I lined up investors."

"Investors," said my mother.

"Yeah," said Porky. "Investors. Backers. People you can persuade to risk their money so you don't have to risk yours." He glanced at me. When he saw the smile on my face, he looked away and said with a shrug, "Or maybe you could borrow some money from the bank." He put his hands in his pockets and looked at the floor, frowning and working his brows.

"We want some clamburgers, Porky," I said, dispiritedly. "I'll help you make them."

"Yeah," he said. "Okay."

We went behind the counter and got to work. Porky filled the french-fry basket with potatoes and lowered it into the fat, put six clamburgers on the griddle, began frying some onions, and lined up six buns to toast. I ladled clam chowder into cardboard containers.

"You could invest, Porky," I said, standing beside him, both of us facing away from the room, away from my mother and Patti.

"Aw, gee, Peter," he said. "I don't think so. I'm not making a fortune here, as you well know, and I've been wondering if maybe I ought to remodel the place a bit, modernize, maybe branch out, too, open a second place in Hargrove."

"I invested in you," I said, very quietly.

"Hey, don't think I'm not grateful, Peter, but let's keep this on a business basis."

"Look at them," I said, nodding over my shoulder in the direction of my mother and Patti, sitting at the counter, staring glumly into their drinks. "Don't you want to put smiles on those faces?"

He looked their way, and then he turned back toward the grill and sighed. "Sure," he said, "I'd like to put smiles on those faces, but you've got to appreciate my position here—"

"I do," I said. "I do appreciate your position, so here's what I've got in mind: Why don't you invest something now, anything, just to give my mother some confidence—"

"I—"

"—and I promise you, as soon as I find some other sucker, I'll pay you back."

He hesitated. "I don't know," he said. He went back to work. He assembled the clamburgers, with fried onions on every one, and I wrapped them in squares of translucent paper, tucking a slice of pickle in the final fold, as Porky had taught me to do. He poured the french fries into a brown paper bag that immediately began to darken with grease. We put the containers of chowder and the clamburgers into one large bag, and added small white paper containers of tartar sauce and cocktail sauce and cole slaw. The bag of french fries went into a second brown paper bag, and that too began to darken with grease.

Porky put the bags on the counter and handed my mother the check. She got her wallet from her handbag and handed Porky some bills. He took them and he went to the cash register and stood there for a moment, with his head down, but I could see that he was looking our way. He hit the key to open the register, took some bills from the money tray, added them to the bills my mother had given him, and brought them to her.

"Here you go," he said.

"Thanks, Porky," said my mother, absently stuffing the bills into her wallet.

"You want to count that," said Porky.

With a look, she said, "Porky, I'm sure it's right," and began to close her bag.

"Mom," I said, "you want to count it."

Reluctantly, with a look for me that told me I was speaking out of turn, she opened her wallet. "Oh!" she said, when she looked at the bills, and then, "Oh, Porky!" She leaned across the counter and flung her arms around his neck, and he turned a brilliant red.

"I figured, why don't I become your first investor?" he said. "After all, Peter was my first investor, and it seems like such a good idea—sound, you know, a solid investment—and—for old times' sake."

Patti shot a look in my direction, raised an eyebrow, and pursed her lips.

I shook my head once and mouthed, "Never. Impossible."

My mother said, "Oh, Porky, darling, thank you, thank you," and she kissed him.

Patti raised the other eyebrow.

22

My Father Bets on My Mother's Horse

MY MOTHER, PATTI, AND I crept up the back porch stairs, reluctant to confront the lion in his den. We paused, and my mother put on a brave smile and crossed her fingers.

"You don't mind going in the back door?" I whispered to Patti.

"Nah," she said. "We're all in this together now."

My mother opened the door and immediately called out brightly, "Hello-ho-ho! We're ho-ho-home!"

We made our way to the living room, where we found my father slumped in his favorite chair, staring blankly in the direction of the television set, where an episode of "Video Rangers" was underway. This was a locally produced half-hour adventure serial set on a spaceship somewhere in another galaxy sometime in the future. It was a kids' show, but my father never missed an episode. The production values were poor; the budget was tiny; the actors were comically inept. (The television picture was, of course black and white, since color television would not be commercially available at a price that a family with my family's budget could afford for years, but color would not have improved "Video Rangers.") Apparently, my father had been sitting in his chair since he got home from work, waiting for his dinner, consoling himself with beer. Several empty cans were on the table beside him, and he was drinking another one. Also on the table were a bag that had held pork rinds, the heel of a wedge of cheese he had found in the refrigerator, and a jar of pickled cherry peppers. He burped and poked around in the jar, chasing the last of the pickled peppers.

"I'll bet you thought we'd *never* get here," said my mother.

My father scowled. "Where the hell have you two been all this—" he began, and then he turned from the television set and caught sight of Patti, who had entered the room after my mother, followed in turn by me.

My father's eyes popped—really, just like the eyes of a cartoon lecher—at least I recall that they did. He blinked, he licked his lips, and, in my memory, his eyes were bloodshot, bulging, and moist with desire.

Patti put her hands behind her back, brought her knees together, and bent forward at the waist, playing at being sweet and shy. "Hi," she said. "I'm Patti. Peter's friend." She fluttered her lashes and added, "Ella's friend."

"Isn't she cute?" asked my mother.

She reached into the bag of wrapped clamburgers, pulled one out, and tossed it to my father, as if she were flinging a steak into a cage. Startled from his fixation on Patti, he caught it.

"Hey—" he began, but then, smelling the burger, he smiled and finished with, "—mmm, clamburgers."

A few minutes later we were all eating and, halfheartedly, watching "Video Rangers." The dialogue was murmurous and mostly unintelligible, though it rose and fell as the actors overplayed or underplayed their parts, and now and then a word or phrase emerged whole and comprehensible: "anti-gravity drive," "creatures from another world," "sabotage," "the ship."

My mother, suddenly eager, said, "That reminds me—Porky White is investing in a new business."

"What?" said my father. "What reminded you?"

"Huh? Oh. 'The ship.' One of them said something about 'the ship.'"

My father drew his brows together and scrutinized my mother's expression. Then, suspiciously and, it seemed to me, enviously, asked, "What sort of new business?"

"Elegant Excursions."

"Elegant Excursions?" He was mystified.

"It's going to be a ship—well, a boat—that takes people on excursions. Cruises to Hargrove and back. On the bay. In the moonlight."

"Eating clamburgers?"

"Oh, no, no. Hors d'oeuvres. Canapés. Little sandwiches on colored bread."

My father seemed to recognize a theme. "What?"

"He's going to work up a kind of clam spread. Cream cheese and chopped clams."

"Don't tell me: the clam spread will come in colors, too."

"What a good idea, Bert!"

"Oh, yeah. I wonder where I got it."

We all ate in silence for a moment. My mother was uneasy. I could see that she was searching for a way to take the conversation where she wanted it to go.

"You know," she said, "you've got to hand it to Porky."

"Do I? Why?"

"Well, he's really making a success of that clam bar."

"Luck. Just luck. *Dumb* luck, in Porky's case."

"Oh, Bert—"

"He just happened to get into the clam-bar business at the right time."

"I don't think there has ever been a right time for getting into the clam-bar business."

"Sure there is. There's a right time for everything. And Porky just happened to start his clam bar at the right time, just before the clam fad hit."

"The clam fad?"

"Sure. Clams are the cat's pajamas now—or whatever it is kids say." He turned to Patti and with an attempt at an attractive smile asked, "What do you say when something's the cat's pajamas—you know, great—terrific?"

"A pump. Or a blow—" She caught herself about to say "job" and stopped.

"What?"

"—blow—" She looked to me for help.

"Torch," I said, suddenly inspired. "A blowtorch."

"Blowtorch," said my father, trying it out. "Clams are a blowtorch—"

"A *real* blowtorch," I said, improvising, showing him how. "Clams are a real blowtorch now."

"Clams are a real blowtorch now," he said, doing his best to imitate me.

"You've got it, Mr. Leroy," said Patti.

"A real blowtorch! Look at us. We're the proof of it. We're all eating clamburgers. Q. E. D., right Peter?"

"I guess so."

My father looked at what remained of his second clamburger, sneered at it, and said, as if he were cursing, "Luck. Dumb luck." He chewed. "It's just a matter of being in the right place at the right time." He swallowed. "And for some reason that I will never understand, Chester White, *Chester White,* who wasn't even in the *right line* when they were handing the brains out, has developed a knack for being in the right place at the right time." He opened another can of beer and took a long swallow. Shaking his head, he said, "The son of a bitch—pardon my French—the son of a gun is a lucky son of a bitch." He took another swallow. "Some people have luck, and some do not. He's got it." Another swallow. "I wish I did."

"Wouldn't it be great if we could find a way to get some of it to rub off on us?" said my mother, dreamily, as if she couldn't for the life of her think of a way to accomplish such a thing.

My father gave her a dismissive look and sucked at his beer. Through the foam on his lips, he said, "Pffff."

"I was trying to remember what it is you say about getting a ride on somebody else's luck. How does it go, Bert?"

"Bet on his horse."

"Oh, yes. That's right." She sighed, as if she couldn't quite see how any of us might get a ride on Porky's luck. She took a bite of her clamburger and shot a look at Patti, who brightened.

"Gee, I might have an idea," she said. She seemed ready to go on, but then she shrugged, bestowed on my father her famous pout, and said, "But it's probably stupid."

My father grinned like a boy and waggled his finger at Patti. "An idea is like a little bird, young lady," he said. "You've got to give it a push out of the nest and see if it can fly."

He pantomimed this, for Patti's benefit, and my mother, Patti, and I managed somehow not to laugh.

"Well, okay," said Patti, as if suddenly shy in the face of such wisdom. Then, with a here-goes-nothing expression, she pantomimed a fluttering little bird and said, "I was just thinking that maybe we could get a ride on Porky's luck if we—oh, I don't know—if we asked him for jobs or something like that."

"That's very good," said my father, with an indulgent smile. Pantomiming again he said, "Let's see it fly."

Patti obliged him and fluttered her little hands. My father locked his thumbs and made his hands flap as if they were the wings of a bird of prey, and suddenly his hands swooped down on Patti's and grabbed them.

"Aw, gee, Patti," he said, almost brutally. "It didn't get very far. I think a nasty old crow got it."

Patti almost looked as if she might apologize.

"It was too little and too weak," my father continued. "Let's try something bigger and stronger." He made another fledgling fly and said, "Suppose *we* invest in Elegant Excursions, too!"

My mother, Patti, and I gasped as if astonished by the temerity of this suggestion.

"Oh, Bert," said my mother, "that sounds risky."

"Ella, you don't know anything about it. I'm going to put in as much as Porky puts in. There's no reason why he should make all the money." With a wink at Patti, he said, "I'm going to bet on Porky's horse."

Patti smiled winningly, but when my father turned aside to reach for his beer, she rolled her eyes and sneered.

MY MOTHER pulled her old car to a stop at Patti's house. She said, as mothers will, or did, "Peter, see Patti to the door."

Patti and I walked to the door.

On the front steps, before Patti went in, she called to my mother, "Good night, Ella!" and then, to me, in a whisper, she said, "Listen, Peter, I think you might be right about the paternity issue. You're too nice a guy to be the son of a—a nasty old crow. Let's try the experiment again, okay?"

"Well, okay," I said, trying to seem blasé. "Sure. If you want."

23
The Fate of Fledglings (Afflatus, Part 3)

ABOUT SIX YEARS AGO, I was invited to speak at the annual meeting of the Philpott Society, a small group of people devoted to improving the literary reputation of John R. Philpott, the author of *Oysters and All About Them,* a work that I have long regarded as a masterpiece of idiosyncratic organization and one that I eagerly acknowledge as one of the inflationary influences on my memoirs.

The honorarium from the Philpott Society paid our expenses and left us a little surplus, so Albertine and I spent a week in London. Nearly every day we visited the discount ticket booth in Covent Garden and got theater tickets for the evening.

One day (I believe it was the day after we saw a performance of Jean Cocteau's *Les Parents Terribles*), instead of waiting in the queue for twofers, we took a boat ride up the Thames to Kew and visited the Royal Botanic Gardens. It was a gray, cold, drizzly day, not the best day for walking, but we do love a ramble, regardless of the weather, so we spent hours divagating through the drizzle, observing and chatting. It was, until the time came for us to leave the gardens and return to London, one of the most pleasant days we have ever spent together, I think, a gem among gems. Distant as we were from our usual life and its quotidian cares, we had nothing to do but enjoy each other's company and see what there was to see. The day did not require sunshine for its pleasure, nor could sunshine have improved the pleasure that it brought us.

Inevitably, though, the time came when we had to cease our carefree strolling and find the shortest route back to the entrance. We stopped where we were to consult a map of the gardens. We were standing on a paved path in a parklike area, where we could see quite a long way across damp and verdant lawns. Several other paths led here and there. We began to study the map, but were immediately distracted from our purpose by the call of a bird—a mother's urgent, anxious cry, if I may so anthropomorphize. Beside us, no more than a few strides away, a long, sturdy branch stretched out from the trunk of an ancient tree, an old chestnut, I think. In the nearly bare branches at its extremity there was a nest. A mother bird, a tiny bird, some type of sparrow, I think, was nudging a tiny fledgling toward the edge of the nest, and as she urged it on she was—I can't think of any way to put this but in human terms—shouting a few final instructions to it. It was her cries that had caught our attention.

"Oh, my gosh," said Albertine. She turned toward me, we smiled at each other, and I put my arm around her shoulders and hugged her warmly. We were thoroughly delighted with the little drama. We shared the feeling that we were witnessing the defining moment in the fledgling's life, a moment bursting with metaphor, a moment that I for one had previously known only *as* a metaphor, never having observed the moment when a fledgling left the nest and braved the hazards of the great world. While we watched, the mother, still shouting advice, lowered her head and gave the fledgling a good shove.

"She's saying something like 'Now, remember what I taught you: carry a clean handkerchief and don't talk to strangers,'" said Albertine.

"To me it sounds more like 'I've had enough of your lying around all day smoking and watching television! Get out and get a job, you bum!'"

The fledgling flopped over the edge of the nest and fell toward the ground. I felt the hollowness—the cold, empty feeling of fear—that a parent feels when a child steps into the street. The little bird seemed to have no idea at all about flying, no notion that it *could* fly. The branch that held the nest was only about twenty feet above the ground, and the thought had just flitted through my mind that the little bird could probably survive such a fall into the longish grass when, suddenly, silently, swiftly, a crow, a very large crow, swept in from our right and snatched the bird in midair.

"Oh, no," said Albertine. She gripped my hand.

The crow made a sweeping turn and took the fledgling to another tree, not very far off, where there were other crows—not that we could see them, but we could hear them—cheering when the catcher in the sky brought dinner home. Crowing, if you will, about their champion's triumph.

"Ain't nature grand?" said Albertine.

Incredibly—to us, who could see the fate that awaited any fledgling that left the safety of home—the mother bird began nudging the next little one toward the rim of the nest.

"Oh, no," I said. We couldn't turn away. It was a fascinating sight.

The bird pushed the second fledgling over the edge, and like the first it plunged toward the grass. Again, the crow swept in, snatched the hapless creature, and carried it back to its own nest.

We watched, dumbstruck, horrified, while the mother pushed two more fledglings out. The crow got them both.

"I can't take this anymore," said Albertine. She put her arm through mine and we began making our way out of the gardens. Our way took us toward the crows' tree, and as we passed the crow flew right over our heads, on its way to snatch another falling fledgling. When it had returned to its nest again, we could hear the fading cries of the mother bird, but it seemed to me that there was a different quality to the cry now, and I supposed that all her offspring must be gone.

So did Albertine. "I know what she's saying now," she said. "I know. She's asking, 'What fucking asshole decided that this is the way life ought to be?'"

FOUR DAYS AGO, while I was still working on the preceding chapter, before I had found a pantomime for my father to perform when he killed Patti's idea, I quit work early to take Albertine to lunch.

While she was trying to decide what to wear, she asked me to step out onto the balcony and bring her a firsthand report on the state of the weather. I stepped onto the balcony, looked to the sky, estimated the temperature, and then looked down to the street to see how lightly or snugly people were dressed. I saw that the area in front of our building was cordoned off by yellow police tape. A small crowd of spectators had lined up along the tape, and a few cops were inside the cordoned area. A body was sprawled face down on the sidewalk directly below me. Some people were looking at the body. Others were looking up in my direction. Some of those looking up were pointing, and after a moment I realized that they were pointing to some floor above ours. I went back inside.

"What's it like?" Albertine asked.

"It's chilly," I said, "and there's a body on the sidewalk below us."

"What?"

"I think that at some time earlier in the day, while we were reading the paper, someone on a floor above ours must have fallen, jumped, or been pushed from a balcony or window. He—at least I think it's 'he'—is lying on the pavement—"

"Dead?"

"It looks that way to me."

She went out onto the balcony and looked down. After a while, she came back in, shaking her head.

We dressed in silence, and we left the building and walked through the crowd in silence, but in the subway station, when we were standing on the platform, waiting for the train, Albertine said, "He must have fallen right past our balcony."

"While we were reading the paper," I repeated.

We looked at each other and burst out laughing. We began making wisecracks about death, about suicide by lethal leap. We were shaken, and we were frightened. We were laughing at the edge of the abyss, trying to be brave, trying to pretend that death held no terrors for us, as if we did not expect to meet the fate that all fledglings eventually must. Nothing we said was funny enough to be worth recording here. When we came up out of the subway, we sobered up, and neither of us said a word about the dead man during our lunch (chicken for Albertine and swordfish paillard for me). Then, after we had left the warmth of Café des Artistes, with her arm through mine, huddling against me in the cold January wind on Central Park West, Albertine asked, "Do you remember the fledglings in Kew Gardens?"

"I've been thinking about them all afternoon," I admitted.

THAT NIGHT, while we were lying in bed reading, at about midnight, when the man who lives directly above us began throwing his furniture around, as he seems to do every night at that time, Albertine gesticulated toward the ceiling and said, "Of course, *he* wouldn't be the one to jump."

24
Testing the Hypothesis, Part 2

I WAS SITTING IN DUDLEY'S CHAIR, looking into the fire, waiting for a visit from Patti. The night was warm enough not to require a fire; it might even have been warm enough to make a fire ridiculous; but I required a fire for atmosphere. I was Dudlifying myself, putting myself through a course of Beakerization to prepare myself for Patti's visit and the resumption of our experimental investigation into the matter of my paternity. The transformation seemed to require my sitting in Dudley's chair before the fireplace, and it seemed to require a fire in the fireplace. The fire hadn't lit right away, so I'd torn pages from the magazines in the rack beside Dudley's chair to keep it going. A haze of smoke still filled the room, even though I'd opened the windows. I had begun reading a story in one of the magazines, but when I followed the "continued" line, I found that the page on which the story concluded had been one of those I'd burned to get the fire going. I was sucking on one of Dudley's pipes and trying to decide whether the struggling young painter in the story would manage to persuade the pretty young waitress—actually a struggling young actress—to pose for him, and, if so, how he would manage to do it, when the phone rang.

"Hello?" I said.

"Dudley?" asked a sweet voice at the other end of the line.

"No," I said without thinking, "this is—"

"*Dudley,* it's Ella."

"Huh? Oh. '*Ella.*' Um, good evening, 'Ella.' How are you?"

"I'm fine, Dud. I was wondering if I could come over and visit you for a while."

"More homework, I suppose?"

"Homework? Oh, yeah, that's it. More homework."

"Of course. I'd be glad to help you. Come right over, my dear."

"I have to change my clothes first."

"Oh."

"I won't be long. I'm just going to go up to my room and change my clothes."

"Okay."

"Just going to run up to *my room*"—a giggle—"and *change my clothes.*"

"Oh. *Your room.* I see."

"I'll bet. Here I go—up to my room. See you later."

I went upstairs to Dudley's study. With the light out, I looked across the way at the window of the room in my grandparents' house that had been my mother's bedroom. Had I understood Patti correctly? Was I, as Dudley, actually going to see the light go on in the room and then see Patti, playing the part of my mother, begin undressing, like the shy girl in the young painter's unheated studio, assuming that he had found the words to persuade her to accompany him there and then had found the words to persuade her to begin unbuttoning her blouse? I stood in the dark wondering what those words would be, when the light did indeed go on in the room across the way, and there was Patti in the doorway with my grandmother by her side, the two of them performing a pantomime, Patti in the role of a distraught young girl bespattered by a passing car, and my grandmother playing a kindly grandmother more than willing to help her. Patti pouted, plucked at her skirt, wrinkled her brow, slumped in exasperation, gesticulated to indicate the madcap driver careering along oblivious to the puddles and to her, and reinacted her leap backward, too late, alas, to avoid the wave of muddy water, and then—with a smile and a shake of her head at the way good luck sometimes comes right along with bad—produced a change of clothes from a paper bag that she was holding; my grandmother pouted in sympathy, patted and petted Patti to comfort and calm her, smiled at the change of clothes, indicated the dressing table, then turned and left the room, closing the door behind her.

Without once looking my way, Patti began unbuttoning her blouse.

WHEN THE DEAR GIRL arrived at the front door a few minutes later, I was in quite a state. All the ardor of a young man in love had set my heart to pounding and sent my blood pulsing through my veins, while the wisdom, propriety, and caution of a middle-aged—oh, let us not say that, not "middle-aged"—let us say rather that the wisdom of a man no longer quite so young nor nearly so foolish as he once had been counseled me to control myself, to still my throbbing heart, cool my ardor, calm my passions: to behave myself.

I opened the door with a trembling hand.

"Hi, Dud," said the innocent darling.

What would she have said, I wondered, if she had known that a thousand heartbeats earlier I had watched with hungry eyes while her schoolgirl's garb fell from her body, the white blouse slipping from her shoulders, the plaid skirt dropping down her creamy thighs, until all, all was revealed, all her charms, more than I could allow myself to recall while she was standing there, so sweet, so pure.

"Come in," I said, trying not to sound like a spider welcoming a fly.

25

Take Me Away; Take Me with You

SLIPPING HER PUCKERED LIPS over the tip of her paper straw, Patti sucked up and swallowed a mouthful of vanilla milk shake and then in a voice thick and soft, milky and sweet, asked, "Well, Peter, did you learn anything new last night?"

I had been expecting this question since the day when Patti had suggested another experiment. I had known that we would meet at the malt shop the day after that experiment, when we were playing ourselves again, to consider what we had discovered while playing my mother and Mr. Beaker. I had, since the conclusion of the experiment, often practiced what I wanted to say to her, and I felt fairly certain that, if I delivered my answer in the way that I had rehearsed it, I could strike just the right note—a chord, actually, of notes that might before I had so cannily combined them have seemed discordant, a chord in which humor harmonized with high purpose, friendship with lust, the offhanded assessment of a dispassionate investigator with the all-but-inexpressible awe of an adolescent, like one of those complex—and, for me, unsingable—chords that ended so many of the doo-wop songs.

"I found," I said, drawing my words out to emphasize the depth of thought underlying them, "that—you—have—beautiful—breasts."

She exhaled a bit of a laugh down the straw and it bubbled richly through her milk shake.

"I always supposed that you did have beautiful breasts," I went on, "but I was very—ah—pleased—to have my supposition confirmed—by direct observation—and—ah—digital palpation."

She pulled her straw from her glass and blew an inch of milk shake into my face.

"Nice shot," I said.

"Was this whole paternity experiment just a way to get your hands on me?" she asked.

"No!" I said quickly, perhaps too quickly.

She rolled her eyes.

"It wasn't," I asserted. "Honest."

She ran her tongue over her lips.

"Patti," I said, in a tone of deepest sincerity, "I really do have strong doubts about my paternity, and strong suspicions about the part that Dudley Beaker might have played in my conception. I meant what I said about conducting an experiment, and I'm grateful to you for being willing to assist me with it." I paused; then, with a shrug, I added, "I never said I wouldn't enjoy it."

She threatened me with the loaded straw again, and I raised my hands to suggest surrender, or at least a truce.

"I seem to recall that you told me we would be investigating certain events that may or may not have occurred in the past, between your mother and Dudley Beaker, not that we would be considering your opinion of my breasts or any other part of my gorgeous little body."

"You're right," I said. "Forgive me for straying from the purpose of our undertaking."

We snickered at each other.

"I learned something, too," she said.

"Yes?" I said, hoping for a compliment.

"Assuming that you're doing a good job of portraying Dudley—"

She paused and cocked her head.

"I think I am," I said.

"Then I think that Ella probably did have a crush on him."

"Really?"

"Yeah. He's kind of cute—and I'm talking about him, you know, not you—"

I hung my head.

"You're kind of cute, too," she said, "but I'm talking about Dudley in the pictures you showed me. He's good-looking, and he's suave—for a small-town guy, anyway—but I think that—if I'm really being honest with myself about this—the thing that I find most attractive about him when I'm with him might be the fact that he's grown-up, especially the particular way that he's grown-up."

I hadn't expected this.

"He's still young," she explained, "and he's got those jazz records and that crazy sports jacket in the back of the closet, but basically he's a grown-up guy, a man, and it's flattering to think that a man is interested in me—as if I were a woman, not just a girl." She poked her straw at the last of her milk shake. "That's it," she said. "He makes me feel like a woman: he makes me feel grown-up, and sophisticated."

This was interesting. He had always made me feel like a little boy, and a bumpkin.

"To tell you the honest truth," she said, "I—Ella, you know, when I'm being Ella—I like that feeling."

"Mm."

"I like the feeling a lot. I like the feeling more than I like him."

"Ah."

"But liking the feeling is enough, I think. Enough to make me—me, Ella—want to go back and see him again. And I might go further than taking my blouse and bra off next time, too. I might. Because I want to be grown-up, and do what grownups do."

She drank the last bit of the milk shake, and then, almost reluctantly, she said, "I learned something about myself, too. I think it was something I already knew, but I wasn't fully aware of it, if that makes sense. I'll tell it to you. It might come in handy to you someday. You can use it to get girls. Some girls, anyway."

"What is it?"

"Girls like to hear guys say, 'I love you'—"

"I think I knew that."

"Patience, jackass."

"Sorry."

"We like to hear, 'I love you,' but it doesn't take long before we begin to understand that the words usually mean something else."

"Oh."

"But there is something that a girl—some girls—this girl—might rather hear, or would find more beguiling—"

"Beguiling."

"Yes. That's exactly the word I want. Beguiling. I would have said seductive, but seductive sounds as if sex is the only motive, and it might not be. Love could be. Even companionship."

"I'm lost."

"Sorry. I'm kind of wandering among my thoughts. What I want to say is that I discovered that I could become a hopelessly giddy gasbag for a man who said, 'I want to take you away from all this.' Do you know what I mean at all? I mean somebody who could—who could and would—take me away from my house and my family and the dark hallway that runs down the middle of that house, with the torn carpet the color of peas, and the smell in the morning when my little brother wets his bed, and the heavy way my mother falls against the other side of the wall beside my bed on nights when my father decides that a good smack will help her sleep, and the way she wheezes in the mornings when she lights her cigarette, and the way she asks me if I want one, with a smile that is an invitation to join her in regretting everything I just listed for you. I'm not saying that Ella felt the same things I do—I just mean that she might have felt the way I do—but for a different set of reasons. I could be very attracted to a man who would take me away from all that, or who seemed as if he would, even if he just seemed as if he might possibly take me away from all that, and I could imagine that Dudley might."

I am embarrassed to record my response to what she said, and I confess that I thought of including here something different from what I said, but I found my attempts at improvement more embarrassing than the original. At least the original was honest in a way, the way that our thoughtless responses to people are, and mine was as thoughtless—may I say guileless—as a reflex.

Here it is.

"My dear," I said, in Dudley's manner, reaching across the table to take her hands in mine, "won't you let me take you—"

"Don't make a joke out of it," she said, pulling away, getting up, scraping her chair on the floor as she did.

"I'm sorry," I said, and I was.

"I'm going home," she said. She walked to the door. At the door, she turned, and, indicating with a sweep of her arm the malt shop and everything that had transpired there, said, "Peter, why don't you let me take

you away from all this?" and I did let her take me away from it, and along
the way to her house I tried to convince her that I was better than I
seemed, and I explained to her that making a joke was my way of clearing
the air, blowing the smell of her brother's piss away, and she laughed at
that, and when I said good-bye at her house she turned her face up to be
kissed, and I kissed her and for a moment she took me very far away, but
then the kiss ended and we were still standing on the unpaved road in
front of her house and it was time for me to go.

26
Traveling by Balloon

THE DESIRE to be "taken away from all this," to be lifted up and out of the life one currently found oneself leading and transported to some other, a desire that was actually a set of more specific desires arising from the particular set of disappointments that fate had chosen from the myriad disappointments offered to the young, became a general yearning of Babbingtonians of my generation, a yearning encapsulated in one handy package in our desire to be blown up, as in, "Aw, man, I am so bored in this town. Nothing ever happens here. I just wish somebody would come along and blow me up, you know what I mean?"

Yes. I knew. We all knew. Implicit in that desire was the understanding that the life we were leading was not the life we would have chosen to lead, the belief that fate, the ill wind that had blown our parents to this dull burg, seeking shelter, perhaps, from a sudden storm, had moored us in this limp life, this empty bladder of a town. It was a *cri de coeur* that we heard often, and I admit that my own heart cried it sometimes, begging fate to send me a wind from another direction, a plea familiar to every sailor.

(I hear in this cry an anticipation of the use of *blow* for cocaine, the use of cocaine as a chemical means of transportation from somewhere boring to somewhere else, and I see that some of my little pals were already, in the realm of desire if not in actuality, on the road from inhaling to snorting.)

We found Babbington boring. I say "we," I include myself in the group, because for a while I *was* in the group; I found Babbington boring, or *claimed* to find Babbington boring. Looking back, I think that I never

actually did find the town boring. I was faking my boredom, showing that
I could pronounce the shibboleths of my tribe, the disaffected youth of
suburbia. Albertine is fond of saying that people who are bored are boring, and I'm sure we were, I was, but it was the fashion to find Babbington boring; in fact, it was the fashion to find life itself—the local,
quotidian life as lived by boys and girls in Babbington with little opportunity to go anywhere else—boring, and to want to be taken away from it.
We were living in a town that was in the process of losing its identity as a
town and becoming just a patch of a pale, monochromatic wash on the
map of the country's socioeconomic bands: the suburbs. We were teach-
ing one another to believe that anywhere but here would be better, would
have a more interesting culture, a more vital life for the soul (the yearning
gas bag within us). How lazy we were! We didn't want to leave this un-
satisfactory place or to run away from it; we didn't want to have to get
ourselves up and go; we didn't want "get up and go" to enter the picture at
all. We wanted to be taken away. We wanted an agent who would not only
pick the destination (that somewhere that was anywhere but here) but also
arrange the journey and get the tickets, and then, with those welcome
words, "let me take you away from all this," stick a tube sharpened at one
end into a certain part of us and blow into us something transporting.

What great admiration and deep affection we felt for the people who
could or might blow us up, the pumps, the gas tanks, the inflators, the
dispensers of lifting gas. The highest praise for such a one was to say,
"Man, you are mad." By *mad,* a reference to the ultimate inflator, the
Madman of Seville, we meant "having the capacity for doing such a sur-
passingly good job of inflation that one could even inflate a dog, give it a
couple of pats and send it on a dizzying flight to somewhere else."

And what deep affection and desire we felt for that transporting something that the pumps filled us with, whatever it might be, however it
might be administered, anything that, beyond simply inflating us, gave us
lift and buoyancy and allowed us to make the trip from here to somewhere else, anywhere, nowhere. We sometimes called that magical stuff
"gas," which could be specified as "helium" (an inert gas, suggesting a de-
tachment in one's elation, a noble aloofness in one's elevation) or "hydrogen" (the heavy-lifting gas of dirigibles, capable of carrying one very far
away, but dangerous, explosive), and sometimes "hot air," a term that car-

ried with it the most exalted compliment to the inflator, because hot air was just air, common and unremarkable, transformed by the arts of the inflator, someone who was "hot," into a lifting agent, a means of transportation, like those sizzlin' hot Montgolfier brothers, Joseph Michel and Jacques Étienne, who in September of 1783, before the eyes of Louis XVI and Marie Antoinette, lofted a duck, a rooster, and a sheep into the skies above Paris, suspended in a basket below a balloon full of nothing but hot air.

There were already among us a few adepts who managed to achieve a kind of transcendental state of inflation. Those who had the ability seemed to be able to get blown up by even the most mundane experience, to find the gas in the commonest things. We called these lucky ones "balloonists." They did not blow themselves up in the calculating way that suckers or inflationalists did, but in an ingenuous way that we called "just breathing." There were few balloonists, but there were many aspirants to the balloonist state. Balloonists had a certain way about them, a blissful knowingness that came from having said yes to everything, to life in general, even to boring Babbington; having found the hot air that was right in their own back yard, they had no need to travel. I wanted to be a balloonist when I grew up, but also a cynic, if such a synthesis could be achieved.

27

A Quiet Family Dinner, on the Eve

ON THE EVE of our taking possession of *Arcinella,* a few minutes before my father was likely to arrive home from work, I was upstairs in my room, idly jotting lines for potential doo-wop songs, trying for ones that rhymed with Patti (drives me batty, is no fatty, sure ain't catty, dresses natty), when I smelled smoke. I went downstairs. My mother was in the kitchen, trying to make dinner.

"What happened?" I asked.

"Oh, Peter, " she said, "I'm a wreck. Look at this mess." In the cast-iron frying pan on the stove there were some crab cakes. From the top, they didn't look bad, but then *Arcinella* didn't look bad from the top either, and I was just about eighteen hours away from discovering that a boat, like a crab cake, could look just fine from the top and be damaged beyond repair on the bottom. My mother forced a spatula under one of the cakes, struggling to free it from the pan, pushing, pushing, in stuttering thrusts, to get the blade beneath the cake, and when she had it loose at last she raised it gingerly, like a poor dead thing. The undercrust was thick and black, as hard and smooth as the venerable seasoned pan. I was disappointed; I liked crab cakes. They were a family favorite; sometimes we had them with spaghetti, and sometimes we had them with poached eggs on top and hash-browned potatoes on the side, which was the way I liked them best.

"Were you going to have them with poached eggs?" I asked.

"Yes," sighed my mother, and she tousled my hair to salve my disappointment. "I wanted something easy—something I could make without thinking, you know?"

I did know. I'd seen her cook without thinking; I sometimes did my homework that way. There were certain dishes that she made as if she were not there, as if she had drifted on a fair breeze to somewhere else and left an hourly employee behind to mix the crab and onions into the batter, shape the patties, and brown them till they were crisp and golden while she was someplace else where she was not required to cook.

"But I got—distracted." She indicated a pad of paper and a list of things to be done after we took possession of the boat in the morning, and I understood that she'd been visiting the future, the place where our hopes take us, and had let tomorrow distract her from today.

"Couldn't you take the burned part off?" I suggested.

She frowned and regarded the crab cakes doubtfully.

"He always puts ketchup on crab cakes," I noted helpfully, as a good sidekick should.

She burst out laughing. We both understood that the only reason the burnt crust on the crab cakes mattered was that my father wouldn't like it. She and I were both more interested in the boat; we had to give him something to eat to keep him quiet while we talked about it.

She hugged me.

"Clamburgers?" I suggested.

"Mm, we did that," she said.

"Yeah, he'd smell a rat. We need something different, like—"

"Hamburgers!"

"Yeah. That'll do it."

She grabbed her pocketbook. "Get some hamburgers, with the works, and french fries, and strawberry shortcake." She opened her pocketbook and hesitated for just a moment. Then she pulled out the envelope that held the financing for her elegant excursions.

"Expenses," she said. "Business expenses."

We heard the crunch of tires in the driveway, and my mother began scraping the crab cakes into the garbage. "Go on," she said. "Scoot."

I was going out as my father was coming in, and before I shut the door, I heard my mother exclaim, "Oh, Bert! You're home! Why don't you make us a couple of old-fashioneds?"

I walked north, up our street, toward the Straight Line Highway, four lanes of concrete that split Long Island lengthwise like a filleted flounder. When I got to the corner where our street was broken by the highway, I could see the metal cladding of the Night-and-Day Diner gleaming in the evening sunlight, as flashy as the chrome grin on one of that year's finny cars. To get to the diner, I had to cross the highway, and the designers of the highway had made no provision to assist the pedestrian in this endeavor. They had apparently assumed that no one would cross the highway on foot, but those of us who lived near it often did so, perilous though the crossing was, because we still had friends and even relatives across the divide and weren't willing to stop visiting them just because the journey had been made artificially difficult. (In time, the highway became a greater divide, wider, running far more swiftly, and effected or completed another socioeconomic partition in the town, demarcating, like a contour line on a topographic map, a small but significant difference in elevation between the lower-middle-class families who bought the cheap little houses just south of the highway and the upper-working-class families who bought the cheaper little houses just north of the highway and a level lower on the social slope.) The fact that I had to do a little car-dodging always made the trip to the Night-and-Day seem like an adventure; it made the buying of hamburgers more like the hunting of a mammoth, the responsibility of getting them home without dropping them in the gutter more like the responsibility of feeding a family wholly dependent on me, waiting for me back in the damp and drafty cave, where they huddled in darkness, cold, frightened, frail, and desperate; it was the testing sort of labor that a stalwart sidekick ought to be assigned, and I made the most of the drama in it, darting and dashing across the traffic in a daredevil manner that wasn't really necessary, since most of the drivers of that time didn't go very fast, and would actually have slowed to allow a boy such as me to cross if I had stood meekly at the roadside and beseeched them with a look, something that, at my important age, I could not have allowed myself to do.

Safely across the highway, I ran through the parking lot, swung the door open, and stepped into the bright fluorescent light of the Night-and-Day. I loved the place, and I particularly loved the moment of entry. Now, right now, sitting here in Manhattan, I can feel the pressure of my palm against the cool door, feel the door yield, and at once I can smell onions frying.

Leon, the short-order cook, shot me a look, grinned, and nodded a greeting. Leon had a talent that I admired and wished that I, and my mother, possessed: he could keep stirring the onions on the griddle and even flip a burger while talking to someone at the counter; that wasn't the talent, of course, merely a single manifestation of it; the talent was for doing more than one thing at once.

"My little man," he said, "how are you doing this evening?"

"I'm just fine," I said. "You?"

"Hm," he said, and he paused to consider the question. After due consideration, he said, "I'm getting along adequately well, thank you. What can I get for you this evening?"

I gave my order carefully and precisely: four hamburgers, two of them rare, two medium-rare, all with fried onions; two large orders of french fries; a medium order of cole slaw; and three strawberry shortcakes. Leon shoveled some chopped onions from the pile that was always ready in a rear corner of the griddle, partially cooked, glistening, sizzling, guaranteeing that the pungent aroma of the Night-and-Day would accompany the diners when they departed, lodged in their coats and sweaters and hair.

"You want anything else on those burgers, Sport?" he asked, and then swung right into the list he liked to rattle off, "Cheese? Lettuce? Tomato? Fried peppers? Relish? Ketchup? Pickles? Chow-chow? Sprinkles? Chopped nuts? Whipped cream? A cherry?" Usually, he continued through a list of pizza toppings, from anchovies to pepperoni, but this time he raised a hand to stop himself, and me if I had intended to join in, and said, "Uh-oh, now we have got to hush up and listen, because that's my man Rolly Dunham coming on the radio." It was the Rolly Dunham Quartet: piano, bass, drums, and Dunham on the tenor sax. He was playing a solo, and its effect was immediate. It lifted me. It transported me. I could feel myself growing larger and lighter. He was playing a version of a tune that I didn't recognize, but one that I would never forget, and even now, whenever I hear it on a recording, the sound of Dunham's saxophone seems to hold within it the thick, earthy aroma of hot fat and fried onions. When the song ended, I was still floating. Dunham was a master of inflation.

Leon went back to his work at the griddle, but he kept shaking his head as if what we had heard could not have been real. "Oh, man," he said, "did you hear that cat blow?"

"I did," I said.

"I tell you," said Leon with another incredulous shake of the head, "that cat could inflate a dog."

He probably could have. He was a gas tank, a dispenser of lifting gas, a madman of the very first rank. His music was a gas, and he was a gasser, and I was a convert. Doo-wop might have had the power to float bright iridescent bubbles on a summer breeze, but jazz could do some heavy lifting; like hydrogen and hot air combined, it was magical and strong and dangerous, and it blew me up.

WE ATE OUR HAMBURGERS in the living room, at the folding tables, "TV tables," that we used when we ate in front of television. My mother picked at her hamburger, took it apart, put it back together, and passed it from hand to hand, but ate hardly any of it. When my father and I had finished, she gave me a look, and I followed her to the kitchen. She lit a cigarette and puffed at it nervously. Together, we read again and again the list of things to be done the next day and the supplies that we had to be sure to have with us, planning the work and our assignments, and when we had done everything that we could do without being down on the Bolotomy, on board *Arcinella,* she said, "We've got to get a really early start."

"I know," I said.

"Do you think Patti will be ready?"

"Sure she will."

"I hope so."

A moment of silence. In that moment, an idea occurred to me; perhaps it would be better, more honest, to say that a desire overcame me.

"I wonder," I said, attempting an attitude of cool indifference to the reception that my mother might accord the proposal I was about to make, "if Patti should spend the night here—you know—so that we could all get up and get going as early as possible."

Another moment of silence. My mother was considering the idea. For this moment, this brief exhilarating moment, I was able to believe that Patti Fiorenza might actually spend the night in my house.

Perhaps my mother was able to hear my heart pumping hot blood at a rapid rate, because she looked at me and rolled her eyes and almost laughed.

"Just an idea," I said, though we both knew that it had been more than that. With a sheepish grin I said, "Well, I'd better get some sleep," and I went up to bed.

28

"No Harm Done, Most Likely"

VERY EARLY the next morning we drove to Patti's, picked her up, and went on to Captain Mac's. He was going to make his last trip aboard *Arcinella,* piloting her from the canal at the end of the street where he lived to the berth along the quay on Bolotomy Road where she would reside as my mother's boat, and he had invited us to be on board for the voyage.

What a great pleasure it was to ride in my mother's old car through Babbington that morning. The town was calm and quiet, but it was waking up, experiencing the moment of pause before great effort, the moment of inhalation and expectation, like the moment before the weight-lifter grunts and lifts, and all the people we couldn't see as we rolled past their houses were pulling themselves together, taking a deep breath, and preparing to go about their business. The air was fresh and light, cool and clear, but it held the promise of heat, and the thrill of possibility. The memory of that early hour and its potential has made me prefer the early morning to all other times of day. A time comes in life, unless we are very lucky, when one day is likely to be much the same as any other, and I have lived through too many days like that, days defined by what must be done and what goes wrong and nothing else, but morning, particularly the early morning, when most people haven't begun the day, still holds all of the promise that it did on that morning when we stepped aboard *Arcinella,* a morning that seemed to hold the promise not only of a full and exciting day, but of a full and exciting summer, and even of a full and exciting life.

It was a pleasant trip. *Arcinella* purred. The captain guided her with a steady hand. The bay was calm and flat. Picturesque ducks swam beside us for a while. Before we entered the mouth of the Bolotomy River, Captain Mac said, addressing *Arcinella,* "Well, old girl, this seems as good a place as any to say good-bye and hand you over." He throttled down, stepped away from the wheel, and let *Arcinella* drift.

My mother recognized her cue. She handed the captain a check for the balance due, and on the roof of the cabin over the engine room he signed a bill of sale and certificate of ownership. The boat was now Ella's *Arcinella.*

"Who's going to take her into her new slip?" he asked, folding the check and putting it into his shirt pocket. He turned a questioning look toward my mother, who turned it toward me. I looked to Patti, who rewarded me with an expression of confidence, even admiration, groundless, but probably based on some remarks I had let fall into one of our rambling afternoon conversations, reminiscences of nautical adventures I had never had.

"Would you like to take her in, Patti?" I asked, absurdly.

"I wouldn't have any idea what I was doing," she said, delivering the line that should have been mine. "I'd probably wreck everything."

Clearly, I was going to have to be the one to wreck everything.

"Here we go, lad," said the captain, taking a grip on my shoulder and steering me toward the wheel. "Let me show you how to bend her to your will." I went to the wheelhouse as to the gallows.

"Take the wheel," he commanded, and I did as he said with a muttered "Aye, Cap'."

"This here's the throttle," he said, indicating a brass fixture shaped like the outline of a wedge of pie that was affixed to the bulkhead just to the right of the wheel. He nudged it counterclockwise a bit, and *Arcinella* began to move forward, toward the bridge across the bay, to the east of Babbington.

"Well, steer her toward town, lad," he said. I did. It was easy. The wheel was a pleasure to turn. Its frame was brass, green and pitted, and from the frame radiated eight spokes with wooden handles worn smooth and stained dark with use. Turn the wheel to the left, and she went to the left. Turn it to the right, and she went to the right. Nothing to it. I recognized the mouth of the Bolotomy, and I headed toward it. The captain stood to one side, but left me to do what I could on my own, and I began to puff myself up with the thought that I was now the captain, and the old man beside me was just a deckhand, someone who might very well have to take orders from me.

"This lever," he said, forgetting his place, "is your gearshift handle." He lowered his voice to a confidential whisper, as if it were important that *Arcinella* not hear what he was about to say. "The old gal's got a few peculiarities, and this here's one of 'em." Pointing to the metal pedal beside my right foot, he added, "That's another of 'em. That's her clutch."

"Ah-ha," I said. He made it sound like the kind of female detail we might be sniggering about in the locker room.

"When my father installed the Champion engine in her, he installed the transmission, too, so she drives her prop through first and reverse gears. When you bring her into the slip—you're gonna want to bring her in bow first, I figure—"

"That's what I thought I'd do," I said, and though I hadn't given it any thought at all before the captain brought the matter up, when I thought about it now I found that very little thought was required to convince me that bringing her in bow first was likely to be a lot easier than turning her around and backing her in.

"Well, then what you're going to need to do when you get a bit of a way out from the slip is set your throttle down so she's just kind of chugging along—"

I reached for the throttle.

"Of course you probably don't want to do that now."

"No, no. Of course not. I was just—um—checking the setting."

"When the time comes, you're going to want to have her just chugging along, but of course you won't want to give her so little gas that she stalls."

"Uh-uh," I said, and chuckled along with the captain, imagining the fun that would ensue if some nameless nitwit were to give her so little gas that she stalled.

"Then when you're at the slip, you'll want to put in the clutch and shift into reverse."

"Reverse?"

"To retard her forward motion."

"Oh, sure. Of course."

"Ideally," he said, drawing it out so that I would understand that it implied a long life's hard-won experience on the bay and on the boat, "you want to slow her down enough so she glides on into the slip sweet and easy and just barely kisses the bulkhead."

He turned away for a moment. At the time, I thought he was gauging the distance to the slip and the kissable bulkhead, but if you were to ask me now I would say that he was hiding an irrepressible grin.

He turned toward me again, gave me a pat on the back, and said, "Treat her gentle," and stepped aside.

I judged that I was near enough to the slip to throttle down, and so I did, turning the wedge of brass by degrees until the engine had reached a speed that seemed just this side of stalling. So far, so good, and a treacherous sense of confidence in my fledgling's wings swelled my little chest. I didn't dare turn away from my work for an instant to check, but I thought it likely that Patti and my mother were watching me with admiring—nay, adoring—eyes.

Though I had throttled her down, *Arcinella* displayed a troubling reluctance to retard her forward motion. Her engine was turning over slowly, but her momentum carried her toward the slip and that looming bulkhead with reckless haste. Time to shift into reverse and calm her down, bring her in sweet and easy.

The clutch. It was a metal pedal projecting through the floorboards in the wheelhouse. I put my right foot on it and pressed. Nothing happened. It didn't move at all. Ordinarily, in a car, the driver would have been given some mechanical or hydraulic advantage so that the effort of depressing the clutch pedal was eased, but here all such landlubbin' frippery had been stripped away, deemed, I suppose, an affront to the masculinity of a clamdiggin' bayman, so that to depress this clutch pedal, I had to stand on it. This I did, and with the clutch in, I shifted into reverse. *Arcinella* raced on toward her rendezvous with the bulkhead. What was required of me now, I knew, was to release the clutch in a smooth manner so that reverse was engaged but *Arcinella* didn't stall. This, I realized as the sweat began to run into my eyes, I could not possibly do, since I was standing on the clutch pedal, with all my weight employed in keeping it depressed. I could remain standing on the pedal and allow *Arcinella* to run headlong into the bulkhead, or I could step off the pedal and hope that she would not stall despite the violence with which reverse would be engaged. Better to do something than to do nothing, I thought, and so I stepped off the clutch pedal.

She shuddered, seemed to hesitate for a moment, as if trying to understand what had happened to her, then with a sound like a sigh she stalled, and in the sudden silence glided smoothly, swiftly, single-mindedly directly into the bulkhead, which she struck with such force that all hands would have been thrown to the deck or perhaps even overboard had not all hands seen it coming, watched, indeed with mounting horror as *Arcinella* raced toward the impact. When she struck, she shook herself like a wet dog, then rebounded in the direction of the opposite bank, which she nearly reached before the captain managed to restart the engine.

With me standing glum and mute in the bow, ready to take a line ashore when we were close enough, Captain Mac brought her in sweet and easy, and this time her bow never even touched the bulkhead.

When we were all ashore, he turned to my mother and with an unwelcome hand on my shoulder said, "There's been no harm done, most likely—but," he added, in a lowered voice, "of course, I can't say for sure that there hasn't, and I can't take responsibility if there has."

29
Trouble Down Below

WHEN THE CAPTAIN was out of earshot, if not yet out of sight, my mother stood on the bulkhead with her hands on her hips, her feet planted firmly, looked out over *Arcinella,* shook her head, and said, "What a mess!"

I felt the sudden onset of fear, like a punch that I hadn't anticipated. Did she regret the purchase, regret everything? Was it all going to fall apart before we even got underway? Was it my fault?

"You said it!" said Patti, and for an awful moment I really thought that all was lost, but then I saw that what my mother had said and what she felt did not match. She was smiling at the boat, smiling at the task that lay ahead of her, and so was Patti. They could hardly wait to get to work. We had brought a thermos of coffee, and the plan was to go through the lists my mother had made and parcel out the work while we drank our coffee, but my mother couldn't wait. She got right to work, and Patti and I followed her example.

In a certain kind of endearingly sentimental movie, a Cinderella story, a moment comes when the Cinderella character is invited to the plot's equivalent of the Prince's ball and discovers that she has nothing to wear, a lack that makes her feel unworthy of the invitation and hopeless of ever being worthy of the Prince character's attentions. Her champions, who should be appalled that she has confused couture and character, instead work miracles to transform her appearance by scrubbing her clean and fashioning the illusion of a fashionable costume. They improvise a gown from a tablecloth and duct tape, and a tiara from a colander and candy sprinkles. The old lady next door, whom everyone had till now shunned as a shriveled harridan, drifts into a bittersweet reminiscence of the days, long gone, when she was the reigning beauty of the block; she teaches our Cinderella how to curtsey and flirt, bestows upon her a treasured brooch, and offers the sort of motherly advice that young girls ignore, as their mothers did before them.

That Cinderella transformation was what my mother hoped to effect. We spent the day trying to persuade *Arcinella* to forget the trying years she'd spent as a clam boat under the callused hand of Captain Mac, removing all the leavings of her years as a working boat, the dirt, the broken bits of clamdigging gear, the trash that accumulates on boats and never seems to get removed until there is a change of ownership, the detritus of one phase of a life, one way of life, cleaning her up and scrubbing her down in preparation for the next day, when the plan was to repaint her and dress her up for a very different sort of life from the one she late had led.

At one point, early in the day, my mother was about to go below and see what ought to be done down there, but she put her head through the narrow opening beside the wheel and immediately backed out with a shudder.

"Peter," she said, "I think that's your area of responsibility, down there, the engine and all that."

"Aye, Mom," I said, and went below to the engine room and the hold, my dank domain. My mother thought it was foul, and I understood her distaste, but I didn't share it. It was a fine place for a boy to work, but not a place where he'd want his mom or his girlfriend to go. They'd get themselves dirty down there, and they wouldn't like it, but I got myself good and dirty down there, and I liked it just fine.

When I crouched to get through the engine-room door (technically called the companionway, I think, but I called it the engine-room door for as long as my mother owned *Arcinella,* and I'll do so here) the engine was immediately to my left. Farther forward, ahead of the engine, there was a small open area, and ahead of that a larger open area, the hold, which was also accessible from a large hatch in the forward area of the deck, where burlap sacks full of clams could be stored out of the heat of the sun. I couldn't stand anywhere belowdecks. In the area beside the engine, I could squat, but forward of that I had to get onto my hands and knees or scuttle sideways, like a crab.

The engine—my engine, I'd begun to consider it—dominated the belowdecks space. While I was cleaning it, removing grease with rags and an old toothbrush, I became aware, gradually, over the course of a few hours, that the bilgewater, instead of being confined to the bilge where it belonged, had risen above the planking. I was standing in it. It sloshed as the boat rocked gently in its slip, and it lapped about my feet. I crouched down and touched the surface of the bilgewater with my hand. It was half an inch or so above the decking. Even as a first-time boat owner I was able to deduce that the rise of the bilgewater over the course of the day meant that the boat was sinking.

I didn't know what to do, but I knew what not to do: I couldn't let my mother know. Knowing that she'd floated her dream on a sinking ship would have destroyed her confidence, dashed her hopes. I suppose that goes without saying.

Before I went up into the sunlight, I resolved to protect my mother from the deflating knowledge I'd obtained and to find some way to keep the old girl afloat. Blinking in the brightness, firm in my resolve, I felt that I had in my time belowdecks become a boy far wiser, tougher, and much more manly than the boy who had gone below in the morning.

"You need a good scrubbing," said my mother, possibly as her way of acknowledging the transformation that I had undergone. I looked at Patti, who was separated from me by the full length of *Arcinella*. She looked back at me in a curious way; perhaps, I allowed myself to think, she was wondering what I would be like as a lover.

"Well," said my mother, "that's enough for today. Tomorrow we can start painting and decorating." She unscrewed the top of the thermos bottle and poured the cold coffee into the bay. She grabbed me playfully by the ear and said, "Let's get you home and into a hot shower."

30

An Act of Sabotage, in Reverse

I COULDN'T SLEEP. I'd worked hard enough and long enough to be exhausted, but I bore the burden of disturbing knowledge, and it kept me awake. I was a kid who knew that he still had a lot to learn, but I felt that when it came to *Arcinella*'s hull, I knew too much: I'd learned something that I'd rather not have known. I lay in my bed, and instead of passing the time before I fell asleep in pleasant recollection of my evening with Patti in Dudley's study, as I had on every other night since the actual occurrence, I found myself shivering with the chilling memory of what I had discovered below *Arcinella*'s decks, which came blowing in like a frigid nor'easter. This mnemonic wind did not blow me up; it was strong, but it brought none of the lovely stuff that memories of Patti did. It brought only the sort of thing that keeps me awake now: anxiety, guilt, and regret—deflationary agents all.

(Writing those words, this morning, April 29, 2000, a gray one in a winter that has decided to stay in town well into the spring, I'm sluggish from a night when all of those things kept me awake. I'm anxious about a couple of the jobs I've taken on: a website based on the Happy Clam animated television series, for which I have done quite a bit of work but for which I have no contract and only an oral promise that I'll be paid the fee, which seems to shrink every time I talk to the management of the publishing house that owns the rights to the Happy Clam series; and a little book for high school science teachers that is intended to give them simple, easy-to-implement procedures for getting kids interested in careers in molluscan biology, which must be fully outlined four days from now.

Those anxieties lie uneasily atop the run-of-the-mill anxieties I have about the two other jobs I'm doing at the same time: a history of the Seventy-Seventh Street Proctology Group, commissioned by the principals in the practice as part of its lavish seventy-seventh-anniversary celebration; and a recruiting website for Stickley and Garnet, Certified Public Accountants, an outfit "where you can make your future add up to something." So, you see, my overarching, all-encompassing source of anxiety is the need to figure out how to do all that work at more or less the same time, assuming that all the jobs actually materialize, a situation that I sincerely desire, since these contract jobs are the way I keep the household in gin, our preferred analgesic against the anxieties of the workaday life of a hack writer who is four years shy of the day when he turns fifty-nine-and-a-half and can at last become a full-time memoirist and part-time flâneur. Do you wonder that I relish the hour or so that I am able to steal each morning for a return to that time when all my anxiety, guilt, and regret was centered on *Arcinella,* when the only thing I had to fear was the possibility that she might sink before morning, when my guilty feelings arose almost exclusively from the suspicion that her sinking was my fault for having rammed her into the bulkhead, and what I regretted most was my having been so foolish as not to have consulted the people I knew who could have told me before my mother bought her whether she was a boat still strong enough to withstand the rammings-into-bulkheads that she was likely to suffer at the hands of a very young captain with a lot to learn? Things were so much simpler then.)

I got out of bed, dressed in the dark, made my way down the stairs, avoiding the ones that creaked, and let myself out of the house. All of Babbington lay between me and the slip where *Arcinella* was asleep and sinking, but because Babbington was shrinking as I grew, and I had a better bicycle than I'd ever had before, I estimated that I could get to the boat in twelve minutes. Surely she would stay afloat that long. I went to the garage to get the bicycle, but the garage was locked. Why? Because my father had finally gotten around to installing doors on it. Having doors, he had thought that he ought to have locks. So he had bought and installed locks. Having locks, he thought he ought to use them. So he had locked the doors. All right. So be it. If I couldn't ride, I would walk. That might take me half an hour, I imagined, starting out at a brisk pace.

The air was warm and soft and gentle. My feet scraped on the side-walk, crunching in the mix of pebbles and sand at the roadside, or thud-ding softly on the tar of the blacktop lanes in the old part of town, striking smartly on the concrete sidewalks. The town was for the most part hushed and still. I heard cats sometimes; a dog now and then; a train whistle off in the distance, the train approaching Babbington, whistling at the cross-ing; and the church clock, which struck twelve not long after I had passed through the village, the clockwork switches in the boxes that controlled the traffic signals; the lapping of the water against the bulkhead along the Bolotomy. I sought the shadows, and now and then when I found a partic-ularly good one, dense, the right size for me, I stopped within it for a while, and just waited and watched to see what would happen. Nothing much did happen, nothing that Babbington would be talking about in the morning, but I found that lights were burning in some of the houses, and when I stopped at the illuminated windows to look inside and see what I could see, my progress was impeded. I went on, walking in the dark, sa-voring the feeling that the night was mine, that in a sense all of Babbing-ton was mine at this hour, when no one else was abroad. I was the night walker of Babbington, the mystery boy who walked the streets in the dark, slipping like a shadow from shadow to shadow. He might be look-ing in your window at any time. Stories would be told about me. Mothers would warn their daughters not to stand too near the window when they were undressing for bed, because the night walker might be out there, you never could tell, and here and there around the town one or another of those daughters, one of the ones who had begun to develop a certain yearning, not simply for sex, but for being recognized as growing up, as beginning to become someone who might figure in someone else's dreams, would say "Yes, mother, I'll be careful," and go to her room and close the door and turn the light on and begin very slowly, standing in a carefully selected spot, to remove her clothes in a graceful dance, an im-provisation that she would improve and polish from night to night, a dance performed for me, the night walker, the boy in the shadows of Bab-bington, watching.

Had my mother performed such a dance when she was a girl? If she had, it wouldn't have been for my precursor as night walker of Babbing-ton, since her window was on the second floor, and the night walker would have had to have used a ladder or climbed a tree to see her. I knew, from personal experience, that we night walkers didn't bother with such things as ladders or trees, because they increased the likelihood of getting caught, and they slowed us down without increasing the odds of our actually seeing any nude girls. No, if my mother had done the undressing dance, it would have been for her next-door neighbor, Mr. Beaker, playing toward the fine view that he had into her bedroom from his study, as Patti had for me.

I made many detours as the night walker of Babbington, and I did actually see some people in their bedrooms, turning a light on to get a drink of water, waking from some unknown anxiety and propping the pillows to read themselves into some other place where the anxieties were not their own, but I saw no naked girls, no dancers. "My timing must be off," I told myself. "I should start out earlier next time." I knew that I would be walking at night again (but I didn't know then that it would become my custom, that I would actually become Peeping Peter, the Night Walker of Babbington).

I suppose it took me an hour to get to the stretch of the Bolotomy where *Arcinella* was. As I came along the bulkhead, I tried to pick her out, and I thought I recognized her up ahead, but then I changed my mind, because someone was aboard the boat I'd taken for *Arcinella*. Mixed emotions arose within me. I felt a kinship with the person, whoever it might be. We were walkers in the night, a breed apart. We might sit on the bulkhead and swap stories of the things we'd seen, I thought, and as soon as I thought of our swapping those stories I knew that mine would be lies, that in my versions of the sights I'd seen, pretty girls would be performing the undressing dance. Immediately there arose a conflicting emotion: jealousy. I was jealous of my position as the night walker of Babbington. There should be only one of us. I was sure of that. The town couldn't have more than one. If Babbington could have two, why not three, and if three, why not a dozen, and if a dozen, why not half the town, and if half the town, why not everyone? If everyone took to walking at night, there would be nothing at all odd about it, and if there were nothing at all odd about it, there would be nothing interesting in doing it, at least not for me. I wanted to be outside the main stream. If there were more than one night walker, then I would have to stay home. "This town isn't big enough for both of us," I muttered.

I slipped into the shadows. There wasn't much cover on the water side of the road, so I backtracked until I could cross the street without being seen by the pretender to the office of night walker. On that side of the street, there were shadows and cover aplenty—hedges, trees, and shrubs, and lawns over which I could creep without a sound. I crept. When I was across the street from the boat, deep in the shadows, behind the trunk of a tree, I saw that the boat was indeed our *Arcinella,* and I saw that the other night walker was Captain Macomangus.

What was he doing? For a moment, it occurred to me that I must be witnessing a poignant scene, Captain Mac bidding a tender farewell to his beloved old boat, and I thought that I really ought to make a silent with-drawal or retreat, absent myself from this touching tableau and leave him alone to make his adieux, but curiosity kept me in my peeping role. Just how, I wondered, did one go about saying good-bye to a boat? Maybe there was an old established ritual that I ought to know. If there was, I didn't learn it. Captain Mac closed the hatch on the forward deck, wiped his hands on his pants (and I took note of that, since it was clearly *comme il faut* in the unwritten book of clamboat-captain procedures and practic-es), and stepped off the boat onto the bulkhead. He glanced around quick-ly—furtively, I thought, checking to see whether anyone had seen him. He didn't notice that I had. Then off he went, on down the road toward the south, toward home, I supposed.

When he had passed out of sight, around the bend that the road took at a canal, I came out of hiding and went over to *Arcinella.* I stepped aboard and gave her a careful inspection. With one exception, everything seemed to be as we had left it. I couldn't see that anything was missing. I couldn't see that any harm had been done. But I did notice that *something* had been done. The bilge had been pumped dry.

31
Night Walker, Night Bailer

PAINTING AND DECORATING *Arcinella,* which my mother had expected to take a day, took a week. Throughout that week, night after night, I would wait until my father, who sat up later than my mother, had turned the television set off and gone to bed, then throw some clothes out the window of my bedroom and creep down the stairs in my pajamas, so that if I were intercepted I could claim that I'd come downstairs to use the bathroom. I'd spend a couple of minutes opening the back door very slowly and quietly and closing it equally slowly and quietly, and then I'd grab my clothes, dress in the shadows, and make my rambling way through sleeping Babbington, pausing at all the lighted windows, coming at last to the slip where *Arcinella* lay at rest, quietly taking on water.

Captain Mac and I seemed to be on the same schedule, because every night I would arrive at the boat while he was still at work. I hid in the shadows across the street to observe him, and when he had finished and disappeared around the bend in the road on his way home, I dashed through the streetlamp light and slipped quietly aboard the boat. After two or three nights, I came to understand what the captain was up to: he was bailing *Arcinella,* but he was pumping a little less water from her bilge each night. He wanted it to seem that she had begun leaking only after we had bought her, so that he would be able to claim that the poor old girl hadn't been leaking when he sold her to us, that we must somehow be to blame for her leaking now (and if we protested, he would certainly invite us to recall that fatal collision with the bulkhead, my fault).

When I found that he was leaving the bailing job unfinished, I began finishing it myself, making sure that the bilge was as dry as I could get it before I returned home. What I knew about bailing came from childhood experiences that had made me think of it as a form of play, part of the pleasure of sailing with my grandfather. He had a dinghy that he sometimes trailed behind the *Rambunctious* when we were going to go crabbing in the waterways that wandered among the islands in the flats on the other side of the bay, and the dinghy often took on water during the crossing. When we reached the flats, we would pull the dinghy to the stern of the *Rambunctious* and clamber into it, and then before we began crabbing we would bail the little boat. My grandfather had fashioned bailers for us from empty cans, adding handles to make them easier to hold and trimming the cans to a scoop-like shape that made them more efficient than unmodified cans would have been, but I knew that a plain old empty can would work, and that was what was available to me, in a trash barrel in the shadows beside one of the houses across the street from the creek, so I used a simple empty can to bail *Arcinella*.

For anyone older than, I'd say, eight, bailing is not play. It's just a chore, and it is one of the chores that brings no satisfaction at all. It is never really completed, for one thing. There's always a little water in the bilge that you can't get out. That bit of residual water is the kind of thing that can bring a compulsive type to tears.

I bailed, and I bailed.

It was slow, and it was boring.

However, it became one of those tasks, like painting the mullions and muntins of windows with many lights, that invite the mind to wander, and during my nights of bailing, I began to think more and more often about how my nights in the bilge might be represented in a story, my story. I didn't think of it as a story that I would tell, though here I am telling it to you now; instead, at the time, I thought of it as a story that someone else would write; specifically, I thought of it as an interview in the series of interviews that appeared in the *Babbington Reporter* under the rubric "We Pay a Call."

We Pay a Call . . .
on the Night Bailer of Babbington
by Egbert Penman,
the Curious Columnist

You haven't seen him. He takes great care to ensure that you do not see him. But he is at work, every night, while you're asleep. He's the Night Bailer of Babbington, a legendary figure who turns out to be an actual person, a fascinating young man—a boy, really—whose name I am not at liberty to divulge. I'll call him Larry, as he suggested. Actually, "Larry" is the current incarnation of not one but two of Babbington's legendary figures: the aforementioned Night Bailer and also the Night Walker of Babbington, who is the lone figure abroad at night, slipping from shadow to shadow and occasionally—legend has it—peeking into the windows of virgins.

"And not just virgins, Egbert," he avers with a laconic chuckle.

"'Larry,' the responsibilities attendant to two legendary roles must really keep you hopping."

"Yes, they do, Egbert, but along with the responsibilities, there are rewards, and the rewards are enough to make the work worthwhile."

"The peeking into windows."

"Heh-heh. No, no. That's really a very minor part of the job. The greatest rewards come from inflating the boats."

"Inflating the boats?"

"Yes. That's what bailing really is, you know, Egbert."

"Huh?"

"A lot of people think only of the negative aspect of bailing—removing water from the bilge of a boat. But the Night Bailers—all of us in the long line of Night Bailers—don't look at it that way."

"You don't?"

"Oh, no. Not at all. You see, Egbert, bailing is an inflationary process; when we remove water from a bilge, we are simultaneously drawing air into the bilge."

"I'm afraid I don't follow—"

"Nature, as you know, abhors a vacuum. So, when I evacuate the water from a bilge, I've made a vacant space for Nature to fill, and she does fill it—with air; in other words, she blows the boat up."

"That's amazing."

"Yes, it is, Egbert, but even more amazing is the fact that inflating these boats gives me the ability to dilate or compress time."

"Really! Just how do you accomplish that?"

"Well, not to be too technical about it, but time is really nothing more than the progress of things from a state of relative orderliness to a state of relative disorder, and ultimately to a state of complete disorder, so every time I empty a bilge I am returning Babbington to a state of relatively greater orderliness than the state that obtained before I began bailing, and so I am, in a very real sense, reversing time."

"Where did you learn to talk like that?"

"Huh?"

"Never mind. Let me just explore the implications of what you said. Are you suggesting that without your nightly bailing, time would actually move more quickly than it now does?"

"Yes, Egbert. That's correct. Each night, by inflating sinking boats, I make up for lost time; that is, for time lost during the day, when the bilges were filling."

"So when I find myself wondering where the time goes, or if I am in search of lost time, now I know where to find it: in the bilges of the boats of Babbington!"

"Right you are, Egbert."

"Ah-ha! Now I think I see the secret to your amazing ability to bail—or I guess I should say inflate—so many boats. By making up for lost time, you find the time to bail all the boats in Babbington— am I right?"

"Yes and no. Yes, making up for lost time is the way I find the time to bail as many boats as I do. With each boat that I bail, I regain a little time, and if I'm very quick about it I even have a small surplus, so that some nights, when I've been very efficient, I actually have time to kill before the dawn comes."

"And how do you do that?"

"I just sit on the bulkhead and watch the Bolotomy flow by."

"So, after you've inflated all those boats—"

"Not all of them, Egbert. I don't inflate every boat in Babbington. Some of them I let go."

"Those are the ones that sink?"

"That's right."

"And do you choose which ones to bail—I mean inflate—and which ones to let go?"

"I do. Yes."

"How do you make that decision?"

"Well, some of the boats that I do not inflate belong to people who are not worthy of owning boats that float."

"And how do you determine that?"

"I gather information in my role as Night Walker of Babbington."

"I see. So your two roles are complementary."

"Yes, to a degree, but only to a degree, and only in one direction. That is to say, the Night Bailer of Babbington makes use of information gathered by the Night Walker of Babbington, but I haven't yet noticed that the Night Walker makes use of any of the efforts of the Night Bailer."

"So the Night Walker doesn't own a boat?"

"Heh-heh-heh."

With another laconic chuckle, the legendary and mysterious Night Bailer (or was it the Night Walker?) turned and sauntered with cool nonchalance into the shadows, where he (they?) melded with the night and disappeared from sight.

In that manner I made the time pass and I got the job done, but I can't say that I enjoyed it, and I doubted that I could keep it up. The captain was leaving more and more water in the bilge each night, and I wasn't succeeding in reversing time. I was spending longer and longer as the Night Bailer, which was making me seem lazy and sluggish at my day job, where I was assistant to my mother and Patti in making *Arcinella* look good on the surface.

I could see that when the captain eventually decided to abandon the work—to abandon *Arcinella,* my mother, Patti, and me—when the night came, as I was sure it would, when I found that he had not bailed *Arcinella* at all, I wouldn't be able to keep her afloat on my own.

Arcinella would sink. That would be bad. Worse, her sinking would seem to be my fault. I had to keep her floating to keep my mother's hopes and dreams afloat, and I had to keep her floating so that I wouldn't look like a fool. How? The Night Bailer needed help.

32

In Which I Swallow My Pride

I KNEW from observing Captain Mac that he had a device that pumped water from the bilge in a steady stream. I never allowed myself to get close enough to see just what this device was, but I assumed that it must be a hand pump. I assumed this because I knew that hand pumps existed that were specifically designed for evacuating water from bilges. My grandfather had a hand pump, and I had seen him use it to empty the bilge of the *Rambunctious*. I hasten to say that the *Rambunctious* did not take on much water, and that the pumping of the bilge was a brief chore before a pleasant day on the bay, less brief if there had been rain. I had even used my grandfather's bilge pump myself. Since this was all I knew about bilge pumps, I jumped to the conclusion that it was all there was to know about bilge pumps, that the hand pump was all there was in the way of bilge-evacuation devices of any sort beyond bailing.

Where could I get a bilge pump? I didn't want to go to my grandfather and ask to use his, because I would have had to admit to my having been foolish not to consult him before buying *Arcinella,* and I would have had to endure his compassionate understanding and forgiveness. The whole thing would have made me miserable.

I had another place to turn for help. My best friend, Rodney "Raskolnikov" Lodkochnikov, came from a family with a long history of clamming, boat ownership, and intimate acquaintance with boats not long for the world on the surface. The Lodkochnikovs lived a short way from where *Arcinella* was berthed, in a house that stood on pilings over the edge of the estuarial stretch of the river.

When Raskol opened the door and found me standing in front of him, he folded his arms in a manner at once challenging and dismissive, and leaned back against the doorframe frowning. I told him my story. He smirked and snorted. A smirk is not the sort of response one hopes that a problem will elicit from a friend. Neither is a snort.

"Dad!" he called out after letting an awkward moment pass. "Peter's here."

"Well, well, well," said Mr. Lodkochnikov from the depths of the dank, dark Lodkochnikov house. I heard the creaking of his easy chair, and in a moment he came to the door and stood beside his son. He folded his arms, displaying the original model of challenging and dismissive Lodkochnikov arm-folding, of which Raskol's earlier example had represented the latest version. "So you've come to talk to us," he said, smirking as Raskol had.

"Yeah," I said. I frowned. I looked chagrined. I shrugged. I hung my head. In general, I tried to look like a whipped dog.

"Mother!" called Mr. Lodkochnikov. "Peter's come to talk to us!"

Mrs. Lodkochnikov appeared.

"Big Ernie! Little Ernie! Ariane!" she called into the gloom. "Peter's here to talk to us!"

The two Ernies and their delectable sister appeared and stood behind their stocky parents. It would have made a good family portrait, with all of them folding their arms and smirking in the same way.

"So you come to talk to us, Peter," said Big Ernie.

"Yeah," I said, looking down at my shoes.

"I'll bet you've come to talk to us about Captain Macomangus's old boat, *Arcinella*," said Mrs. Lodkochnikov.

"Yes," said Mr. Lodkochnikov, twisting his smirk into a sneer. "I'll bet you've come to tell us that Captain Mac's old *Arcinella* is sinking."

"That's right," I said, surprised.

They laughed. They actually laughed.

"It's widely known, Peter," said Little Ernie.

"It's been widely known for quite some time," said Big Ernie. He snorted.

"The poor old thing's been on the way to the bottom with unseemly haste for upwards of a year now, Peter," said Mr. Lodkochnikov.

For a moment, I was relieved. It wasn't my fault. She wasn't sinking because I had rammed her into the bulkhead; she'd been sinking for a long time before that. Whew. Then, of course, the truth dawned. We'd been swindled, and it *was* my fault. I'd inspected *Arcinella* and pronounced her sound. I should have known. More to the point, I should have asked. Six clamboat experts, any one of whom could have told me what I had needed to know, stood there with their arms crossed, smirking, inviting me to realize that I had done a foolish thing, several foolish things, actually, and that the first of those several foolish things had been not asking for their help and advice. I understood, standing there looking at them smirking at me, that within a certain segment of Babbington everyone must know that I had done a foolish thing. All of Babbington along the waterfront must have known that *Arcinella* was sinking, certainly all the clamdiggers. I recognized it now, but, of course, too late.

"What a jerk," I said, shaking my head.

All six Lodkochnikovs emitted nearly identical snorts.

Mrs. Lodkochnikov asked, "Why didn't you come to us before you bought the boat, Peter?"

The tone of voice in which she asked this question told me that she was far more hurt than annoyed, and I realized that I had hurt her. I understand now, and I think that I understood even then, at that moment, when I raised my head to look at them and saw them with their brows knit, waiting for an explanation, that I'd committed a terrible sin of omission against our friendship: I hadn't come to them for advice in the one area in which they could lay claim to having mastered all the mystery.

They were poor people. Because they had so little, they must have found it particularly hurtful not to have been asked for one of the few things they possessed in abundance, their knowledge of sinking clam boats. My not asking them, my apparently disparaging the value of their counsel in the one area where they were rich, must have called into question my entire attitude toward them, made them wonder whether, behind my smiles and apparent demonstrations of friendship, I didn't think they were worthless. I hung my head again. I had betrayed my friends.

"Well, I—I don't know," I lied.

"Yes, you do," she said, "but even though you already know why, I'm going to tell you why, just so that we will both be aware that we both know why you didn't come to us for advice when it could have been most useful to you. Are you ready?"

"I guess."

"You fell victim to the sin of pride."

"I did?"

"Yes. And arrogance."

"That too?"

"You've reached that point in life when you think you know more about the world than you actually do. A little knowledge is a dangerous thing, Peter."

"Yeah, I've heard that."

"A little knowledge tempts one to ignore the advice of people who have more than a little knowledge. Do you know what I mean?"

"Yeah." She was beginning to sound like Dudley Beaker.

"You have let the arrogance of the ignorant get you into trouble."

"Yeah," I said, wondering how much more of this I'd have to endure.

"If you'd come to us, we might've had an opportunity to warn you against letting the arrogance of the ignorant get you into trouble."

"I know, I know," I said. I hung my head lower still, and shook it at my folly, and scuffed my shoes on the worn planks of the porch. I hoped that this was nearly over now, that in another moment they would be slapping me on the back and telling me all was forgiven and inviting me to borrow their bilge pump. That didn't happen. Instead, Mrs. Lodkochnikov pointed out another of my failings.

"And it wasn't only our advice that you eschewed," she said. "You should have gone to your grandfather Leroy before you even looked at a boat. You should have asked him to come along with you when you looked at boats. You should have asked him to negotiate for you when you were striking a bargain—"

All of that was true.

"You're right," I said.

"You were pig-headed," said Big Ernie.

"You were a fool," said Little Ernie.

"You can always count on my boys to sum up a complex argument in a few words," said Mr. Lodkochnikov, pounding his huge offspring on their backs, "a few words that even a pig-headed fool can understand."

They turned and disappeared into the dark of the house, leaving me with the terrible feeling that I had lost the best friends I'd ever had, and the likeliest source for the loan of a bilge pump.

33
Pride, Vanity, and Folly

THE LODKOCHNIKOVS wouldn't help me, so I was going to have to go to my grandfather Leroy and admit that I had been a fool when I advised my mother to buy *Arcinella,* and, worse, admit that I had dismissed as irrelevant or useless all that my grandfather had over his long life learned about boats and their tendency to sink, most of it probably learned the hard way.

My grandfather knew boats, really knew boats. He had built three: the sailboat *Rambunctious,* aboard which I had passed many happy summer days; the nameless little dinghy that he pulled behind the *Rambunctious,* which I rowed while he searched for crabs hiding in the shadows of the overhanging grasses at the edges of the islands in the flats on the far side of the bay; and a smaller sailboat, a little catboat called *Bumper,* which he had built for his boys, Buster and Bert; he allowed me to sail *Bumper* alone, and once I sailed her all the way across the bay and back.

We've established that I had a lot to learn, but I had learned some important lessons, and among them was the lesson that an unpleasant task like acknowledging a mistake is better done sooner than later, so I set out for my grandfather's house right away. From the Lodkochnikovs' it was only a short walk alongside the Bolotomy, in the upriver direction. I made the walk with my head down, kicking the dust at the roadside. I was reluctant to go, and I certainly wasn't hurrying on my way, but I was resolved to do what I had to do and to do it like a man. As I walked along the way toward Grandfather's house, I resolved to be truthful with him. That seemed very fine of me when I made the resolution, but when I began thinking about it, I realized that it meant that I was going to have to tell him that I had not sought his advice because I hadn't wanted it.

I began to muse on vanity and pride and folly and the way that they get a boy—particularly an adolescent boy—into trouble. My thinking, which I recall as remarkably keen and insightful for an adolescent boy, went something like this:

> I am an adolescent boy, and an adolescent boy has his pride, and his little vanities, and his misplaced affections, his follies.
>
> His pride develops when he recognizes that he is beginning to be someone. What is this thing called pride? It's the boy's own estimate of his awakening self, the degree of esteem in which he holds his forming self. (Pride's opposite is said to be humility, but from what I've seen in my life so far, most of what people claim as humility is really just another form of pride, the pride of people who hold themselves in high esteem for not being proud.) To the extent that pride influences a boy's actions, it will be an influence in the direction of wisdom and right choices if it is based on a real and accurate assessment of his merits and abilities, but it will be an influence in the direction of foolishness and error if it is based on a fantastic assessment, and an adolescent boy's estimate of himself is likely to be more dream than fact. So, his fantastic self-esteem will be one force nudging him toward folly.
>
> The vanity of an adolescent boy is his perception of the figure that his boy-self cuts in the world, his estimate of the estimate that other people make of that person-in-the-making, their placement of him along a line from respect to contempt. This awareness may be based on careful observation and sound reasoning, or—more likely—on fantasy, illusion, wishful thinking, despair, and fear. There are boys whose pride makes them want to be worthy in their own eyes, to be able to look themselves in the eye in the morning, in the mirror when they check to see whether this might be the day to begin shaving, and tell themselves that they're fine fellows, no matter what the world thinks; there are those whose desire for the regard of their fellows is grand and noble, those who seek true fame, the esteem of the worthies; and there are those who court the mob, who will do anything to be known, to be known for anything, just to be known.

When we—we adolescent boys—are deciding a course of action, we think first about what others will think of us and only second about what we will think of ourselves. We are vain first and proud second. We would rather be admired—or famous, the vain boy's dream—for some quality that we do not actually possess or do not in our hearts think worthy of admiration, than to be ignored though we know in our hearts that we are good and right and able.

That's a boy's vanity at work, but if he's granted some unearned admiration—let's say that he comes to be known as a boy who "knows boats"—he'll find that his pride is at work, too, and his pride will tell him that he's a fake, and so the vain boy will live in fear of discovery. He will fear that the people he has fooled will discover that he's fooled them, and so to avoid having to listen to the voice of his pride he begins fooling himself. He begins to give himself the credit that the credulous world gives him. He does not ask the questions that should be asked, does not seek the help that should be sought.

His actions often seem, from the outside, bold and confident, but he is standing at the brink of folly. Another step, and he falls. Once he has fallen, there's no pulling him back onto solid ground. He won't allow it. He won't even allow his friends to remain on solid ground. "If you're going to be my friend or keep my affection," his thinking goes, "you will have to join me in my folly, because I've decided to live in this fool's paradise, and I am inviting you to join me here. I feel—"

(Note the word that the young fool chooses: *feel,* not *think.*)

"—I feel that I will be happy here, and I don't want you to tell me that I won't. If you're willing to join me, then jump, friend, but if you will not jump, if you turn and walk away, then we are parted, we are citizens now of different lands, speakers of different tongues, and you are no longer my friend, cannot be my friend."

I reached my grandparents' house and stopped at the edge of the front yard, where I was still out of sight, behind a hedge. I thought about the conversation that my grandfather and I would have if I went inside.

I would be contrite.

He would be kind.

I would feel like a fool, ashamed of the folly that my pride and vanity had brought me to.

He would do his best to make me feel that I was no more foolish than he had been at my age.

I would not be convinced.

He would tell me a story involving some petty foolishness of his.

We would laugh together, and I would pretend to be relieved.

He would give me sound advice.

I would go on my way, wiser but humbled.

I would turn to wave good-bye, and I would catch him smiling indulgently, thinking that I still had a lot of growing up to do, a lot to learn.

I decided against it. I turned around and went on my way. I was on my own.

34
Arcinella, *All Fixed Up*

MY DUTIES as the Night Bailer of Babbington left me tired every morning, and my secret knowledge of *Arcinella*'s secret status as a sinking ship made me glum, but my mother and Patti were full of energy and hope, and they began each day chipper and chirping. They worked at a furious pace throughout the day, hardly pausing for lunch, just grabbing a bite of a sandwich now and then, and several times during the day their excess of hope and energy would inflate them to such a dangerous degree that they would burst into song as a way of letting off steam.

They went over *Arcinella,* topside, from stem to stern, fixing her up, making her look good—trim, shipshape, and, above all else, elegant. My mother from the very beginning had imagined the boat looking elegant, and for her the concept of elegance was encapsulated in the words "a black-tie affair." So she dressed *Arcinella* in a tuxedo. She and Patti painted her black and white—I should say that they painted her a rich, gleaming black and a pure, shining white, because those were the terms they invariably used—and an elegant job they did, too. In a week, *Arcinella* looked good. She really did.

Her hull and deck and the roofs over the cabin and the hold and the hatch cover forward were shining white. All her vertical surfaces and all the trim were gleaming black. The exhaust pipe that rose straight up from her engine was glossy black, gleaming, and the bucket that capped it to keep rainwater out when the engine wasn't running was gleaming black, too. On the starboard forward corner of the cabin, Patti and my mother had mounted a long pole, gleaming black, and from the top fluttered a satin pennant, white, with EEE embroidered on it in black satin script.

Throughout the week, while they were working abovedecks, I worked below. I had no idea what I should be doing, so I began doing what they were doing, fixing things up. This meant that from time to time Patti and my mother saw me bringing an armload of something damp and dirty up from *Arcinella*'s innards. They would wince at the sight of the load of muck I was carrying and shrink away from it. I could see that they were grateful to me for being willing to take on such a task, and they left me to my dirty work. Sometimes they asked how it was going, but they never came below to take a look, so they didn't discover the awful flaw that I had found.

While I worked, I praised myself, often, for enabling them to stay above in the sun where they could remain happy and hopeful, praised myself for working below, hiding the misery that came from knowing what I knew, suffering in silence so that they could enjoy the bliss of ignorance. (I discovered, then, that self-praise, in the form of silent fantasies about receiving unlikely rewards, from medals to money to murmured declarations of awe and affection, can keep a guy going during a disagreeable job, and that discovery has served me well throughout my working life.)

Once during the week, and only once, my mother paused in her work as I was passing on my way to the trash barrel at the roadside, sighed, and said, "Peter, are you sure you wouldn't like us to give you some help down there?"

"Oh, no," I said. "It's hot and cramped and dirty down below, no place for you and Patti. You two just go on fixing things up abovedecks, and I'll fix things up below."

She didn't ask again, and I did as I had promised, after a fashion, although, to tell the truth, I didn't work all the time. Sometimes I snoozed in the area forward of the engine and aft of the hatch, where I wasn't likely to be discovered.

What did I accomplish? I disposed of everything I found that didn't seem likely to be useful during an elegant excursion. I swabbed and scrubbed. Most of all, I cleaned *Arcinella*'s engine as thoroughly as I could. When I had finished, I thought the old Champion Six was a thing of beauty. That may not have been so to eyes other than mine. Beautiful it may not have been, but it *was* clean. However, I have since come to understand that in the case of *Arcinella*'s old engine cleanliness may not have been a good thing. Old engines acquire a protective coating of dirt and grease that shields them from the harsh reality around them the way that certain old people acquire a coating of beliefs and prejudices that they use to shield them from the annoying actualities of the changed world in which they find themselves stranded. To the eager lad who has learned a little bit about solvents, washing all of that away seems like a good idea, but sometimes the patient suffers for it.

I want to be clear about an essential fact: I didn't *fix* anything down below; I just fixed things up. In most phrasal verbs, such as *blow up, do in,* and *buy out,* the particle intensifies the base verb, often suggesting that the action is brought to a state of completion. In *fix up,* however, the particle weakens the base, suggesting an action performed only on the surface, something that falls well short of the simple power of *fix* alone. Just compare

I don't want you driving that old wreck until I've fixed it, Mom.

with

Let's fix up that old wreck and sell it to some sucker.

Instead of merely fixing *Arcinella*'s engine up, I could have asked Patti to entice one of her drag-racing admirers to come over and give the engine a thorough overhaul, to fix whatever needed fixing, change the oil, give it a ring job, adjust the carburetor and the timing, replace the points and plugs, and all of that. I knew the words, and the small part of me capable of a detached, logical assessment of our situation told me that bringing in expert help would be a very good idea, but all the rest of me resisted it, and the rest of me won.

So, at the end of the week, *Arcinella* looked neat and elegant, trim and sound, but while we stood on the bulkhead admiring her, her pennant fluttered in the stiffening breeze, straightened, and displayed the initials of Ella's Elegant Excursions, so that she seemed to wail, "*EEE*," and I knew why.

35
My Confidante

THE NIGHT BEFORE the shakedown cruise, I excused myself from the dinner table and said that I was going to walk over to the Purlieu Street School to see if I could get into a handball game, but I didn't head for the school. Instead, I crossed the highway and went to the diner, to use the pay phone there. I dialed Patti's number and listened to the ring. My hand was shaking, my heart was pounding, and my throat was dry.

"Hello?" said a voice.

"Hello, Mrs. Fiorenza, it's Peter." I could hear the tremor in my voice. "May I speak to Patti?"

"It's *me,* Peter," said Patti. "What's wrong? You sound upset."

"I am," I admitted. "Can you meet me tonight, late? Can you slip out of the house?"

"Sure," she said. "What time?"

"Midnight."

"I like the sound of that. At Dudley's?"

"Huh? Oh. No. At the boat."

"Arcinella?"

"Yeah. If I'm not there, wait for me, okay? Sometimes I have trouble getting out of the house. But wait for me. I'll be there."

"What's this about?"

"It's about *Arcinella.* She's—" I hesitated. The desire to have someone share the burden was strong, but I couldn't quite bring myself to tell Patti the whole truth.

"She's what?"

"She's—um—she's kind of like a person, don't you think?"

"Yeah. I do. She's very sophisticated, you know?"

"Sophisticated?"

"Yeah, now that she's all dressed up and elegant, ready for a night on the town?"

"Oh. Right. But—um—what about beneath the surface?"

"Hm?"

"What about—well—her heart?"

"You mean her engine? You've got that all fixed up."

"Oh, sure. That's no problem. That's all fixed up. Maybe I don't mean her heart. Maybe I mean what about—what about—her soul?"

"Her soul? Does she have a soul? She's a boat. Do boats have souls?"

"For that matter," I said, seeing and seizing an opportunity to step aside from the issue that had prompted me to call, "do *we* have souls? And what, exactly, do we *mean* by a soul? Let's omit the religious notion of a soul, since, as Dudley always used to say, 'That's a mythical quality, very much like the unicorn's horn.'"

"Ahhh, *Dudley*," she said knowingly.

"Personally," I went on, "I think that what we mean by the soul is the essence of the self—what we boil down to—not the us we know at this moment, right now, or at any other single moment, but what we are when we ignore the daily variations, the distortions of the self caused by temporarily strong but essentially fleeting influences, such as those brought on by joy or vexation."

"The essence of the self."

"Yes. But I wouldn't say that the soul is the ideal self, because some people have souls as rank and nasty as the viscous gunk that I cleaned from the bottom of *Arcinella*'s bilge."

"Ick," she said.

"However," I continued, "even though we have to factor out the distortions of transitory influences, I don't think we should deny the fact that the soul can be altered by experience."

"Like when people say that something is 'good for the soul'?"

"Right," I said.

"So a charitable act is good for the soul."

"Right."

"But some other things are bad for the soul."

"Like vicious acts, or miserly acts."

"I think you're saying that the soul is a container—"

"Yes! Yes! That's what I think!"

"A gas bag."

"Yes. A gas bag. And it enlarges or shrinks as we fill it or empty it."

"And the things in it can be good or bad—or a mixture—and each of us has a mixture that's unique."

"Yes, but remember that the soul doesn't hold everything. That's the self. The soul is within the self, but it is smaller than the self, since it is only the heart of the self. I should say the soul of the self."

"Like the nucleus of a cell if the self is the whole cell."

"Um—yeah—okay."

"You were going to say something different."

"I was going to say that it's like the living clam inside its shell."

"Of course!" said Patti. "The shell is just the outward self, the protective coating."

"But the innards are the real person, and the clam makes both of them, the inner and the outer, by sticking its neck into the soup of stuff around it and drawing it all in—"

"But then keeping only what it chooses to use—"

"And expelling the rest back out into the soup."

"It blows itself up, doesn't it?"

"Yeah, in a hard-shelled clam-like way, it does."

We were silent for a while, satisfied with ourselves, congratulating ourselves for being such clever kids.

"Of course, that's just an analogy," said Patti after a while. "But what about the human soul? What did you call it, the essence of the self? Where is it? Where does the soul reside?"

"I guess we will eventually discover that it resides in a set of minute chemical imbalances at the synaptic clefts in the brain," I said.

"Yeah, I guess you're right," she said, and I heard her pop her gum.

"But," I said, and as I said it I could hear myself slipping into Dudley's voice and manner, or perhaps I should say slipping even more deeply into Dudley's voice and manner, "even thinking about the electrochemical states of all those neurological interstices is so difficult that we prefer to think of the soul as intangible, and even when we as a species someday succeed in mapping all of the brain's neuronal highways, byways, switch-backs, crossroads, and dead ends and can at last see the so-called soul for exactly what it is, most of us will go on thinking of it as intangible, in a manner similar to the way in which we go on thinking that the sun rises and sets though we know that it isn't so."

"We are rational beings only when we remember to be."

"Um, yeah," I said, hearing from her what I had intended to say myself. "That's right."

"In other words, most of the time we don't think: we feel, and our feelings guide us."

"Right," I said, a little annoyed that she should be making my points for me.

"We twitch and twist and lash out without reason, like dogs dreaming, always a comical sight, and we would be every bit as comical as dreaming dogs if we didn't turn our nightmares into excuses for perpetrating horrors upon our world and upon our fellows."

"I begin to suspect, my dear," I said, as Dudley would have, "that you have been reading my notebooks, my diary, my private animadversions on what we laughably call human understanding."

A giggle. "I have peeked at it," she said, "when you're not looking."

I cleared my throat and said, "Well in that case I suppose that it will come as no surprise to you to hear that I think that the reason for mankind's being so readily inclined to believe that there are forces at work in the world beyond *all* comprehension is the fact that there are *some* forces at work in the world that are beyond our comprehension, or because the effort to comprehend them is too much for us."

"They give the entire species a headache."

"Yes. I—ah—couldn't have put it better myself."

"It *is* easier, and in a way more exciting, to allow oneself to believe that the world is full of mysteries that we will never understand, that there is a spiritual side to life that is insubstantial but all-pervading, and forever unknowable."

"Yeah," I said, myself again, "like that gas bag we call the soul—and that brings me back to the subject of boats."

"It does?" she asked, as herself.

"It does, because—I'll tell you this, and you can think I'm crazy if you want—while I was working inside *Arcinella,* down in the hold, cleaning the engine, I felt that I was ministering to a being, that she was a soulful thing, a thing with a spirit, like something alive, and that she had a soul. We—we fixed her up. We cleaned her up, spiffed her up, put a good face on her, made her up so that she looks as if she's ready to go out to a party, but the buoyancy's escaping from her soul, and it's being replaced by something denser and darker; she's melancholy; she's in the grip of a deep and abiding pessimism, and I get the feeling that she's weary of this life."

"What the heck are you getting at, Peter?"

"She's sinking."

"Oh," she said. "That. Yeah. I know."

36
The Night Bailer Gets Some Help

PATTI WAS ALREADY ON BOARD *Arcinella* when I arrived, sitting on the deck forward of the hatch, crosslegged, with her shoes off. She waved silently when she saw me coming. With barely a word, we went below. Patti was fastidious about touching anything greasy, and seeing how careful she was not to touch anything, I realized how dirty everything still was down there. I'd fixed it up to my standards, but they weren't Patti's, or my mother's.

Patti crouched alongside the engine and, almost immediately, pointed at a particular part and asked, "What's that?"

"That?" I asked, stalling for time, since I didn't know.

"Yeah, that."

It was a protuberance with a handle on top of it. It looked like a valve of some kind, so I took a chance. "It's a valve," I said.

"A valve," she said, with a teacher's mirthless smile, "and what's that valve for?"

"I don't know," I said. When she pouted at that, I added, "I mean, it's probably—"

"—a way to pump the bilge dry when the engine's running," she added for me.

"What?" I said, amazed.

"Sure," she said. She leaned closer to the valve and examined it, tilting her head from side to side. After a moment, she pointed to a short length of tubing that protruded from one port of the valve. "See this?" she asked.

"Yeah," I said. The tube extended downward from the valve to a point about half an inch from the centerline of the hull, into the bilgewater at a low point near the heavy timber of the keel.

"And see this?" she asked, pointing to another tube that extended from the valve and ran to a fitting in the hull, from which it could draw water from the bay.

"Mm-hm."

"And see this?" She rose and pointed to a length of hose that was clamped to a domed housing at the upper front of the engine and ran to an outlet at the side of the hull, above the waterline.

"Uh-huh."

"Here's the deal," she said. "This valve controls the flow of cooling water through the engine block. If you turn it the way it's turned now, bay water comes in down there, flows through the block, and then exits there. That's the way it's supposed to be set up normally, for a boat that's not sinking. But if you turn the valve the other way, the engine will pump the water out of here—"

"Bilgewater."

"What?" she said, glaring at me in wonder and incipient anger.

"The water in here—it's bilgewater. That's the bilge."

"Oh. I thought you were saying you didn't believe me. When you said, 'Bilgewater.' It sounded like the nautical equivalent of 'bullshit.'"

"I guess it is, actually."

"Anyway, the engine will pump the bilgewater out of here and send it out into the bay—*back* into the bay, I guess you could say."

"How do you know this?"

"I asked."

"Asked?"

"I asked your grandfather."

"Oh."

"I was talking to your grandmother, doing some research."

"What?"

"Doing some research. I'm still working on the question of your paternity, you know."

"Oh. Thanks."

"Anyway, we were talking, and your grandfather came by, and I told them both about *Arcinella* and asked if they'd like to see her all fixed up.

Your grandmother didn't come, but your grandfather did, and he spent about an hour with me, looking her over."

"Did he tell you she was sinking?"

"No, but he did point out the valve, and told me what it was for, and told me how to use it."

"Knowing that you'd tell me."

"Yeah," she said sweetly and softly. "And from that I figured out that she was sinking, but he didn't want to tell me that she was—" She hesitated, but then went on to add, "—because he didn't want me to think that you were a jerk."

"I should have asked him to take a look at *Arcinella* before we bought her," I confessed. "If he had—"

She put her hand on my arm and said, "You're right. That's what you should have done, but it's too late now, so you might as well forget about it," describing in a few words an attitude toward life that I wish I had adopted at the time and maintained without alteration ever since, instead of the attitude I did adopt, the one that makes me wake in the night and lie there sleepless and fretful, my memory full of every mistake I have ever made, every misstep, every folly, my anxiety asking which among my little ships is sinking fastest.

"I wonder why Captain Mac hasn't been using the engine to pump the old girl dry," I said, to get us off the subject of my culpability.

"He probably didn't want to attract attention. It's awfully quiet down here along the river at night, and there are houses right across the street. Somebody would be sure to wake up and call the cops, don't you think?"

"You're probably right," I said. I had been thinking that I would start the engine and use it to bail *Arcinella,* to pump her full of air, but I understood that I couldn't, and I said so. "I guess I don't want to attract attention, either. If somebody did call the cops, they'd want to know what I was up to, and my mother would find out that the boat's sinking." I sighed and said, "I'd better start bailing," hoping that Patti might offer to help. She didn't.

I bent to my work, and a voice from over my shoulder said, "Bailing is for chumps."

I knew who it was without looking. It was my old friend Raskol. When I did turn and look, I found that he was squatting on deck, looking in at us through a porthole, grinning. In another moment he was down in the hold beside us.

He was smiling. He had a couple of lengths of garden hose coiled over his shoulder, and in his hand he held a small metal device. He handed the device to me and said, "If you knew enough about old clam boats to know what to pray for when yours is sinking, this would be the answer to your prayers."

It was a length of tubing, threaded at both ends, with an opening along one side.

"What is it?" I asked.

"It's a jet pump," he said.

I looked at it carefully.

"It has no moving parts," I said. "How can it be a pump?"

"Give it here," he said.

I did, and he went to work. In a few minutes, he had connected a garden hose to either end of the jet pump. One hose he ran through the hatch and into the Bolotomy. The other he attached to the nearest of the faucets that sprouted at intervals along the docks and supplied boat owners with fresh water from the town tank. Then he did what I had been telling myself he surely didn't intend to do. He turned the water on.

"You're putting her out of her misery?" I asked, and I tried to sound as if I were kidding when I said it.

"Nope," he said, soberly, "I'm bailing her out."

"By filling her up?"

"Come here," he said, and he led Patti and me onto the foredeck. He bent over and pulled the end of the other garden hose from the dark river. Water was rushing from it.

"Now come below," he said, dropping the hose into the river again.

When we were below, he lifted the pump from the bilge and held it so that the opening was just at the surface of the bilgewater. We could hear, and even see, the bilgewater rushing into the opening and out into the Bolotomy.

"What a little sucker!" exclaimed Patti.

"That's amazing," I said. "How does it work?"

Raskol gave me a look. "Very well," he said drily.

"But I mean, what makes it work?"

"I don't know," he said. "It's one of the great mysteries of life."

37

The Mysteries of the Jet Pump Revealed

GATHER ROUND, Saturday-morning documentary viewers. Move right up close to the television screen. You can bring your bowl of cereal with you. Today we're going to learn about fluid dynamics. We'll begin by conducting a little experiment. Ready? Okay, here we go.

First, you're going to have to find a small piece of paper, the sort you might use for taking a telephone message. Go on, get that piece of paper, and hurry right back.

Now hold that piece of paper in front of your mouth, grasping it only by the edge nearest your mouth, leaving the far edge free to flap. Note that the piece of paper curves downward toward the far edge, bending under its own weight.

Blow briskly and steadily across the top of the piece of paper. It rises, straightening until it is nearly horizontal.

Why does that happen? Well, by blowing across the top of the piece of paper, you create a stream of air that is moving very rapidly relative to the air below the piece of paper. Because the pressure within a moving fluid decreases as the speed of the fluid increases, the pressure above the paper becomes less than the pressure below the paper, and the greater pressure lifts the paper, pushes it up.

The statement that the pressure within a moving fluid decreases as its speed increases is known as Bernoulli's principle, because it was formulated in 1738 by the Swiss mathematician and physicist Daniel Bernoulli, who showed that the total energy in a steadily flowing fluid system is a constant along the flow path. Because the total energy is constant, an increase in the fluid's speed must be matched by a decrease in its pressure.

Bernoulli's principle explains the working of an airplane's wing. The shape of an airfoil creates an upper surface that is longer than the lower surface. Because the entire wing moves through the air as a unit, air flowing over the longer upper surface has to flow faster to get from the leading to the trailing edge, with the result that the pressure is reduced on the upper surface, making it less than the pressure on the bottom surface. The resulting pressure difference sustains the plane in flight. We call this phenomenon lift; that is to say that the conventional name for the phenomenon is lift, but I contend that we might as well call it suck. From one point of view, the wing is lifted, pushed upward, by the greater pressure below it—a kind of blowing—but from another it is sucked, pulled upward by the lower pressure above it. I submit that this is an equally valid explanation, but perhaps you disagree. Perhaps you feel that in claiming an equivalent between blowing and sucking I am just "playing with words." If you feel that way, I invite you to perform another experiment. Assemble the apparatus shown below:

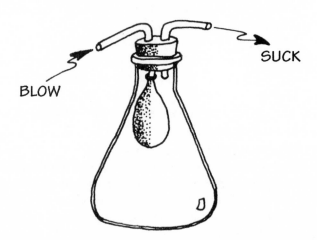

Ready? Okay. Now blow into the tube that leads to the balloon. The balloon will inflate, of course. As it inflates, hold a finger very near the end of the other tube, and you will feel that air is being driven from the flask as the inflating balloon occupies more of the interior volume. Stop blowing, and allow the balloon to deflate. Now suck on the other tube, the one that leads to the interior of the flask, not to the balloon. As you suck, the balloon will inflate. So, you see, under the right conditions, sucking is an inflationary force, and so the Night Bailer was quite right to characterize his nocturnal mission as inflation rather than evacuation.

Enter G. B. Venturi, Italian physicist, who discovered that the speed of a fluid flowing through a tube could be accelerated by introducing a tapering constriction into the flow path. Bernoulli's principle tells us that Venturi's constriction will also lower the fluid pressure, since an increase in velocity must lead to a decrease in pressure, and so we come at last to the jet pump.

A cross-section of a typical jet pump is shown below. Water from an

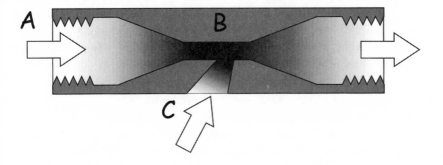

outside source (the "drive water") enters inlet section A under pressure. As the water passes from the inlet to the throat section B, its velocity increases and its pressure decreases. Then, depending on your point of view, either the relatively lower pressure within the throat section sucks or the relatively greater pressure outside the pump blows water from the bilge into the extractor inlet C. Finally, the drive water and the bilgewater are ejected into a discharge hose and carried away.

The claim is often made for jet pumps that they have no moving parts, therefore nothing to maintain, and nothing to break, but that isn't so. The drive water must come from an outside source, under pressure, which means that the pump must be incorporated in a system that provides the water and the pressure, the medium and the motive force, and that system must having moving parts, must be subject to wear, must, inevitably, eventually, break. Everything does. The mind. The heart. The bowels. Everything.

38
A Brief Aside on Hope

OF ALL THE LIFTING GASES, the lightest and loftiest is hope, the best of gases and the worst of gases. It swells your soul and sends you soaring. It gets you up there, where the air is rarefied, but then, when you need it most, when you are suspended so high above the daily difficulties that we call "it all," hope has the most annoying way of leaving you flat. You cannot hold it in forever. Your lungs cry for a fresh breath, even though you know that what surrounds you is not the lifting gas of hope but the ambient air of quotidian care and disappointment, a gas with no lift at all. Unable to sustain yourself any longer, you let the last of hope escape in a sigh, and, sighing, sink.

> What makes hope such an intense pleasure is the fact that the future, which we dispose of to our liking, appears to us at the same time under a multitude of forms, equally attractive and equally possible. Even if the most coveted of these becomes realized, it will be necessary to give up the others, and we shall have lost a great deal. The idea of the future, pregnant with an infinity of possibilities, is thus more fruitful than the future itself, and this is why we find more charm in hope than in possession, in dreams than in reality.
> Henri Bergson
> *Time and Free Will,* "The Aesthetic Feelings"

Every dream remains one by virtue of the fact that too little has succeeded, become finished for it. That is why it cannot forget what is missing, why it holds the door open in all things. The door that is at least half-open, when it appears to open onto pleasant objects, is marked hope. Though . . . there is no hope without anxiety and no anxiety without hope, they keep each other hovering in the balance, no matter how far hope outweighs for the brave man, through the brave man. However, hope too, which can deceive with will-o'-the-wisp, must be of a knowing kind, one that is thought out in advance.

Ernst Bloch, *The Principle of Hope*

39
The Art of Starter-Whacking

IT MUST HAVE BEEN Thursday or Friday when I began to think that Ella's Elegant Excursions really might be a success, and the shakedown cruise on Friday night convinced me.

My mother was full of confidence, and Patti and I caught it from her. That's not quite right. I began by faking my confidence, to please my mother, and to please Patti, but like so many affectations, this one became real enough after a while for me to lose the distinction between confidence faked and confidence felt. When Patti and I caught each other's eye, we exchanged no winks or secret smiles to indicate that either of us was indulging my mother in her folly. We were with her. Her folly was ours.

My mother emerged from my parents' bedroom wearing a raincoat, said a quick good-bye to my father, asked him to wish us luck, waited a moment, accepted a grunt as good wishes, and hurried out to the car. When we stopped at Patti's house, she was waiting on the porch, also wearing a raincoat, and she ran to the car and slid in beside me, breathless with anticipation. We exchanged looks, took a deep breath, drove to the dock, and boarded *Arcinella*.

Patti and my mother busied themselves abovedecks, and I took the bucket from the exhaust pipe and went into the wheelhouse to start the engine.

I pressed the starter button. From the engine room, I heard a dull metallic click, nothing more.

I pressed the button again. Another click.

"Third time's the charm," I said, as my grandmother would have in the circumstances, and pressed the button again. Not even a click.

I went below. I looked at the engine. What could I possibly do to make the thing start? I knew nothing about its innards, so I wiggled its wires and flexed its fan belt. I thought about giving it a good whack with something, and the hatchet that Captain Mac had left behind came immediately to mind, but I dismissed the impulse as childish and went back to the wheelhouse.

I pressed the starter button, and nothing happened, nothing at all. The sun was beginning to set, and I was beginning to sweat. Panic was setting in. I hurried below, not because I had any idea what I might do down there to get the engine running, but because I didn't want my mother to see me in the wheelhouse and ask me if anything was wrong.

Squatting there, staring at *Arcinella*'s engine as if it might tell me what to do, I began to realize that Patti and my mother didn't seem to be moving around much abovedecks. They must have finished whatever they had to do, and now they were just waiting for me to start the engine. The thought made me begin to wring my hands, and I had nearly decided to go above and confess that I couldn't get the engine to start when I heard a deep male voice say from the quayside, "Good evening, ladies. Don't you look nice."

"Why, thank you, sir," said my mother, coyly, in the manner of the Southern belles in movies.

I looked through one of the forward-facing portholes and saw that the man onshore was Mr. Lodkochnikov, Raskol's father.

"Where's young Peter?" he asked.

"He's below," said my mother, "getting the engine ready for our shakedown cruise."

"I haven't been aboard *Arcinella* for a very long time," said Mr. Lodkochnikov. "Do you suppose I might have permission?"

"Oh," said my mother, surprised by the fact that it was she who had the right to grant permission to board, "why, of course."

Mr. Lodkochnikov, a short, thickset man, lumbered aboard.

"Very nice," he said. "Very, very nice."

Patti giggled; apparently he hadn't been talking about *Arcinella*.

"Mind if I go below and get a gander at the old gal's innards?" he asked.

"Not at all," said my mother. "See if you can get Peter to hurry up. The sun's already starting to set."

Mr. Lodkochnikov made his way into the wheelhouse and through the little door, wheezing and grunting all the way, until he was beside me. Without any greeting, he asked in a whisper, "Want some help?"

"Yes," I said, with a sigh of relief. I thought, for a moment, of apologizing to him, telling him that I had learned my lesson and felt the full weight of my error in not having sought his advice, the savvy of the entire Lodkochnikov clan, before my mother ever bought the boat, but he grinned, winked, and grunted, and I took that to mean that he understood everything, that he forgave me, and that he didn't want me to embarrass myself by saying a single word about it, so I didn't.

"Bat'ry's dead," he said, as if it were the kind of arcane knowledge that would ordinarily have been revealed only after a secret ceremony involving blood.

"Oh," I said, despondently, since a dead battery was so, well, fatal.

"We'll use the bat'ry from your mother's car," he whispered, and then, loudly, he said, "Good idea, boy! Very good idea! I'll get it for you." He grabbed a wrench from the box of rusty tools the captain had left behind, went above, where he told Patti and my mother that I'd had the inspired idea of replacing the dead battery with the one from my mother's car, then removed the battery from her car and carried it belowdecks, where he installed it in place of the dead one.

"Give her a whirl," he said when he was done.

In the wheelhouse, I pressed the starter button, and something whirled, but the engine didn't start.

I bent over and peered down into the engine room.

"Well," he said, grinning for some reason, "the pinion gear on your starter motor is not engaging the rack on the flywheel."

"Ah-ha!" I said, as if I knew what he was talking about. "I thought it sounded like that. Is there anything we can do?"

"Oh, sure," he said, still grinning.

"What?"

"Well, old Mac used to whack her with a hatchet. Didn't he leave you the hatchet?"

"The hatchet? Yeah. He left a hatchet. I keep it in the cupboard in the wheelhouse, with the slickers—just in case." (Secretly, I had assumed that the hatchet was for battling sharks. I had never seen a shark in the bay, but when I discovered the hatchet, I came, through an erroneous process of reasoning, to the conclusion that if Captain Mac had carried a hatchet there must certainly be sharks in the bay but that through a lack of coincidence they just never happened to be around when I was around.)

Mr. Lodkochnikov, without asking "in case what?" said, "Well, you get that hatchet."

I did.

"Now," he said, "you give a couple of whacks on the end of the starter motor—not too hard—here, wait a minute. I'll show you."

He said all of this as if it were as it should be, as if everyone ought to know that the captain of a clam boat kept a hatchet for whacking a recalcitrant starter motor, as if he were surprised that I had not mastered a skill that every boy my age ought to have mastered, and perhaps he was right in thinking that I was insufficiently educated, but starter-whacking wasn't the sort of operation that I ever saw in the industrial documentaries I watched on Saturday mornings.

He demonstrated how to whack the housing of the starter motor with the flat end of the hatchet. "Not too hard, now, because you don't want to knock the damn thing right off the bracket, but you got to give her enough of a whack to free up the shaft in the starter and get it to engage."

He gave it a whack. He gave it another.

"If a couple of whacks don't do it," he said, "then you give her another spin with the starter button up there so's you get the teeth into a different position and then you whack her again."

"Uh-huh," I said.

"Do that," he said.

"What?"

"Hit the starter again."

"Oh. Okay."

I pressed the button, and almost as soon as I had he called out, "That's enough. Come on back down here."

He handed me the hatchet.

I gave the end of the starter motor a timid whack. He made a sweeping motion with his hands to indicate that I ought to give it a less timid whack. I did, and I was rewarded with a metallic clunk from the opposite end of the housing, a clunk that, even to a neophyte starter-whacker like me, clearly meant success.

When I pressed the button, the starter engaged, and the engine started. My mother and Patti cheered.

40

The Shakedown Cruise

MR. LODKOCHNIKOV made his way through the wheelhouse and was headed for shore when my mother stopped him with a hand on his arm. "Mr. Lodkochnikov," she said, "won't you accompany us on our shakedown cruise?"

Embarrassed, awkward, he said, "Oh, I couldn't—I—"

"Please," said my mother.

"You can stand in for all the paying excursionists who'll be aboard when we begin regular service," said Patti.

"I'm not very elegant," he said, offering as evidence his callused bayman's hands.

"Tonight," said my mother, "you are."

When he was seated comfortably in a deck chair forward of the hatch, drinking a glass of champagne, we made our way downriver and onto the bay through the stillness of the evening and its fading light, the Champion Six rumbling easily, just loafing, and the slick smooth hull of the sleekest and prettiest clam boat on the bay hardly parting the water, barely leaving a wake. *Arcinella* was a smooth thing, and she rode gently on the water when her bilge was dry. She seemed confident and capable, ready, a reliable underpinning for our venture. So she seemed.

My mother and Patti, dazzling in long, slinky, bias-cut satin gowns of a silvery moonlight-white, were busy, going through the motions of providing the attentive service that they hoped would bring to Ella's Elegant Excursions admiration, renown, and paying customers, offering Mr. Lodkochnikov little pastel sandwiches from a silver tray and working through my mother's checklist of policies and procedures, circulating among the phantom excursionists and chatting them up, offering almonds, which my mother considered the only really elegant nut, and lengths of celery filled with cream cheese tinted rose and mauve, like the picturesque clouds that floated along the horizon, pouring invisible champagne into invisible glasses, making mock introductions, priming silent conversations, pointing out landmarks on the shore, and encouraging the proper admiration of the summer sunset, but although they were in constant motion they never gave the impression of working hard. They were as smooth as *Arcinella*. All of us were gliding, enjoying our buoyancy and the beguiling belief that from now on life would be like this for us, that the way would be easy, the tide would always be in our favor, we would have a broad-beamed sturdy ship beneath us and the soft air of summer evenings in our hair and the gentle bay glowing golden in the evening light. At one wonderful moment, just before we came to the place where the river broadened and lost itself in the bay, Patti and my mother slipped into the wheelhouse, and we all stood together in the little cabin, savoring the flavor of our coming success, as if it were the sweet custard in a yeasty doughnut, and my mother put her arms around Patti and me, and it was such bliss that I almost forgot that the boat was sinking.

"People are going to love this," said Patti.

"Do you really think so?" asked my mother. She wasn't concerned or doubtful; she just wanted to hear Patti say it again, and like a good acolyte, Patti did.

"Oh, yeah. They are going to love it. It's going to blow them up."

"It's really going to change this town," I said. "Everything's going to be much more elegant from now on." I said it because I knew what my mother wanted to hear. She had in her mind's eye and in her heart a vision of what an elegant excursion ought to be. It ought to be as elegant as a cocktail party in a black-and-silver movie from the 1930s. I suppose that no one could make a clamboat seem to be as elegant as that, which may explain the complete absence of clamboats from the sophisticated comedies of the 1930s. However, my mother had the vision, and she had infected us with it. She had the confidence that it could be done, that we could do it, and she had infected us with that, too.

"Where should we go?" I asked.

"Anywhere," she said, blithely. "Anywhere you like. You're at the wheel. *Arcinella*'s in your hands. You take her wherever you think she wants to go. Patti and I will keep the excursionists happy." I think I expected her to wink after she said that last bit, to make it clear that what she'd said was just a joke, that this was only practice, but she didn't. Instead, she tapped Patti on the shoulder, and the two of them returned to work, moving around the deck as if it were crowded with elegant excursionists who had to be kept happy.

I turned *Arcinella* toward the east and the broader part of the bay, keeping her moving along just fast enough for a smooth ride, but not fast enough to suggest that we had anywhere special to go, since the idea of a destination or the threat of a deadline can suck the air of elegance out of any excursion. At the leisurely pace of people with no particular place to go, we chugged our way under the bridge that crossed the bay, and into the waters off South Hargrove, where, with decorous elegance, I swung *Arcinella* in an arc as broad as the width of the bay, till she was turned west, toward home again.

The sun was down, and the stars were out, but there was still enough of a glow in the sky to silhouette Mr. Lodchochnikov in the bow, in his deck chair, where he sat smoking, looking at the stars, accepting with a nod of his head Patti's offer of a little cognac: the very picture of an elegant excursionist and a satisfied customer.

WHEN WE REACHED *Arcinella*'s slip, I brought her in perfectly, so smoothly and gently that the bow barely touched the dock, and the champagne glasses on the tray that my mother had left on the roof of the cabin didn't even jiggle. Mr. Lodkochnikov lifted himself from his chair, stretched, declared with a contented sigh that it had been "a lovely excursion, just lovely—the sky, the stars, the champagne, the beautiful ladies, the steady hand at the helm—everything," kissed the hands of Patti and my mother, saluted me, and left for home.

We watched him walk away, then silently turned to cleaning up after him and his phantom companions. We said nothing to one another as we worked. I think that all of us shared the same desire: to savor our success personally, focusing on the part of it for which we felt individually responsible. For me, it was that perfect landing. I didn't want anything to

interrupt that period of self-congratulation. I had done well, and knew it,
and I was proud.

WHEN WE HAD FINISHED, we stepped from the bow to the bulkhead
and then to the margin of the roadway, and when we were all ashore, we
turned to look at *Arcinella*. She was a little wet with dew. Her glossy
paint glistened in the yellow streetlamp light and the silver moonlight.
She looked neat, trim, elegant, and beautiful.

"She's beautiful," said Patti.

"Yes," I said. "She is. I thought she was beautiful that first night we
saw her, but now—"

"It shows what a little spit and polish can do," said my mother.

"And paint," I said.

"And the right clothes," said Patti. She raised her arms and pirouetted.
"The right clothes, the right walk, the right talk, and you can turn a tramp
into a lady. Thank you, Ella."

She had embarrassed all of us, including herself. We looked at the
ground for a while, and then my mother said, "Well," and Patti and I said,
"Yeah," and we got into the car and drove to Patti's house.

AT PATTI'S HOUSE, I got out of the car, walked to Patti's door, opened
it, and held it for her. She slid out, holding the long satin dress with one
hand, and taking my hand with the other, and we held hands all the way to
her door, where I said in a voice deeper than the one I ordinarily used,
more like almonds than peanuts, "May I be permitted to tell you how very
beautiful you look in that gown, Patricia?"

She kissed me, slowly and affectionately, and said, "Tomorrow night?
At Dudley's?"

"Yes," I whispered into her little ear. "Tomorrow night."

MY FATHER was sitting up, watching an old movie on television.

"Well?" he asked, turning briefly toward my mother.

"Mr. Lodkochnikov loved it."

"Good," said my father. Then, a moment later, "What? Who?"

"I'll tell you all about it tomorrow, Bert. I'm too tired now." She went to him, leaned over and threw her arms around his neck, and hugged him. "But it was a great success, a wonderful success."

"Any sandwiches left?" asked my father.

"In the refrigerator," she said, "in waxed paper."

I went upstairs to my bed, undressed, masturbated, and fell asleep. It had been a wonderful day, a wonderful night, the best night that Ella's Elegant Excursions would know, my mother's greatest success.

41

Testing the Hypothesis, Part 3, in Which I Discover Certain Magic Words of Great Value to a Seducer of Young Girls

Do we show the public . . . the mechanism behind our effects? . . .
Do we display all the rags, the paint, the pulleys, the chains, the
alterations, the scribbled-over proof sheets—in short, all the horrors
that make up the sanctuary of art?
  Charles Baudelaire,
    quoted by Walter Benjamin in *The Arcades Project*

PATTI (AS ELLA) AND I (AS DUDLEY) sat facing each other in the
chairs before the fire, but I hadn't lit the fire. It was summer, after all.

"Dudley," she said, "can I tell you a secret?"

"Of course you may tell me a secret," I replied, supposing that I knew
the sort of secret she intended to divulge.

"Okay—"

"I hope, Ella, that you will consider all your secrets safe with me."

"Oh, sure—"

"And it is also my hope—my fervent hope, I might say—that you will
be as frank and forthcoming in disclosing your secrets to me as you would
be if you whispered them to your pillow in the privacy of your own bedroom." Here I winked a wink that went unnoticed, or at least unacknowl-
edged.

"Yeah. I will. So—"

"In short—"

"Dud!"

"Yes, my dear?"

"Shut up and let me tell you!"

"Of course."

"When I grow up—"

"Ah, my little darling, I almost wish that you would never grow up."

"When I grow up, I want to be famous."

"Ah, fame." I brought the tips of my fingers together and nodded. "There are many species of fame, Ella, but most of them are not worthy objects of your desire. I would much rather you said that you wanted respect, or admiration, than fame."

"But I do want to be famous. I want people to know who I am. I want them to nudge one another when I walk by and say 'That's Ella. She's a big success.'"

"Success, too?"

"Yes. Fame and success, that's what I want. And I know how I'm going to get them, too."

"Do you, now?" I asked with the slightly amused, slightly weary, slightly wary tone of condescension that Dudley had used with me when I told him that I thought I could probably build an airplane out of a wrecked motorcycle and some scrap metal if I took a correspondence course in welding.

"I'm going to buy a boat," she began, and, slowly, hesitantly, as if some of the details were coming to her on the spot, she laid before me the whole plan for Ella's Elegant Excursions, from the purchase and conversion of the clam boat to the pastel sandwiches and champagne. When she had finished, she sat for a moment, flushed with excitement, a little out of breath, and then sank, as if the lifting gas of hope had been displaced by denser stuff, the murky waters of doubt, and without looking at me she came to the point, asking meekly, "Do you think it will work?"

To tell the truth, sitting there in my chair with years of life lessons behind me and my cupped hand warming the last shallow swallow of cognac in my snifter, I didn't. I don't know when the shadow of doubt had first fallen over the charming fantasy she laid before me, but I do know that by the time she had finished I saw the enterprise for what it was, or

what Dudley would have considered it to be, a quixotic undertaking, and I
saw the principals in the effort—Patti, my mother, and me—for the poor
deluded fools they were.

Patti raised her head and turned her eyes toward mine. She wanted an
answer.

"I don't think it will work," I said, and I swear to you now that I could
see the tears well up in her eyes with each word I spoke. Seeing those
tears standing in those dark eyes, hearing her breath catch, seeing her
chest heave, something came over me, a change so profound and complete that I would not be exaggerating if I said that in the interval between
two heartbeats I became another man. Who could have been or remained
so hard a man as to stick to the truth of his thoughts when a little lie could
dry those tears, ease that breath, return a flutter of hope to that sweet bo-
som? Not I, not I. I leaned toward her, extended my arm across the space
between us, put my hand beneath her darling chin and raised it so that she
was looking into my eyes again. "Unless you *make* it work," I concluded
with enthusiasm.

She brightened. Seeing the effect of a mere five words that did no
more than offer the *possibility* of a future success, I searched for something that would inflate her further. I understood, somehow, that I had to
proceed with caution. I couldn't use a jet pump. I had to use something
gentler, a method of inflation that Patti-playing-Ella wouldn't detect or
would be willing not to detect. I chose parable.

"I know how very many things young people wish for," I began, slowly. "After all—"

I paused, picked up my pipe, peered into its bowl, and allowed a wistful chuckle to escape from me.

"—I was young once myself, you know."

This she rewarded with a bit of a smile, her small hand on my knee,
and a squeeze.

"So I know that the thought arises in a young person's mind that he—
or she—can do something that will make the world take notice, and become famous—rich and famous."

Now at this point a very odd feeling began to come over me, a revela-
tion, perhaps, or inspiration, perhaps, but whatever it was it really did
come over me, creeping over my skin, warm and tingling and exciting, as
if it had entered the room on a breeze rather than arising from within me,

and I shuddered—not from fear or cold, but from sheer excitement, because at that moment I relived with vivid immediacy the moment years
earlier when I had admitted to Dudley that I thought that if I did manage
to build an airplane out of a motorcycle and scrap metal and flew it across
the country, I would certainly become famous as the first boy to fly solo
across the country in a plane that he had built from a motorcycle and
scrap metal after learning how to do his own welding.

"Forget it," he had said, in many more words than that, specifying for
me all the difficulties that I would have to overcome if I were to succeed
and specifying as well all the character flaws that would in my case turn
the difficult into the impossible.

In a kind of trance, speaking as Dudley, speaking to Patti, to my mother, and to myself, I said, "It will in all probability not be easy. Do you
remember the old story about the droll madman who attracted crowds by
inflating a dog?"

"Sure I do."

"Think, for a moment, about the part of the story that you have *not*
heard."

She drew her brows together and pursed her lips. "What part is that?"
she asked.

"It is the part that is never told, the part that the listeners would not sit
still for, the part about all the effort that the madman put into making himself the famous dog-blower of Seville. Just think what that took! Think
about all the hours that our clever madman spent learning to inflate a dog,
hiding in a shed somewhere with a poor stray upon whom he practiced.
Think of the failed attempts, the disappointments, the disappointments
piled on disappointments, the dogs that ran away, the ones that bit him,
the ones that burst like overstretched balloons and sprayed themselves
across the walls of the miserable isolated dwelling where he sequestered
himself while he was mastering his art."

"Ooh," she said, grimacing in sympathy with the overblown dogs.

"Think of the anguished bouts of self-examination, when the madman
held his head in his hands and asked himself whether he shouldn't have
chosen some other path to fame, when he despaired of ever developing
the skill to inflate a dog, doubted that anyone would be interested in witnessing the inflation of a dog even if he succeeded in accomplishing the
feat, and the times when he questioned his underlying motive, his thirst

for fame, asked himself whether fame was a thing worth pursuing and wondered whether he wouldn't be happier abandoning the pursuit and settling into a comfortable obscurity."

"Gee," she said. "It sounds—almost impossible." I had brought her to the brink of tears again, but I knew what I was doing.

"Oh, no," I said at once. "Not impossible. The madman of Seville *did it,* remember. And *you* can do it, too. You *can* succeed at this. You *will* succeed at this. You'll be famous for it. I know you will. I *believe* in you."

I barely managed to get the last words out, because she was in my lap, kissing me, running her tongue into my mouth, slipping her hand into my pants.

LATER, UPSTAIRS, in Dudley's bed, I lay on my back smiling at the ceiling in a state of goofy bliss. I was keeping my silence, because the only word left in my lexicon seemed to be *wow.* Patti was propped on an elbow, leaning over me, running her fingertips along my penis as if it were a pet.

"Where did you learn to talk like that?" she asked.

I drew a long, deep breath, reclaimed myself, and said, "From listening to Dudley, sitting in the chair where you were sitting. I guess it's a case of 'like father, like son,' except that he never offered me any encouragement. Just the opposite, in fact. He never said that he believed in me."

"Mmmm," she said, and then, after taking a moment to consider whether she would say anything else, she added, "About that 'like father, like son' business? I don't think so."

"What?"

"I've been doing lots and lots of research, much more than you know, and I'm beginning to have some other ideas."

"Really? Even after tonight?"

"Even after tonight. Tonight was—well—fantastic."

I smiled—beamed, to tell the truth—and said, "Aw, shucks, ma'am, twern't nothin'," as movie cowboy heroes did after they'd singlehandedly liberated a prairie town from a band of desperadoes.

She squeezed my penis; it was the equivalent of poking me in the ribs with her elbow. "I mean 'fantastic' as in 'probably never happened,'" she said.

42

Splash! Flash! Ella's Opening Night

MY MOTHER STOOD IN THE BOW, holding a clipboard that she had painted white and decorated with tiny edible silver balls that were meant for decorating cakes. "Ohh," she wailed, checking her guest list. "Do you think anyone will show up?"

"Sure," said my father, still struggling with his tie. "It's a free meal with all the booze they can drink. They'll show up."

"The mayor? Do you think the mayor will come?"

"That fathead? Any chance to make a splash, he'll come. And I guarantee you he'll try to grab the spotlight. Mark my words."

"Oh, Bert, stop fussing with that tie. Let me fix it for you."

She swatted his hands aside.

"I don't know why I let you talk me into this," grumbled my father.

"It's only for this one time," she said, "just the opening night, the grand opening. How would it look if Elegant Ella had to greet the cream of Babbington society without her elegant fella?"

I saw a car come around the bend from the direction of town.

"Hey," I said. "Here comes somebody."

"Oh, my God," said my mother.

A car pulled up, but it wasn't what we'd been hoping for: it was a wreck, a jalopy. Out of it rolled a distinctly inelegant little man, rumpled and sweating in a baggy brown suit, with a porkpie hat pushed back on his head, a cigarette dangling from his mouth, and a big Speed Graphic camera in his hand.

My mother glided to the bow with a walk I'd never seen before. My father's expression suggested that he'd never seen it before, either.

"Good evening, good evening," she gushed in a voice not quite her own. "Welcome to Ella's Elegant Excursions. I'm Ella."

"Winky Wills," the little man announced, extending his pudgy hand toward my mother. His cigarette bobbed as he spoke. "Ace photographer. *Babbington Reporter.*"

"Oh!" said my mother, thrilled, scared, flustered. She shook his hand vigorously, then turned to us and nearly screamed, "This is Mr. Winky, everybody!"

"Wills," he said, struggling aboard. "But it don't matter. Winky'll do."

He shook my father's hand, and mine, then turned to Patti and gave her a professional appraisal. "How's about a little cheesecake before the boat gets crowded, toots?"

"Gee, I—"

"Great advertising, kid."

"Well, okay."

He got her to perch on the low cabin over the engine, cross her legs, and pull the hem of her dress up over her knees.

A car crunched to a stop in the gravel beside the bulkhead. Then another, and another. Doors opened, doors slammed.

My mother said, "Good evening! Good evening! Welcome to Ella's Elegant Excursions. I'm Ella," and "Welcome, welcome, welcome," again and again. She cried it, she gushed it, she giggled it. She was so grateful to them all for showing up.

And more and more excursionists did show up. For a while there was an unbroken line of them, stepping aboard, being handed aboard by my mother, getting their pictures snapped by Winky Wills, standing beside my mother in her slinky satin gown, or beside Patti in her slinky satin gown. With every arrival, my mother checked her guest list, and despite the fact that there were so many eager excursionists, she worried that the mayor would not show up.

"Ohhh, Peter," she said. "Do you think he'll come?"

"Sure he'll come," I said, though I had no reason for thinking that he would. "Don't worry, Mom."

"I don't know," she said. "He may have bigger fish to fry."

"Oh, Ella," said Patti, laying a hand on my mother's bare shoulder, "don't you worry. Tonight you're the biggest fish in Babbington."

My mother gave Patti a hug of thanks for that encouragement, and as she did so the mayor's car pulled up. How did I know it was the mayor's car? The mayor's was the only car in town driven by a chauffeur, a miniature of the Babbington town flag flew from the radio antenna, and the license plate said MRMAYOR.

My mother's eyes widened, she stood tall, and she glided to the bow. "Why, Your Honor!" she said, as if his arrival had been the last thing on her mind. "Mr. Mayor!" she said, as if he hadn't ever been invited to sample Ella's Elegant Excursions gratis. "My goodness," she said, consulting her clipboard with the merest suggestion of a frown, as if she didn't expect to find his name there. "Welcome," she said, as if despite his having blundered in uninvited he was indeed welcome, as any stray would be welcomed by so generous an outift as Ella's. Where had she learned all this? From the magazines she read? Were there articles about running your own aquatic excursion business? How to dress? How to speak? How to handle the arrogant late-arriving big shot?

The mayor at that time was L. D. Gerber. He was short, fat, and vain. His wife was a head taller than he, and she thought herself slim. It may have been an issue of perceptual distortion. For this occasion, Mrs. Gerber, to her everlasting credit in my mind, had dressed herself in a pink gown accented by a feather boa. She struck a particularly festive note, and unlike the mayor, who seemed to want to treat the evening as a re-election rally, she seemed inclined to have a good time.

"Oh, my dear," she said, clasping both my mother's hands as she lumbered aboard, "what an elegant fantasy you've created!"

Patti arrived with champagne. For a while, she and I circulated among the excursionists, pouring champagne and passing out pastel sandwiches. The excursionists greeted one another and sipped and chattered. More than once, as Patti squeezed through the growing crowd, I saw men and women alike turn and crane their necks to get a look at the glorious way white satin slid across her bottom. Everywhere there was an air of eager anticipation. *Arcinella*'s deck was becoming more and more crowded— overcrowded.

My mother caught up to me and tugged my sleeve. "Peter," she said, "you'd better cast off and get the show on the road before anybody else shows up. We've got all we can hold—and then some."

"Aye, mom," I said.

With the assurance of an old hand, somebody who's been through it before and actually does know what he's doing, I cast off the bow and stern lines and backed *Arcinella* out of her slip. I took her downriver toward the bay, smooth as, well, silk sliding across a nubile bottom. When we reached the broad waters of the bay, my mother leaned in through the wheelhouse window. "Patti and I can't keep up with them," she said. "Is there any way you can give us a hand? Pour champagne or pass hors d'oeuvres?"

"Um, sure," I said. "I can tie the wheel for a while."

I throttled *Arcinella* down to an easy glide and tied the wheel so that she'd scribe a broad arc across the widest part of the bay. I was on my way out of the wheelhouse to lend a hand in the attempt to keep the guests supplied with food and drink, when Winky Wills, ace photographer, leaned in and said, brandishing his impressive camera, "Think I could get a picture of you behind the wheel, kid?"

In a flash, a mental image formed in my eager little adolescent brain: the image of young Peter Leroy, me, on the front page of the *Reporter*, guiding *Arcinella* with a steady hand. "Sure!" I said, but a glance at my mother showed me how overworked she was. "Um, but, can we put it off a little, just till things calm down? I've got to help with the hors d'oeuvres."

"Sure," he said. "Do what you gotta do. But—tell me somethin'—if you're gonna be handin' out hors d'oeuvres, who's gonna be driving the boat?"

"Ah!" I said, feeling like a very clever lad indeed. "I tied the wheel. She'll just scribe a broad arc across the widest part of the bay. Should be a nice smooth trip."

At that point, one of the guests stuck his head through the wheelhouse window and asked, "Hey, kid, any more champagne?"

I shrugged at Winky and hustled off to pour champagne. Winky snapped a picture of me on the job, as a waiter.

The boat was crowded to the very edges of the deck with guests. "Freeloaders," muttered my father as I passed. It was hard to squeeze through the crowd without disturbing people, who disturbed other people, and so on, so my passage caused a ripple, and when the ripple reached the edge of the crowd at the edge of the deck, the ripple effect made people grab at the nearest someone to keep from falling overboard. In one group, while I was refilling glasses, a corpulent braggart telling a golfing story mimed the motion of a swing and the resulting ripple nearly knocked a woman overboard—on the opposite side of the deck.

Fog began to creep in. It grew thicker and thicker. My mother and Patti and I were busy serving and amusing the guests, but I think we were all aware of the fog. I know I was. I kept peering forward apprehensively to see if there was anything like an iceberg in our way. There wasn't, so I stayed on the waiting job, pouring and passing.

Then, from a group standing in the bow, came cries of alarm.

"Oh, my God!"

"Oh, no!"

"Look out!"

A channel marker had suddenly materialized on the starboard side, so close that it could have been another person in the group.

The fog had kept me from noticing that the current of the outgoing tide had drawn us off the course that I had set, out of the broad and open part of the bay and into the archipelago beyond the clam flats, where the shallow waters were cut by channels for larger boats that drew more water than *Arcinella* did. These channels were narrow, not the aquatic superhighways that are marked by bell buoys, but the equivalent of two-lane blacktop roads, maintained by the county. They were marked with wooden posts, painted black along their shafts and white on their rounded tops, which resembled the miters on the bishops in my plastic chess set. Panels painted white and carved to resemble herring gulls' wings projected from the sides of the posts to indicate the direction of deep water.

As the marker slid harmlessly by, Mayor Gerber shouted, "Iceberg!"

His group laughed at that, because he was, after all, the mayor.

"A regular comedian," muttered my father.

Before the laughter died, and before I managed to squeeze through the crowd to the wheelhouse, another channel marker emerged from the fog on the port side. *Arcinella* struck that one, not quite head-on, making contact about two feet back from the bow, sending the boat veering violently to starboard and pitching the mayor's wife overboard.

Flash! Winky Wills was in the right place at the right time, and he got a shot of her going bayward to port.

"Sweetie?" said the mayor as she vanished. "Oh, my goodness. Sweetie! Somebody do something!"

Flash! Winky got a shot of Porky White, gallantly, fearlessly, and unhesitatingly diving in to save Sweetie while the mayor cried for help. Flash! Winky got a shot of Porky standing in about three feet of water holding Sweetie in his arms. Flash! A shot of Sweetie back aboard and clinging to Porky.

"My darling Sweetie," cried Mayor Gerber, "are you all right?"

"Oh, yes," she said, batting her lashes at Porky. "I'm quite all right—thanks to this gallant corsair."

"This is really outrageous," said the mayor, smarting, I think, more from having been put in a position where he looked indecisive and cowardly than from Sweetie's attentions to Porky. "Mrs. Leroy, you really ought to have hired an experienced bayman to captain your craft—rather than entrusting the wheel to a—a—witless incompetent."

He glared at me so that there would be no doubt which witless incompetent he meant. I hung my head.

My father, standing tall, said with a sneer in his voice, "Just a minute, there, 'Your Honor.'"

All eyes were on him. I was surprised and pleased that he was going to defend me, and I wondered, fleetingly, whether Mr. Beaker would have done so had he been there.

Throwing a protective arm over my shoulder, my father said, "He may be a witless incompetent, but he's doing the best he can."

That brought him some laughter and applause. I almost laughed myself.

Noticing that he had everyone's attention, my father went on. "When it comes to being at the helm, if you want my opinion, the voters of Babbington should've entrusted the governance of the town to a man like—"

For a heady moment I thought he might say "my son, Peter," but he didn't, of course.

"—Chester White!" was what he said. More laughter, with Mayor Gerber leading it. "You can laugh if you like," said my father, nodding his head, "but Chester leaped in while you stood there spluttering like a—a windbag—and a blowhard!" That occasioned much nervous laughter among the excursionists, who sensed a town scandal in the making.

My mother handed Sweetie a couple of towels, and I squeezed through the crowd to the wheelhouse. Mayor Gerber followed me. I was expecting a lecture—or worse, since the thought had occurred to me that as mayor he might be able to command bailiffs to clap me in irons and throw me in the pokey when we got back to town. Instead, he took a bottle of champagne out of the bucket, popped the cork, sank onto the deck, and begin drinking it as if it had been prescribed. I set to work, untying the wheel and turning *Arcinella* toward home. In a while, I heard the mayor begin singing "Nobody Knows the Troubles I've Seen." I allowed myself a quick glance backward. He was at the stern, sitting on the deck, his shoes off and his pants legs rolled up, his legs dangling overboard, swishing his feet in *Arcinella*'s wake.

A few well-dressed, good-looking people, the very sort my mother wanted to attract to her elegant excursions, were standing beside the wheelhouse. One of the men in the group raised his glass in the direction of the drunken mayor and said, "Isn't that elegant?"

His audience tittered.

A second man said, "Oh, very elegant, very, very elegant, but—" and he held aloft a little sandwich on bread tinted robin's-egg blue "—this is the very *heighth* of elegance."

His audience roared.

My mother, far enough away not to have heard the remark but near enough to have heard the laughter, turned toward the group and smiled. Her eyes shone. The second well-dressed man raised his sandwich again, in her direction, and leaned toward her in a suggestion of a bow. She acknowledged it with the suggestion of a curtsey, and the group laughed again.

43
The Morning After

MORNING SUN FILLED the dining room, but to me the day seemed gloomy, despite the fact that I found Patti at the dining room table across from my mother.

(An aside, before I allow the morning after the grand opening to continue, on the subject of moods and weather: Why does the weather so rarely conform to our moods when our moods are so often willing to conform to the weather? Having written that, I realize that my moods are no longer as willing to conform to the weather as once they were. Maybe the weather no longer has any influence on my moods. Maybe the weather has only a negative influence on my moods, all weather. A sunny day doesn't inflate me, despite the promises in songs, but a cloudy one can certainly deflate me; so can a sunny one, now that I think about it. More to the point, perhaps, is the fact that I am so rarely blown up and buoyant these days that I seem to be slowly sinking all the time. Maybe, at fifty-six, I have become a grumpy guy.)

Though I was gloomy, my mother's mood was as sunny as the day. . . .

WHEN I WAS READING a draft of this memoir to Albertine, she interrupted me at this point to say, "You should take that out, Peter. The whole aside."

"Should I?" I said, surprised and, to my additional surprise, disappointed to hear her say so.

"Yes, you should."

"Why?"

"Because it isn't honest."

"It's not?"

"No. I have been silent about this for a long time, but now that you seem to be about to misrepresent yourself in print, I cannot remain silent any longer."

"Yikes," I said, if I recall correctly.

"For some reason—and I suspect that I know the reason—it has become one of your cherished self-delusions to think that grumbling and cursing and beetling your brows and gnashing your teeth will erase your reputation as a happy screwball and turn you into a respected and awful curmudgeon. Face it: the moment you enter a room people start giggling. You scatter hilarity in every gloomy corner of this painful kingdom."

"I do?"

"Yes. You do. You're inflationary."

"Gosh."

"You blow people up."

"They couldn't be persuaded to think of me as deep?"

"No."

"Weighty?"

"No."

"Not even if I affected the dark foreboding grumbling of a thundercloud? If without a warning, without any cause or provocation that anyone could see, I sucked the sunlight out of the day—"

"That would be very dramatic, but no."

"But I have some sad tales to tell, and I have some verbal sludge to sell. If people would only go down below and look, they'd see that my bilge is full of turbid—"

"No," she said, "they wouldn't. They wouldn't see it. They'd only see the glint of silvery light shimmering on the surface of your bilgewater."

"But if I took them down there, down belowdecks—"

"They'd think you were being whimsical."

"Shit."

"Droll."

"God damn it."

"Charming."

"Fuck."

"You're just not any good at playing the sinking ship," she said, slipping a consoling arm across my sagging shoulders. "You might as well float."

MORNING SUN FILLED the dining room. My mother's mood was as sunny as the day.

"Wasn't that a wonderful night!" she said.

Patti and I exchanged a glance. My mother really seemed to think that the night had been a success. On the table in front of her was a copy of the *Babbington Reporter* with the banner headline

"ELEGANT EXCURSIONS" MAKES A SPLASH

On the front page there was a large photograph of Sweetie Gerber going overboard. There was a smaller photograph of Porky White, standing in the water, holding Sweetie. Inside, an eyewitness account of the episode filled most of the gossip column, "Bruited About Old Bolotomy," since my mother had had the foresight to invite Deirdre Perkle, who wrote "Bruited About," and another version of it had aired on "Wake Up with Ann 'n' Andy," the morning show on WCLM, since my mother had invited Ann and Andy, too.

My mother picked the paper up and beamed at it. "I bet all Babbington is talking about us this morning!" she said.

"I—um—well—I guess you're probably right," I said, but I couldn't imagine that Babbington would be saying anything very flattering about us. Would the mayor's wife be telling everyone what a wonderful time she had getting thrown into the bay?

"What we have to do this morning, first thing," said my mother, flipping her pad to a clean sheet of paper, "is make a sober assessment of our first excursion. We're going to do this every morning—take a cold, hard look at how well we did and think about what we can do to make the next night's excursion even better. That way we'll be getting a little bit better every time, and we're sure to succeed."

"Okay," said Patti, and I nodded, though I wasn't sure about "sure to succeed."

"First, let's look at how much money we took in."

"Wait a minute," I said, hating myself for having to say what I had to say. "We didn't take in any money. Nobody paid anything. Everybody was an invited guest."

"Yes, of course," said my mother, "but let's figure out how much we would have taken in if everybody *had* paid."

"Why?" I asked.

"You silly!" said my mother, reverting, I think, to some slang from her teenage years. "Because that way we'll know how much we *will* take in when the boat is as full as it was last night."

"And people *are* paying," Patti added.

"And people *are* paying," my mother agreed, and both nodded their heads to make it clear that they understood each other perfectly.

"Okay," I said.

So we went through it, all of it. We added up what would have been our gross, and we deducted the cost of food and drink, gasoline and oil, salaries for ourselves, and what seemed like reasonable payments for our investors. We had made a profit, a handsome profit.

"Wow, that sounds pretty good," I said. I can see myself as I was then, at that moment. My eyes were wide and bright. I was running a series of mental multiplications, carrying the night's profit out across the summer, all the summer nights, each a little better as word of mouth did its work, each enjoying an incremental increase, puffed up a bit by a factor that floated into the equation on a gentle zephyr from Shangri-la. I completed my calculations, and though I didn't announce the astonishing figure, I did summarize the results, in this manner: "Wow! We're gonna be rich!"

My father came into the room at that point. It was his habit to sleep late on weekends, and when he woke up he would walk with the dullness of sleep into the kitchen in his underwear and pour himself a cup of coffee. He winced when he heard my prediction, as if I'd foretold a disaster.

My mother smiled the smile that mothers use when they want to dampen but not douse their children's exaggerated hopes, "If," she said, and to emphasize it she said it again, "*if*—we can keep it going as well as it went last night."

My father sighed. He turned toward us, opened his mouth, and stood there with it open. I know—and I knew even then—what was going through his mind. He was thinking of enumerating the very many ways in which "it" had not gone at all well last night. There was so much that he might have said that he didn't know where to begin. Mentally he tried several beginnings and rejected them. Finally, exhausted by the attempt to begin, he gave up. But still he wanted to say something, to get himself on record, so that when my mother failed he would be able to say that he told her so that morning in the dining room after the opening night, when Peter predicted that we were going to be rich, and so he said:

"You can't build a business on ifs, Ella."

There was an awkward and painful silence.

Patti broke it: "Oh?" she said. "I think all the best businesses are built on ifs."

"Oh, yeah?" said my father. "Name one."

"The Studebaker Corporation," said Patti.

"What?" said my father.

"Henry and Clem Studebaker went into business together on February 16, 1852, with no more capital than sixty-eight dollars and two sets of blacksmith tools," she said, reciting a lesson that every Babbingtonian who had passed through Mrs. Tillnell's civics class knew by heart, "and forty dollars of that they had borrowed from Henry's wife. On their first day in business, they made twenty-five cents. Twenty-five cents! But did they give up? No, they did not. They said to themselves, 'If we can just do ten percent better tomorrow, and ten percent better the day after that, and so on and so on—we're gonna be rich!' And just eight years later they were turning out thousands of the Conestoga wagons that carried hopeful settlers westward, looking for a place to plant their future, and today—well, you tell me, Mr. Leroy—is there a single working stiff in America who doesn't dream of putting a Golden Hawk in the garage? I know my pop does."

"Well," said my father, rubbing the stubble on his chin, "maybe you're right, but—"

He paused, searching for some little thing that might reassure him that he, not she, was right, because he knew he must be right. He found it. I could see that he had found it.

"—but if you want to sell excursions to the average working stiff, you've got to have the common touch."

"The common touch?" said my mother, not quite gagging.

"Yeah. Your father may dream of driving a Hawk, Patti, but the last time I saw him, he was driving a Transtar Deluxe half-ton pickup. People may have their dreams, but they don't buy dreams. They buy pickup trucks. You're not selling pickup trucks, the way it is now."

"Pickup trucks are not—" my mother began.

"—elegant," my father finished for her. "I know. But take it from me, if you want to fill that boat, you're going to have to—"

"—not be elegant?"

"Well, maybe you don't have to go that far—but you should think about dropping those little sandwiches."

My mother knit her brows and exhibited a pout remarkably like Patti's.

"Well," said my father, "at least get rid of the colored bread."

44
Six Days

SATURDAY: When we arrived at the dock that evening, there was a crowd waiting for us. People were snapping pictures of one another standing at the edge of the bulkhead smiling, with *Arcinella* in the background.

"The power of the press!" declared my mother, and she and Patti and I were exultant as we piled out of the car and went about the business of preparing for the evening's excursion.

Our work was interrupted often by questions from the assembled multitude, most of them about the dunking of the mayor's wife.

"Where was she standing, exactly, when she went over?" asked a man about my father's age.

"Oh, just over here," said my mother, indicating the approximate spot.

"Mind if I get a picture of Doris standing there?"

"No, of course not," said my mother.

She handed Doris aboard, and Doris stood in the spot where Sweetie had stood.

"Make like you're going over, Doris," called the man, raising his camera to his eye. Doris widened her eyes and opened her mouth and threw her arms in the air and leaned over the side and very nearly lost her balance, but her husband got the shot he wanted.

"Great! Thanks!" he said. My mother extended a hand to him, assuming that he would want to come aboard, but instead Doris squeezed past her, grasped her husband's hand for support, and hefted herself back onto shore. They walked to their car, got in, and drove off. Some of the other curiosity-seekers drifted off, too.

I think that there must have been thirty or forty people in the crowd when we arrived at the dock. When we set out on the excursion, only eight of them came along. The rest snapped pictures from the shore as we chugged downriver.

My mother whispered to Patti, as they began passing sandwiches and pouring champagne, "I thought we'd have more."

"Tomorrow night," said Patti. "You'll see."

SUNDAY: We were ready, we were nervous, we were hopeful, and we were anxious. We were, all of us, still full of hope for our enterprise, my mother's enterprise. My mother's dream was still our dream, and it was still a young dream, still a dream that held the door at least half-open, still offering a view of pleasant prospects, but I had begun to suspect that hope was full of trickery and I had to wonder whether the pleasant prospects weren't illusions, like the cardboard dioramas in sugar eggs.

Only two couples arrived at the dock to embark on an elegant excursion that evening.

"We heard it was quite an adventure," said one of the women as my mother handed her aboard.

At the end of the evening when my mother handed the woman back onto the wharf, she said, "It was very nice," but she sounded disappointed.

We were silent for quite a while, making *Arcinella* shipshape and packing up for the drive home.

"It was because it's a Sunday night," I said, because I felt that somebody had to say something. "That's why only two couples showed up."

"Right," said my mother, eager to agree. "We've learned something: Sunday is not a night when people go on nautical excursions."

"After all," said Patti, "they've got to be at work Monday morning."

"That's why the couples who did show up were so old," I added.

"Over seventy!" guessed Patti.

"They were retired!" said my mother, in the manner of Archimedes discovering displacement, "They don't have to go to work on Monday!"

"But just about everyone else does," said Patti.

My mother nodded her head and then, raising a finger to underscore the lesson we had learned, said, slowly and emphatically, "So, it would probably be best not to sail on Sunday nights in the future."

The three of us smacked ourselves on the forehead simultaneously and on the ride home we repeated the lesson several times and each time laughed about our failure to consider the unique nature of Sunday nights.

MONDAY: On Monday, we saw no excursionists at all. We sat on the hatch cover and waited, and with each passing minute hope closed that open door another fraction of an inch, and we grew a little bit gloomier.

I looked at the sky. It was clear overhead, with a thin sketch where the moon would later shine. The sun was beginning to set, and in the distant west a cloud or two stretched lazily above the horizon.

"It's the weather," I said.

Patti and my mother looked up, looked around, looked at me, looked skeptical.

Pointing westward, I said, "See that bank of clouds in the west? People probably figured that they might drift over here, bringing rain. One of those summer downpours. One of those sudden summer downpours."

"But," said my mother, "they didn't."

"No," I said, "but they might have."

"Most people are very concerned about not getting their good clothes wet," Patti offered, looking at my mother, hoping she'd accept the offer.

"Overly concerned, if you ask me," I said. "Especially when you think about how little damage water actually does to clothes."

"And rain," said Patti, making another offer, "puts a damper on things, even just the chance of rain."

"You said it," I said. "The notion of rain as an agent of depression is so ingrained in our culture that we can't really expect people to rise above it."

"Oh, yeah," said Patti. "Rain is so deflating. Getting wet, being wet. It's all deflationary. Just think of the things people say, like, 'Don't rain on my parade.'"

"Or, 'Don't be a wet blanket,'" I said.

"Or, 'It's a washout,'" said my mother.

"Yeah," I said.

"Yeah," said Patti.

The three of us frowned as one. We began packing up. We were glum. I wished, in the inarticulate way that one wishes for things, that I could make us all happy, and I happened to glance upward, at the sky, at the clarity of the sky, the glaring emptiness of it that threatened to expose our hopes as delusions, ourselves as self-deluded fools, and in the mysterious manner of all inspiration, its accusatory clarity afflated me. Pausing to look at the sky, holding my hand out as if to feel the rain, I burst into song: "Trickle, trickle—"

Patti understood at once; to my call she responded, "Splash, splash—"

We were off, singing "Trickle, Trickle," a song recorded by the Videos, now recognized as a doo-wop classic, and a favorite of Patti's and mine from the moment we first heard it, but a commercial flop when it was released. We packed up and drove home in the mood of people whose summer picnic plans have been disappointed by a downpour, people who are singing to keep their spirits up but singing as if they were singing because their spirits are up, floating quite well on their own, undampened by that downpour, needing no songs to keep them up.

TUESDAY: On Tuesday, as departure time neared, I saw a couple walking toward us along the road from the area near the Lodkochnikovs' house. They were clamdiggers, with the look of peasants—good, sturdy, honest folk, but not the sort that one would ordinarily expect to be interested in taking an elegant excursion. However, as they drew nearer, it began to seem to me that they really were headed for *Arcinella*. "Hey," I said to my mother, not much above a whisper, "I think we might have some customers."

She looked down the road and said, doubtfully, "Really? You think so?"

"I guess you must be Ella," said the woman when she reached us.

"Why, yes," said my mother. Certain now that she really did have a couple of customers, she added, formally, "Good evening. Welcome to Ella's Elegant Excursions."

"We heard that the trip was very restful and romantic," said the woman, who didn't seem to notice my mother's offer to hand them safely aboard and clambered onto the foredeck unaided. "That's what old Lord Caught-yer-cough told us."

"Lord—? Do you mean Mr. Lodkochnikov?" I asked.

"Lod—? Say it again?"

"Lodkochnikov."

"Is that how you say it?" She seemed astonished.

"Well, I think it is," I said. "It's how Mrs. Lodkochnikov says it. And it's how I say it when I'm talking to him, and he's never corrected me."

"Never corrected me, neither," she said, "and I been calling him Lord Caught-yer-cough ever since I've known him, which must be"—she became coy and gave me a poke—"let's just say quite a few years."

"That's all anybody ever calls him," muttered the man.

"Maybe I've got it wrong," I said. "But I'm really glad he suggested that you come for an excursion."

"He said it's restful and romantic," the woman said again, nodding her head.

"But be sure to bring your own food, he told us," said the man, "because otherwise you don't get enough to stuff a guppy." He held up a paper bag.

We gave them the full treatment. They drank the champagne, refused the caviar, sampled the little sandwiches out of politeness, ate the fried chicken and potato salad they had brought, and held hands and smooched in the sunset.

WEDNESDAY: On Wednesday, while we were loading supplies on board, the harbormaster came by. I knew right away that he was the harbormaster because he came chugging up in a launch with HARBOR-MASTER painted on the side in big red letters.

"Ahoy, *Arcinella*," he called out.

My mother said, "Oh, hello," and then rather self-consciously corrected that to, "Ahoy—um—Harbormaster."

"Permission to come aboard?"

"Oh, yes, of course," said my mother.

He swung the launch alongside with consummate skill and nonchalance, hopped aboard, and looked around. After a while, he said, "Nice job you did on the paint. Very nice."

"Why, thank you," said my mother. "Would you care for a glass of champagne?"

"No, no. I couldn't do that."

"How about a sandwich?" asked Patti.

The harbormaster considered the plate of sandwiches very carefully, and very carefully selected a pink one. Juggling the sandwich and his

clipboard, he said, "Happens that I've got something for you. Mm, delicious. You see, *Arcinella* is still registered to Captain Macomangus." He
began filling out a form. "Doesn't really taste pink, if you know what I
mean. Tastes like clam dip."

"It is," said my mother.

"No kidding. Well, she'll have to be re-registered in her new owner's
name before next Wednesday." He finished filling out the form on a pad
that made four copies, tore the bottom one off, the one that was almost
illegible, and handed it to my mother. Then he saluted us briskly and
hopped back into his launch.

"What'd you do, use those Tintoretto's Tints to get it pink like that?"
he asked, with one hand on the wheel and the other on the throttle.

"Yes," said my mother.

"Cute idea," he said, and chugged off, waving what remained of his
sandwich.

My mother, Patti, and I huddled over the form.

"It's expensive," said Patti.

"Oh, not that expensive," said my mother.

"More than we've brought in so far," I pointed out.

THURSDAY: "Somebody in Babbington has got to be looking for a good
time," said my mother, pacing the deck.

"You're right!" said Patti. "Here they come!"

Four carloads of noisy people pulled up and began spilling out of their
cars. They'd already been drinking, and they'd brought their own liquor.
They were not an elegant bunch.

"Uh-oh," said my mother.

By the time we had reached the bay it was clear that the group was
indeed looking for a good time, but their idea of a good time was getting
good and drunk and tossing their inhibitions into the bay. One of the
women—tipsy, voluptuous, and, to be frank about it, thrilling—cornered
me in the wheelhouse while *Arcinella* was on her long arc at midpoint in
the excursion.

"Hi there, Captain," she purred.

"Hello," I said. "Hi."

"I think you're doing a great job."

"Um, thanks."

"You haven't hit anything yet."

"Yeah," I said. "I mean no. Not yet."

"Do you suppose you could show me how to drive the boat?"

"Um, well—"

She wriggled in between me and the wheel. After a minute or so of moving the wheel a little this way and a little that way, she turned herself around so that she was facing me and asked, "Can you keep your mind on your driving and on me at the same time?"

I was flattered, excited, flustered, and suddenly shy. Here was a grown woman showing the kind of interest in me that grown women ordinarily exhibited only in my dreams, and, on top of that, admiring my boat-handling skills.

"I can try," I said, and she snickered lasciviously.

Wham! Patti slid the window glass aside. "Peter!" she spat. "Would you tear yourself away from what you're doing and turn this damned boat around? I'm black and blue!"

"Um, sure, yeah," I said.

Patti glared at the drunken bimbo I was more or less embracing, and the drunken bimbo glared right back. Patti stormed off. I began turning the boat slowly toward home.

In another moment, my mother was at the window. "Peter!" she said. "Take us home! Full speed!" She turned away, shaking her head and saying, "This is not what I had in mind, not at all." I assumed, of course, that she was talking about my conduct in the wheelhouse, conduct unbecoming the helmsman of an excursion boat, a young man in a position of trust.

"You'll have to go now," I said to the woman.

"Game called on account of mom?" she said. Then she raised both eyebrows, winked, and shrugged, and ducked under my arms and wobbled out of the wheelhouse.

When *Arcinella* was secure in her slip and the drunken excursionists were all gone, we climbed into my mother's car and went home without a word.

45

My Mother Aphorizes

THEN FRIDAY CAME AROUND AGAIN. We were to sail at seven, and as seven approached, we preened (and, secretly, we prayed; at least I did, and I suppose that Patti and my mother did; I was still a believer then, and the god I believed in was a god of gifts, omniscient, avuncular, and capricious, who could give or take, and despite his apparently total lack of interest in my needs and desires, his complete unwillingness to give me help when I asked for it, I asked him for help now; I asked him to make this night a success for my mother, and I promised to keep my room neat and clean if he would; I probably should have offered more).

Aboard *Arcinella*, preparing her for the evening, we anxiously asked one another whether we looked all right, whether everything was ready, whether we had enough supplies, and so on, and so on, never asking whether anyone would show up. I started *Arcinella*'s engine and nudged the throttle as low as I dared go, so that she rumbled low, ready and steady.

Patti and my mother paced the foredeck in their satin gowns, striking poses, adjusting each other's hair, and pretending not to watch the road for signs of excursionists.

In time, some excursionists did arrive. There were only four of them, but they were two young couples with stars in their eyes, and Patti and my mother greeted them enthusiastically and for the next few hours did a very good job of pretending that four excursionists were ideal for *Arcinella,* that everything was as it should be, and that they would consider Ella's Elegant Excursions a success if those two couples left the boat happy, but the look in my mother's eyes whenever she glanced in my direction told me that it wasn't so.

When the night was over and the two couples had driven off, we were sitting in my mother's car, and I was silently congratulating myself for having kept *Arcinella* afloat for the entire week, when my mother and Patti burst into tears.

"Now, now, what's all this?" I said, leaning forward from the back seat and giving each of them a comforting squeeze. "Don't let it get you down. I grant you that it wasn't the night we'd been hoping for, but don't let a little setback make you lose heart. We're going to use tomorrow and Monday to figure out how to bring lots and lots of excursionists on board next week."

They continued to sniffle and blubber miserably.

"Come on, chin up! And stop crying now. We've got a lot of work to do, you know. Let's see some gumption!"

More tears than gumption, I'm sorry to say.

"Please stop crying. Please? Aw, come on—hey!—I've got an idea! What do you say we stop at the malt shop and have a strawberry soda? That'll cheer you up, won't it? When you get a strawberry soda into you, everything's going to look different. You'll see that we're really not that far from being a success, a big success, a *huge* success. All we have to do is make some adjustments. We've got to roll up our sleeves, and—"

They turned toward me with nearly identical expressions, in which weak smiles showed their gratitude for my attempt to cheer them up, but their fallen faces and sad eyes betrayed the overwhelming sorrow that we feel when we have experienced a crushing failure, when we can see nothing in the past but the path that led to that failure, each of the thousand minor misfortunes that brought us to our current sorry state seeming now, upon reflection from the position of failure, to have been inevitable, and our future looming now not as the sun-dappled beckoning path it ought to be but as nothing but a continuation of that pattern, a series of new misfortunes, equally inevitable, a path so unappealing that we recoil from following it, and so we either return to the past, where things were certainly bad, but not as bad as we are now convinced they will be in the future, revisiting the history of our misfortune again and again, poking at each painful memory like a sore tooth, or we freeze in the present, surrendering

to defeat, unwilling to try again, unwilling to continue the struggle, convinced now that there is nothing at all that we could possibly do to reverse
our fortunes because the task we have undertaken is not only beyond our
ability, but beyond anyone's ability, that, as my mother put it that night,
with a twisted smile, "You can't inflate a dead dog."

46
A Dead Dog, Beached (Afflatus, Part 4)

"YOU CAN'T INFLATE a dead dog." My memory of my mother's saying that, looking at me with teary eyes and a bittersweet smile, lay dormant for very many years—nearly forty—until one wintry morning when I was walking along a deserted beach on East Phantom island, the largest in the Phantom archipelago that stretches between Montauk Point and Block Island, and came upon a dead dog in the surf. That encounter triggered the memory of what my mother had said that night, and that memory led to my writing this book about my mother and her lunch launch, but not directly, because the course of book-writing never does run true, never along a predictable line, but much more like the meandering course of a man walking with no particular motive for walking other than to see what he will discover and what may befall him, who is diverted here by a shadow, there by a little crowd of people, or by an unusual way that one building juts out and the next stands back from the street—finally arriving at a place that he had never intended to reach. Inherent in the development of any book that its author intends to be a book about its author, which is to say any book whose author recognizes the truth that every book is about its author as much as it is about any other subject that its author might decide to explore, is a certain likelihood that the author will stray from the course that he intended or expected to follow when he began it. I began this book intending to tell the story of my attempt to earn money for my college expenses by digging clams during the summer following my graduation from Babbington High School, and I was well along in telling that story when Albertine and I accepted an invitation from friends to get away to the splendid off-season isolation of their house on East Phantom.

I took the book with me, on a laptop computer, and spent the first day working on it, feeling throughout the day that the work was going well, enjoying the reconstruction of some of the memories of that summer, the leaky clam boat that my friend Raskol and I bought, the days on the bay in the sun, our clownish ineptitude as clamdiggers, and our struggles to keep the boat afloat, but I finished the day nervous and anxious because somehow in the course of that day that had from moment to moment seemed so successful, I had lost the thread of the work. I didn't know what to do next, didn't even in a sense know who I was, who I ought to be next in the story that I was telling, who I wanted to be. I couldn't even tell what had gone wrong, or where it had gone wrong, or why the story that I had set out to tell no longer appealed to me.

Our friends' neighbors, people unknown to us, knocked at the door. They were on their way to a party and invited us to come along. It was the annual winter-solstice party thrown by the owner of the East Phantom Inn, who went by the sole name of Stanton, for all the stalwarts who were still on the island when winter arrived. It was held not in the public portion of the inn, which was closed now, but in Stanton's quarters, in a barn behind the inn that had been made into a rather nice house, unless, perhaps, it had been built to resemble a barn that had been remodeled as a house, which I thought a possibility. A number of little old ladies, relatives of Stanton's, were performing hostess duties. It seemed that every time I turned around there was another one of them, cleaning up, or just sitting there, watching. Two or three of them were in the kitchen, handing out beer and wine and making snacks.

Stanton took us on a tour. A young woman, short, a little chubby, pretty in a bland way, tagged along. Stanton hardly seemed to notice her. The highlight of the tour was Stanton's description of what the master bedroom, downstairs, had been like when he first saw the place, several years earlier. The owner had been a crack addict, dying of AIDS, who hadn't left his built-in bed in months. According to Stanton, he had spent his last winter lying in bed and shoving two-by-fours into the fireplace, shoving them in a little more as they burned. Listening, I asked myself whether that technique would work, and I concluded that it could only work for a short while, when the two-by-fours were long enough to push. As they burned, they would become too short for the dying man to push any further. And then I asked myself who delivered those two-by-fours to him?

Who stacked them beside the bed? Some AIDS support group? Friends?
The lumber yard? If they went to that trouble, why didn't they keep a
proper fire burning for him, with decent hardwood logs? And, the most
important question of all, why was Stanton telling us this implausible story? What was his motive?

I WAS STILL ASKING MYSELF that question later that night, lying
awake at two o'clock, reading a brochure about colonoscopy. I was
scheduled to undergo the procedure when we returned to Manhattan, and
I wanted to know what I was in for.

You and Your Colonoscopy

Straight Talk from Nurse Nanci

Nurse Nanci

So your doctor has recommended that you have a colonoscopy.
That's a *good* thing! Colonoscopy is an important way to
check for colon cancer and to treat colon polyps—abnormal
growths on the inside lining of the intestine. This brochure will
help you understand how a colonoscopy can bene-
fit you and what you can expect before, during,
and after the procedure.

The term *colonoscopy* means "looking inside the
colon." Your doctor examines the lining of the colon for abnormalities by inserting a flexible tube
about the thickness of your finger into your anus
and advancing it slowly into your rectum and colon. (It's not as bad as it sounds, honest!)

During the procedure, you'll be given a very nice
drug through an intravenous drip. You'll feel relaxed and drowsy and "floaty." (Sorry! It's not available for rec-
reational use!) The drug will enable you to remain awake and
cooperative, but it may prevent you from remembering much of
the experience. Once you are fully relaxed, your doctor will do a
rectal exam with a gloved, lubricated finger; then the lubricated
colonoscope will be gently inserted. The scope bends, so the physician can move it around the curves of your colon. The scope
also blows air into your colon, which inflates the colon and helps
the physician see better (though it may cause you some public
embarrassment due to post-procedure flatus).

VERY LOUD country-and-western music, very loud *live* country-and-western music, suddenly came from next door, *burst forth* from next door. Someone was playing a harmonica, someone was playing a guitar, two people were singing, and I could hear them all very clearly even though our windows were closed. They performed a couple of songs and began a third, but they stopped abruptly before finishing it.

"Somebody must have called the cops," mumbled Albertine.

"And the cops called the musicians and told them to cease and desist?" I asked.

"Mmm."

"Maybe, but I think not."

"Mmm."

"Want to know what I think?"

"No."

"Aw, come on."

"Make it short."

"I think that the musicians rented the house next door specifically for woodshedding, to get their act together before taking it on the road, and that it took only two and a half songs to convince them that they are going to have to pursue alternative career paths if they want to win fame and the love of beautiful women. I think that they have discovered that it's not as easy as it looks, that, as Cervantes put it, it is not so easy a thing to inflate a dog, and that the inflation of the particular dog that they have chosen is more than they can manage, and that they have retired in their misery to silent drinking."

"Which means that we can go back to sleep."

"Yes," I said, and she did go back to sleep, but I lay there, awake, thinking about motivation, failure, the inflation of dogs and men, and the hundred trillion neutrinos passing through my body without even the slightest detectible effect on any part of me but my mind, which, once it had begun thinking about them, would not stop.

THE NEXT MORNING, I went for a walk on the beach, for my health. While I was walking, I came upon the body of a drowned dog. At first, from a distance, I thought that it was a fender, the protective pad hung over the side of a vessel to prevent chafing when it rubs against a dock, bulkhead, piling, or another vessel, an old-fashioned fender made of braided rope. When I came upon it, I saw that it was instead what had been a dog, stiff-legged now, its body bloated to the shape of a sausage, its eyeballs gone, and insects crawling over it, but still wearing a vivid red braided collar, a festive note, the brightest object on the beach, and I immediately remembered my mother's saying, "You can't inflate a dead dog," and right then, standing there on the windswept beach, I gave her my leaky old clam boat, to use in some venture at which she could succeed.

47

The Common Touch

MY MOTHER started the car and began driving slowly home. She hadn't gone far when she said, "You know what I wish?"

"Yeah," I said.

"Hm?"

"I think I know what you wish."

"Oh—no—I mean, yes, I do wish that everything had gone the way I wanted it to go, but I know that I can't change that—what I wish right now is that I could go to Dudley Beaker and ask him what I should do. I think he would know."

Patti and I exchanged a look.

"But, of course, I can't ask him because—"

She didn't finish.

I waited a couple of heartbeats, then took a deep breath and said, "I think I know what he would say."

"You do?" she asked.

"Yes," I said, "because I spent a lot of time listening to him tell me what *I* should do, and I think I know what he would say."

It was my mother's turn to let a few heartbeats pass and take a deep breath.

"What?" she asked.

In Dudley's manner, I said, "So you have a thirst for fame, do you? You want the admiration of the mob? It isn't difficult to win. There is only one real requirement."

"What's that, Dud?" asked Patti, as she would have if she and I had been alone in Dudley's living room.

"What is it?" I said with a chuckle. I regretted not having a pipe with me, because this was the point at which Dudley would have spent some time lighting it, and only when smoke wreathed his head would he have said, as I did now, "I think that if you just ask yourself why it is that one man might labor for years to write an elegant treatise on the birth of stars and win only a single admirer, but another can stick a bamboo pole up a dog's ass, blow the poor cur up like a balloon, and thereby not only delight all the halfwits in the town square, but fill his pockets with their silver, you'll know the only requirement for winning fame."

"A dog?" asked Patti.

"No," I said with another chuckle.

"A bamboo pole? A talent for inflation?"

"No, dear girl," I said with a wink. "What is required is a talent for vulgarity."

"Of course!" said my mother, truly startled, turning to look, wide-eyed, at me. "The common touch!"

"I wouldn't have put it quite that—" I began.

"You're right!" said my mother. "The common touch. Good for you!" For her, the Dudley Beaker impersonation was over; she was talking to her son, her little boy. After a moment, she added, "Bert was right," and after another moment, she added, "Like father, like son."

48
Launching Ella's Lunch Launch

IT TOOK JUST TWO DAYS (and some more borrowed money) to get *Arcinella* out of her elegant clothes and into something more comfortable. This time, we didn't work alone. We recruited friends and neighbors, even my father. Together, we repainted her in tropical colors, fitted her out with a primitive galley (let's be honest about this—we bolted a barbecue grill to the deck), rigged a canopy for shade, flew bright pennants from a dozen poles, and mounted loudspeakers so that we'd have doo-wop with us wherever we went.

Porky White, at his own expense, had flyers designed for us, printed, and distributed around town.

I think I knew from the moment we left the dock on the first day that we were going to succeed this time. My mother was wearing shorts and a sailor's middy blouse, and she looked quite attractive, but Patti was wearing a bright red bathing suit that dipped to the dimples above her buttocks in the back, and she looked sensational.

We started our day early, chugging around the bay from clam boat to clam boat, selling coffee, doughnuts, rolls, hard-boiled eggs, and beer to clamdiggers. At noon, when pleasure boats began to crowd the bay, we cruised among them, purveying hot dogs, hamburgers, potato chips, pickles, and beer. We were always busy, and when evening came on and we found that we had farther to travel between boats, we didn't push our luck. We headed for home in the golden light, glowing, counting the profits.

ONCE WE HAD MASTERED the common touch, the enterprise rose like a bubble on a warm breeze. Every morning we catered to the clam-

mies, and every afternoon we catered to the vacationers. Little by little we
expanded the menu, and we eventually offered the three best-selling
brands of beer. Now and then some witty vacationer would ask for caviar
or champagne or "one of those funny little sandwiches." We always
laughed.

For quite a while, it seemed that we could do no wrong, and the rest of
the summer bid fair to add one success after another, but the future never
unfolds perfectly smoothly, and even a bubble rising on a summer zephyr
has its ups and downs.

49

When You Dance (Doo-Wop a Wadda Wadda)

AFTER A MONTH OR SO of doing very well by giving Babbington's boaters what they seemed most likely to want, my mother, perhaps suffering from some form of addiction, tried tinting potato chips a pale yellowish green. She didn't give us any warning. She just started setting out little brown bags of something on the roof over the engine room one morning when we chugged onto the bay. She tore one of the bags open and poured the contents onto a tray. I had never before seen potato chips tinted pale yellowish green, which may be an example of the famous limitations of suburban life. I picked up one of the little bags and read the name that my mother had hand-printed on it.

"'Ella's Chartreuse Chips,'" I read.

"'Sheeps,'" said my mother. "'Ella's Chartreuse Sheeps.' With a French accent."

Patti and I exchanged a look. Neither of us had the heart to suggest that chartreuse sheeps were a bad idea.

She tried throughout the day to interest people in Chartreuse Chips, holding her tray out to them when their boats were alongside, offering free samples. Reactions were varied. Some people took one look and refused to try them, others grimaced while taking a tiny bite, and still others pretended to like them, but they all voted with their wallets. They did not buy.

At the end of the day, when we were on our way home, my mother held her tray full of unsold Chartreuse Chips over the side, shrugged, grinned, said to Patti and me, "I guess I just had to give it one more try," and let the chips fall to the bay, where they attracted a flock of herring gulls and were gone before we were out of sight.

"Ha!" she said, pointing toward the gulls. "Success!"

WE MADE THE MISTAKE, once, of going out on a morning when the bay was choppy. The clammies were out, so we tried to make our rounds and sell them some coffee and doughnuts, but the transactions were difficult under those turbulent circumstances, and a lot of coffee, doughnuts, and change ended up in the bay.

"Bit rambunctious today," said one clammy when we pulled up.

"Yeah," I said. "Bit rambunctious. What can I get you?"

He and his partner perused the menu that Patti presented on a chalkboard. This always took a while.

"Guess I'll have the clamdigger's breakfast," he said at last.

"Me too," said his partner.

"Egg-on-a-roll, twice, and two beers," I called out to my mother.

She tossed the first beer at me. *Arcinella* pitched, and I missed it. It went into the bay. She tossed the second beer. *Arcinella* rolled. I went into the bay.

"Bit rambunctious today," the clammy said again when he hauled me out.

"Yeah," I agreed. "Bit rambunctious."

We returned to shore that evening wobbly and wretched, and from then on the crew of Ella's Lunch Launch were strictly fair-weather sailors.

ON ANOTHER DAY, we were chugging happily along when, little by little, we became aware that we were being enveloped by fog. In a remarkably short time, we couldn't see anything in any direction but whiteness. It was a delightful sensation, and it turned us into children, laughing and giggling and calling into the fog for any customers who might be out there.

"Hello-o-o out there," called my mother.

"Where arrrrre you?" called Patti.

"I can't seeee you," called I.

"It's so strange—and wonderful," said my mother.

"It's like being inside cotton candy," said Patti.

"You know," I said, because the idea had just occurred to me, "I do think that we are in some danger of being run down by a larger boat."

"We don't have a fog horn!" said my mother.

"My fault," I said, feeling guilty. "I should have—"

"We don't need a fog horn!" said Patti. She turned the music up— way up.

The three of us danced on the deck in the fog, and when it lifted we found that we were alone on the bay. Not a boat in sight. No clam boats. No pleasure boats. The businesslike thing to do would have been to call it a day and go home, but we went on dancing.

(We danced to "When You Dance," a song written by Andrew Jones and sung by the Turbans, a group from Philadelphia composed of Al Banks, Matthew Platt, Charles Williams, and Andrew "Chet" Jones, issued as a single on the Herald label in July of 1955. Mark Dorset, author of *Deconstructing the American Pop Canon,* considers "When You Dance" to have been the first song to include in the chorus the word *doo-wop*. The Turbans' recording was already about three years old when we played it in the fog, over and over, that delightful day.)

TOWARD THE END OF THE SUMMER, my father took a week off from work at the gas station, "to help out." He didn't announce his plans. He just showed up one morning.

"Bert!" said my mother when he pulled up to *Arcinella*'s slip.

"I thought maybe I could, well, give you a hand," he said, getting out of the car.

"What about the garage?" said my mother.

"A guy's gotta take some time off. I thought I'd take a week—see if I could help you out."

"Well—ah—thanks," said my mother, "but we've really got every-thing—um—under control."

He looked around, and I watched him. I could see that he was begin-ning to feel awkward, and I realized that he wanted to be part of what my mother had accomplished.

"I—I could use—you know—the engine—the engine could sure use a good going-over—by somebody who knows what he's doing," I said, "in-stead of me."

"Hey!" said my father, rolling up his sleeves. "Good thing I'm here!"

I think he enjoyed himself during the week he spent with us, but I know for certain that we didn't need his help, and that knowledge allows me to say that my mother had succeeded at last.

I saw how much his attitude had changed when, at the end of the week, he tried to tell my mother that he admired what she had achieved. The attempt went something like this:

"Ella," he said, "you—"

My mother saw from his shuffling shamefaced hangdog look what might be coming if he could manage to say it and decided to head it off.

"Let's dance, Bert," she said.

"Ella, I just want to say—"

"Doo-wop da wadda wadda, doo-wop da wadda," she sang.

"Please, Ella, I'm trying to tell you—"

"When you dance—"

"Ella—"

"—be sure to hold her close to you—" she cooed, and, swaying invitingly, held her arms out to my father, who accepted the invitation and waltzed her around the deck, while Patti and I looked on, smiling like approving parents.

50

The Son of Second Best (Testing the Hypothesis, Part 4)

I WAS SITTING in Dudley's chair. Patti was sitting on my lap. We were pretending that she had come to see me to discuss the meaning of life, but I had pulled her skirt up around her waist, and I was rubbing her through her panties while I said, "But my dear, there is no inherent meaning in any of it. The only meaning is the meaning we add to it, like chocolate sauce and chopped nuts on a quite meaningless scoop of vanilla ice cream."

She squirmed a little, rearranging herself so that my erection fit more comfortably between her buttocks, stayed my hand, and said, "There's something wrong with this."

"Scruples at this late date, my little darling?" I said, nuzzling her neck.

"I can imagine it all," she said, "and I can even think of things to say to you, like 'Oh, Dud, you can't mean that there's no meaning to it at all?' and that kind of thing, but you know what?"

"What?"

"I'm not having any fun."

"Oh," I said, crushed.

"I mean as Ella," she said, and gave me a consoling squeeze. "When I'm being Ella, I'm not enjoying myself."

"Oh."

"Do you understand what I mean? I mean that she's not enjoying herself with Dudley."

"To tell you the truth," I said, "I'm glad to hear that. It's very tiring being Dudley. I think it would get pretty tiring being the son of Dudley, too."

"Here's what I think," said Patti. "I think she might have let Dudley snuggle her a bit. She might have let him feel her up, maybe unbutton her blouse, and I think there might have been some kissing, maybe even a lot of kissing, and romantic words—a *lot* of romantic words, since I have found that it is very hard to shut Dudley up—and I think that she might have liked all of that, that it might have been thrilling for her, the forbidden aspect of it, and the kinkiness of it, with an older man and all, and that it would have felt flattering, since he was sophisticated, and so on—but I think that's as far as it went, because that was where she stopped enjoying it."

"But why did she stop enjoying it at that point? What makes you think that she didn't go on enjoying it long enough to conceive me?"

"I think—I just think—that the only reason she got into any kind of amorous entanglement with Dudley—if she actually *did* get into something with Dudley at all—was because she would rather have been with somebody else."

"What?"

"She was longing for someone else, and she let herself take some consolation from Dudley."

"Who was she longing for?" I asked. "Who's on your list?"

"Do you know much about your uncle?"

"My uncle?"

"Your father's brother—Buster."

"Oh. No, not much. He was a year or two younger, and he was killed in the war."

"He was smart, clever, funny, charming—and very good looking. I've read the letters he wrote to your grandparents after he joined the navy. I think you would have liked him. I think I would have liked him. Most important, though, I got the impression from talking with your grandmother that Ella *definitely* liked him—liked him more than she liked Bert—though apparently she was smitten with both of them. The three of them used to go out on dates together."

"But he couldn't be my father. He died long before I was born."

She put her hand over my eyes and said, "Let's suppose that the war is over. Buster Leroy has not come home. But Bert has. Your mother is despondent over the loss of Buster, and his death has made her realize how much she loved him."

"Yeah."

"But she's also happy—because Bert has come home."

"Right."

"She and Bert meet. They're awkward at first. Bert feels guilty about having made it through the war when Buster didn't. Ella is worried that her feelings for Buster show."

"Mm," I said.

"And then it happens."

"What?"

"I don't know exactly, but it's something as small as a shrug or a laugh, something that makes Ella see how much of Buster there is in Bert."

"Oh," I said. "I'm beginning to see what you mean."

"I'll be Ella. You be Bert."

"Aw, no," I said. "Not that."

"Come on," she said. "It's an experiment, remember?"

"Okay," I said, with no enthusiasm for this particular experiment at all.

"Oh, how I missed you, how I missed you," she whispered. She held my head in her hands and looked deep into my eyes and said, "I am so happy to have you here with me," and then she began proving that she meant it.

What followed was bliss. She threw herself into the experiment with a reckless passion that I hadn't seen before. I was delighted to accept every gift she gave me, and it never bothered me once that she kept murmuring, "Oh, Buster, Buster."

51
Chance Brings an Opportunity

Chance, my friend and master, will surely deign to send again, to help me, the familiar devils of his unruly kingdom! l have no faith, except in him—and in myself. Particularly in him, for, when I sink, he fishes me up again, and grips and shakes me like a rescuing dog, whose teeth every time meet in my skin! So that every time I sink, I do not expect a final catastrophe, but only some adventure, some trivial, commonplace miracle which, like a sparkling link, may close up again the necklace of my days.

Now this is faith indeed, with all its half-sham blindness and its jesuitical renunciations—faith which makes me hope even at the very moment when I cry, "Everything fails me!"

Renée Néré in Colette's *La Vagabonde*

WE COULD SEE the end of summer coming. Mornings began to turn cold, and there were fewer boats on the bay. School would be starting soon. It was time to decide that the season was over.

We spent a couple of days preparing *Arcinella* for the winter, and while we worked I made a troubling discovery.

"She's sinking faster than ever," I said.

"Is there anything you can do?" asked Patti.

"I don't know. During the summer, the engine bailed the bilge in the daytime, and I did a little jet-pumping at night, so it was pretty easy to keep her afloat, but now, while she's just sitting here, and we're in school—she's going to sink."

"If you could get the jet pump to work on its own—"

"Yeah, after I take a correspondence course in hydraulic engineering."

"You could ask somebody who lives around here to run the pump for you while you're in school."

"But then that somebody would know that she's sinking, and—wait a minute. There is something I could do. I could install the jet pump somewhere out of sight where it could rest in the bilge—maybe under the planks inside the hull—and run the two hoses to concealed locations where I could get at them easily. Then I could start the pump every morning on the way to school and turn it off every afternoon."

"Sure!"

"Of course, the docks aren't on my way to school—"

"I could—I think I can persuade one of—somebody—to give you a lift."

"Yeah," I said, reluctantly. "Okay."

"I'll pick somebody too stupid to figure out what you're up to."

"Let's get to work."

An hour later, we were well into the work, with the front hatch off, the planking removed and stacked on deck, the pump in place and water running through it to test it, when a delivery truck pulled up at the side of the road and Mr. Yummy got out. Mr. Yummy was not his real name, but it was what my friends and I always called him because he made deliveries for the Yummy Good Baked Goods Company and his truck said on the side, in large blue letters, "Here comes something yummy!" Many of Babbington's housewives considered the slogan an understatement.

He got out of his truck and stood on the bulkhead for a couple of minutes, watching Patti and me at work, and then he cleared his throat and asked, "What are you doing?"

"Cleaning the inside of the hull," I said.

"Cleaning the inside of the hull?"

"Sure. To get her ready for the winter."

"Oh."

"Not everybody goes to this much trouble," I said.

"Yeah. I guess not," he said.

"Personally," I said, shaking my head, "I just don't understand how people can be so lax."

He watched us for another couple of minutes, and then, in a flat voice, in a matter-of-fact manner, he asked, "You know if there are any boats like this for sale around here?"

"ANY BOATS LIKE THIS for sale around here?" I would like to be able to report to you that my first impulse was to say to him, "Oh, sir, you wouldn't want a boat like this, because it's sinking," but I had no such impulse. My impulse was to laugh, out of relief, and out of gratitude to the great god, chance, the only one I believed in by then, for having sent Mr. Yummy our way. The impulse was so strong that I actually did laugh, and when I had myself under control again I said, "Forgive me for laughing, sir, but it's just that, well—first of all—there aren't any boats like this."

"Huh?" he said.

"Oh," chuckling indulgently, "I suppose to the casual observer one clam boat looks pretty much like another—but this boat—this boat is something really special."

"Oh, yeah," he said. "Sure. I can see *that*. I didn't mean—"

"As far as I'm concerned, after owning *Arcinella* here, I couldn't even imagine owning another boat."

"She's something, all right," he said. "She sure is."

With a sigh, I said, "I just wish I could keep her."

"You can't keep her?" he asked hopefully.

"I'm afraid not," I said. "My girlfriend thinks I spend too much time with *Arcinella* and not enough with her."

Patti jumped right in: "I said to him, I said, 'Pete, you gotta choose. It's that boat or me.' "

"Hey, if I was you," said Mr. Yummy, giving me a wink and a nudge, "I'd sell the boat."

"I—I—I just can't," I claimed.

"Why not?"

"Because she's—she just means too much to me, that's all." I gave *Arcinella* a long appreciative look, then turned back to Mr. Yummy. "Isn't she a beauty?" I asked. "Tell me—if she were yours and I came along and asked you to sell her to me, would you sell her?"

"Well," he said, "in your position—"

"Huh?" I said, as if I didn't understand him.

He raised his eyebrows and nodded in Patti's direction. Patti had folded her arms across her chest and was stamping her little foot on the deck.

"Oh," I said. "I see what you mean." To Patti I said, pleading, "Do I really have to sell her?"

Patti pouted and said, "I already told ya. It's her or me."

I thought that the pout brought her perilously close to overplaying it, but it didn't really matter. I knew we had the hook in Mr. Yummy. All we had to do was reel him in, just the way Captain Macomangus had reeled us in, and we did.

WE WERE DOING SO WELL as we neared the end of our negotiations, when we came to the handshake that sealed the deal, that I hated to see it end—or maybe I wanted to show off for Patti. Whatever my motivation, I said to Mr. Yummy, "Of course, you'll want to have her looked over by somebody who really knows boats—unless you really know boats yourself." I think I expected him to bristle at the implied conclusion on my part—the conclusion of a kid so savvy about boats that he actually cleaned the inside of his boat's hull—that a baked-goods deliveryman would not be a person who knew much about boats, however much he might know about baked goods, and to tell me that there wouldn't be any need for him to bring in an expert since he actually knew quite a lot about boats himself.

Instead, he said, "Who me? All I know is bread and muffins! But don't worry about that. I've got a couple of partners in this venture, and one of them really does know boats."

"That's swell," I lied.

52
Moderne Stylizing

"ALL I HAVE TO DO NOW," I said to Patti, "is persuade my mother to abandon the one business in her whole life that was a success for her."

"Let me do it," she offered.

"I should be the one," I said. "She's my mother."

"She's my friend," said Patti. "I wish you'd let me do it."

"Okay," I said. "You do it."

We walked to my house, and Patti went to work as soon as we opened the kitchen door.

She sang out, "It was a great summer, wasn't it, Ella?"

"Oh, yes, it was, it was," said my mother.

"I wish every summer could be like that, don't you?"

"Wouldn't that be wonderful?"

"Yes, out on the bay every day, chugging from clam boat to clam boat in the morning, then chugging from pleasure boat to pleasure boat in the afternoon."

My mother sighed.

"Day in and day out."

My mother smiled.

"Day after day."

My mother's smile slipped a bit.

"Seven days a week."

My mother's brow furrowed, though she was still smiling.

"You know—I was just wondering on the way over here."

"What's that?" asked my mother.

"Now that you're famous, I wonder if Ella's Moderne Hair Stylizing wouldn't succeed."

"Oh, well, I don't know," said my mother.

"Just think about it for a minute," said Patti. "Why did it fail?"

My mother cast her eyes downward. I could see that she would really rather not think about the failure of Moderne Stylizing.

"It was because nobody knew who you were," said Patti. "You were nobody."

I said, "Patti!"

She waved my objections away. "I mean in the eyes of the average Babbingtonian," she said to my mother. "Nobody knew you. You were an unknown woman who launched a wonderful business, but it—"

"Sank," said my mother.

"Um—yeah," said Patti. "It sank. But I think that if you had been well known in Babbington—as you are now—"

"—and I had launched that very same business, it would have been a howling success?" said my mother.

"I think so," said Patti.

"I think she's right," I said.

"I'm sure I'm right," said Patti. "I have some experience with the power of a reputation," she added modestly, "and I think now that you're the famous Ella, of Ella's Lunch Launch, people would be falling over one another to get their hair done by you."

"You mean that if I launched Ella's Moderne Hair Stylizing all over again, now that people know me as Ella, of Ella's Lunch Launch, instead of launching it as I did, anonymously, almost in the dark, that this time Moderne Stylizing would become a shimmering success because the sun of fame would shine on it?"

"Well," said Patti, "something like that."

"It would be an interesting experiment," I said, and then added with a sigh, "Too bad we won't have any time to try it."

"Why not?" asked my mother, who had begun to sketch hairdos on her pad.

"Because we've got to keep the lunch launch going."

"Oh, that. You know, I've been thinking about that. It was a great summer, it really was, out on the bay every day, but you have to ask yourself: is next year going to be as good? Think about it. Back and forth on the bay, every single day. Day in and day out. Day after day. Seven days a week. This summer was an adventure, but next summer might be just a job."

Patti and I mumbled some weak protests, but quickly slipped away, leaving my mother to her plans.

53
Selling Arcinella

I HAD THOUGHT that I would have to persuade my mother to stay away from the sale of *Arcinella*, but she was so completely occupied with the resurrection of Moderne Stylizing that she hardly noticed.

Patti and I were at the docks at dawn. We went over the boat from stem to stern, making shipshape everything that we could and hiding everything that we couldn't. Then we waited.

It was a fine morning. The heat of summer had broken, and the air was lighter, the thin air of fall. (What is the scent of that autumnal air? Two parts chalk dust, one part pencil shavings, I think. Of all the things that I learned in the Babbington public schools, the most enduring is that hope never comes unadulterated by anxiety, but, to even the balance, anxiety is never pure either, but always sweetened at least a bit by hope, and I learned it just by starting a new grade every year, in the fall air, with its mixture of hope and anxiety.)

Patti and I paced the deck, awaiting the arrival of Mr. Yummy and his partners. When we heard the sound of motors, and wheels on pavement approaching, we tried not to look, lest we betray our eagerness, our schoolkids' hope and anxiety, but we couldn't keep ourselves from looking. We glanced quickly in the direction of the sound, then went back to our pretense of nonchalance, then glanced in the direction of the sound again. Then we glanced at each other. We raised our eyebrows. What we saw was not what we had expected.

Three vans pulled up in front of *Arcinella*'s slip. One was Mr. Yummy's Yummy Good Baked Goods van, the second was an Immortal Hilarity Ice Cream van, and the third was a Dew-Kissed-Meadow Milk van. Mr. Yummy and his partners hopped out of their respective vans, eager and not even trying to hide it. They converged on the Immortal Hilarity van and from it extracted a huge cooler that two of them carried, with difficulty, aboard *Arcinella*.

"Welcome aboard," I said when they had set the hefty cooler down.

"These are my partners," said Mr. Yummy. "That's Sam, and that's Dave."

"I'm Peter," I said, shaking the hands of Sam and Dave in what I hoped was the manner of a straight-shooting guy who would never try to sell them a sinking boat.

"And I'm Patti," said Patti, extending her hand.

"Oo-ee, Patti. Aren't you something!" said Dave. "Gimme the full three-sixty." He made a rotating gesture with his finger. Patti obliged by turning slowly around. "Yow!" he said, employing the technical terminology of a connoiseur.

Sam squatted beside the cooler, said, "We brought lunch," and flipped the top open. The cooler was entirely full of beer, on ice. Sam laughed, took a can out, and opened it with an opener that he kept in a handsome leather holster on his belt. The opener was silver plated and engraved with "SAM" in a stately typeface of the kind used for chiseling Latin mottoes in the granite pediments above the imposing entrances to government buildings. Sam guzzled about half the can and wiped his mouth on his sleeve.

"Are you the one who knows boats, Sam?" I asked, hopefully.

Sam, tossing the empty can into the Bolotomy and scooping another from the cooler in a single fluid motion, said, "That would be Dave."

"Well, then, Dave," I said, taking care not to permit myself a single note that might be considered ironic or patronizing, "I expect you'll want to get into her." I indicated the way to the wheelhouse with a be-my-guest gesture.

Dave shrugged and said, somewhat reluctantly, I thought, "Right."

We all watched Dave as he made his way gingerly along the deck to the wheelhouse, fumbled with the latch, crouched to crawl through the opening that led below, and disappeared from our sight. Although we could no longer see Dave, I felt fairly certain that I knew what he was doing down in *Arcinella*'s hold. I think he spent some time running his hands over her engine and wiggling its wires and belts. Then, I imagine, he began inching forward, picking up whatever he found and putting it back down, making as much noise as he could to show that he was on the job. I may be wrong, but I very much doubt it.

After he had been gone for what seemed long enough for him to get greasy enough to be able to say that he'd given her a good going over, I called out, "What do you say, Dave?"

"Looks good to me," he said, as if he knew.

Sam and Mr. Yummy slapped each other on the back and opened two more beers. I got behind the wheel and took *Arcinella* downriver, guiding her with a steady hand, heading toward the bay.

When we reached the open bay, rain began to fall. It fell straight down. It began gently but increased steadily. Sam, Dave, and Mr. Yummy responded to the rain with a beery version of a child's version of an Indian rain dance, whooping and prancing around the deck. Suddenly, a bolt of lightning struck a channel marker just a few yards off *Arcinella*'s bow. Sam, Dave, and Mr. Yummy jumped about three feet straight up in the air and dashed into the wheelhouse, where Patti and I had already taken shelter.

In the crowded wheelhouse, Sam, Dave, and Mr. Yummy made repeated attempts to sing "The Wiffenpoof Song," though they could agree on only a few words here and there. Patti and I added incongruous doo-wop flourishes. When they finished singing, or gave up trying, a silent moment passed. Then Mr. Yummy took a long pull at his can of beer and sighed. With a drunk's deep seriousness, he said, "Y'know, we're gonna call this boat Three Guys . . . 'cause we're three guys . . . and that makes sense . . . I'm not saying it doesn't . . . but we ought to call her Freedom . . . 'cause that's what she's going to bring us. From now on, we're our own bosses. No more working for somebody else. We're gonna be on our own! It's a dream come true."

Patti and I exchanged a guilty glance, then quickly looked away.

Mr. Yummy made a clumsy attempt to get his arms around everyone in the wheelhouse, grasp us all in one beery hug, and for a moment I thought he was going to launch into "God Bless America," but the emotion must have overwhelmed him because he broke away and lurched through the wheelhouse door and over the stern into the bay.

When Sam and Dave had him back aboard again, I throttled down, shifted into neutral, gave the wheel a pat, and, addressing *Arcinella* in a voice that I meant to carry, said, "Well, old girl, this seems as good a place as any to say good-bye and hand you over."

I stepped away from the wheel and let *Arcinella* drift.

The three guys looked around in bewilderment for a moment, not recognizing their cue. Then Mr. Yummy realized what was expected of him, pulled a folded check from the pocket of his pants, and flourished it. The others, with some hesitation, followed suit. I took the checks and signed a bill of sale and certificate of ownership. Mr. Yummy waved the documents in the air, let out a whoop, and poured a can of beer on Sam's head.

Folding the checks and putting them into my shirt pocket, I asked, "Who's going to take her into her slip?"

I turned a questioning look toward Mr. Yummy, who turned it toward Sam.

Sam held his hands out, palms forward. "Hey, not me," he said. "I don't know how to drive a boat. I'd probably wreck the thing somehow. Let Dave do it. He's the one who knows boats."

I got a grip on Dave's shoulder and steered him toward the wheel. "Here we go, Dave," I said. "Let me show you how to bend her to your will."

Dave looked at the wheel, but he didn't touch it.

"Take the wheel," I said, commandingly.

Dave did as he was told, reluctantly.

"This is the throttle," I said. I nudged it, and *Arcinella* began to move forward. Dave had his hands on the wheel, but he didn't move it.

"Well, Dave," I said. "Steer her toward town."

He turned the wheel, little by little, inch by inch, until she was headed toward town, and then he began to relax a little. The rain stopped, and the day began to brighten. Mr. Yummy, Sam, and Patti left the wheelhouse. Mr. Yummy and Sam immediately headed for the beer cooler.

When Dave and I were alone, I said to him, as one guy who knows boats to another, "You know, Dave, I've got to tell you that *Arcinella*'s got a few peculiarities."

"Yeah?" said Dave, apparently under the impression that he was going to hear a dirty joke.

"She drives her prop through first and reverse gears of the gearbox from an old Champion," I said, and Dave grinned as if he figured the good part would be coming along any second now, "so when you bring her into the slip—" I interrupted myself to say, "I'm assuming you're going to bring her in bow first."

Dave said, just as I had when Captain Mac played the trick on me, "That's what I thought I'd do."

I rewarded him with a nod to acknowledge the wisdom of bringing her in bow first and said, "Well, then what you're going to need to do when you get a bit of a way out from the slip is set your throttle down so she's just kind of chugging along—"

Dave reached for the throttle, and I swear that for a very brief moment I had an out-of-body-out-of-time-out-of-mind experience and saw not Dave but myself, younger by a summer, standing there at the wheel, reaching for the throttle, as if I were Captain Mac.

"Not yet, Dave," the Captain and I said.

"No, no. Of course not," said Dave, recoiling from the throttle as from a flame.

"When the time comes," I continued, slipping further into the fraternity of duplicitous bastards, "you're going to want to have her just chugging along, but you won't want to give her so little gas that she stalls."

Dave, trying desperately to commit everything I said to memory, said, "Uh-huh. Uh-huh. Got it."

"Then when you're at the slip, you'll want to put in the clutch and shift into reverse."

"Reverse?"

"Yes, reverse. To retard her forward motion."

"Oh, sure. Of course."

"Ideally, you want her to glide on into the slip sweet and slow and just barely kiss the bulkhead."

I turned away for a moment to hide the frown I was wearing. I wasn't pleased with myself. I would rather not have been doing what I was doing, joining the evil fraternity of all those since time immemorial who have sold leaking boats to gullible suckers, but I decided to press on with it. I turned back to Dave and said, "Treat her gently."

With that I left the wheelhouse and joined the group on deck. Mr.

Yummy held a can of beer out toward me, and I took it. *Arcinella* approached her slip. She was going too fast. I almost started for the wheelhouse, but I caught myself. I took a pull at the beer and managed to keep myself from even looking in Dave's direction. I knew what I'd see if I looked. I'd see Dave reaching toward the throttle, trying to decide the right moment to throttle down. His hand would be trembling, as mine had. He'd be sweating, as I had.

I felt the engine slow. Dave had throttled down, just a bit, not enough. *Arcinella* continued toward the bulkhead with undiminished speed.

Right about now, Dave would be eyeing the shift lever, then the clutch. He would step on the clutch, find it stiff, stand on it to depress it, and with the clutch in, he would shift into reverse.

He did. I felt the engine race when the clutch was in. *Arcinella* rushed toward her rendezvous with the bulkhead. Then Dave must have released the clutch pedal, because *Arcinella* shuddered, seemed to hesitate for a moment, then stalled, and silently glided smoothly, swiftly, single-mindedly toward the bulkhead.

Mr. Yummy looked at the bulkhead. He looked at Dave in the wheelhouse. He looked at Sam, who was watching the bulkhead grow ever nearer and opening and closing his mouth without making a sound. He looked at me. "Hey," he said, and by that I think he meant that *Arcinella* seemed likely to strike the bulkhead with force sufficient to do some harm. "Hey!" he said again, louder, and by that I think he meant that this was trouble.

"She's gonna—" came out of Sam.

"Somebody—" said Mr. Yummy.

"Do something!" said Sam.

Impulsively, desperately, Mr. Yummy reached out for a piling as *Arcinella* glided past it. He threw his arms around it and tried to brace his feet to slow the boat, but the momentum was too great and he was swept from the deck and left clinging to the pile.

Arcinella struck the bulkhead, shook herself like a wet dog, then rebounded in the direction of the opposite bank. I dashed into the wheelhouse, restarted the engine, and, with Dave standing glum and mute beside me, brought her in sweet and slow, and this time her bow didn't even touch the bulkhead.

A FEW MINUTES LATER, we were all on shore. We stood there, lined up along the bulkhead, looking at *Arcinella*. I had my hands in my pockets, and I was rocking on my heels a bit. If I had had a pipe—not a briar, like Dudley's, but a corncob pipe like Captain Mac's—I would have been puffing it.

"Well," I said, breaking the silence after a while, "she looks okay. I doubt that you've done her any real harm." I paused, and then added with a shrug, "Of course, I can't say for sure that you haven't, and I can't take responsibility if you have."

54

Good-bye, Old Boat

FOR TEN MORE NIGHTS I played the part of the Night Bailer of Babbington, slipping through the shadows and pumping *Arcinella*, bailing her out, blowing her up, keeping her afloat, but I did what Captain Mac had done, leaving more water in her bilge each night, and on the tenth night, leaving the water above the planks, I coiled my hoses over my arm, pitched the jet pump into the bay, said good-bye, and walked away.

Not long after, probably at night, some night while I lay in my bed at home, sleeping in a stream of neutrinos, baywater rose in *Arcinella*'s bilge until it filled her, and, unattended and alone, she sank.

I learned about it from Raskol the next day, at school.

"Hey," he said, rushing past me in the hall, "Captain Mac's old boat sank. Right at the dock. I heard that the guys who bought her from you aren't even going to bother bringing her up."

THAT THANKSGIVING, when we had finished dinner, after my grandparents had gone home and my father was snoozing in his chair, my mother said, "I'd like to see her."

I knew who she meant. "So would I," I said.

We got into my mother's car and drove to Patti's, and then the three of us drove to *Arcinella*'s slip. We got out of the car and walked to the edge of the bulkhead, where we stood looking down through the murky water at *Arcinella*'s graceful shape and muted pastels. The thought occurred to me that if I had a few dozen inner tubes and an air hose I could probably raise her, but I kept it to myself.

"I feel that we ought to say something," said my mother. "Like something over a grave, or a burial at sea."

To the great surprise of my mother and me, and perhaps to Patti herself, Patti began to sing a doo-wop version of Stanza XI of Wallace Stevens's "Esthetique du Mal." I improvised backup as well as I could.

A vessel sinks in waves	Dum doobie doo-wop,
Of people, . . .	Dum doobie doo-wop.
. . . as big bell-billows from its bell	Wop wop,
Bell-billow in the village steeple.	Doo da wop bop.
Violets, . . .	Dimma nimma nim nim.
Great tufts, spring up from buried	Doo-doo-wa-da,
houses	Doo-doo-wa-da-doo.
Of poor, dishonest people, . . .	Sho-dote-n-sho-be-doe,
. . . for whom the steeple,	Sho-dote-n-sho-be-woe.
Long since, rang out . . .	Boop shoo,
. . . farewell, farewell, farewell.	Shang-a-lang-a jingabop.

This left the three of us quite choked up. My mother, who was standing between us, put her arm across our shoulders and gave us a squeeze. She sighed and smiled and shook her head and said, "She gave us quite a ride."

"Yes, she did," I said.

"She blew me up," said Patti, "filled me full of hot air."

"She was truly inflationary," I said, "a gasser—a *jet pump*!"

"A *blow job*!" said Patti impulsively, and the three of us burst into adolescent laughter.

"Oh, I loved it all!" said my mother, sobering, hugging herself, and shivering a bit. She turned and started for the car, and Patti and I followed. Along the way, she asked, "But do you know what was the best of the best, the best part, the very best part of all?"

"The day we were lost in the fog?" suggested Patti.

"The day—" I began, and then stopped. I had intended to suggest the day when my father had tried to tell my mother that he admired what she had accomplished, but I could feel my embarrassment before I even said it. "I don't know," I said. "What was the best part?"

We got into the car.

"For me," said my mother, "it was the night 'Lord Caught-yer-cough' sailed with us. He really enjoyed himself!"

She started the car and put it in gear.

"He even ate the sandwiches," she said. "He ate them all!"

She drove off.

"He probably would have eaten the Chartreuse Chips if I'd had them," she ventured.

She drove on for a couple of blocks in silence.

Then she said, "Maybe not."

55
And Then . . .

FOLLOWING THE SUCCESS of the lunch launch, my mother seemed unable to fail. She had succeeded once, and that was all fate seemed to require for entry into the successful-business club. On the scale of businesses that she could run from the spare room or the basement, she had one triumph after another, moving on to a new venture whenever inspiration blew in and blew her up. She had become famous, within Babbington, for Ella's Lunch Launch, and people wanted to know her. As Jasper Milvain, a writer who learned how to tailor his work to the tastes of a lucrative market niche, famously said, you have to become famous before you can secure the attention that would give fame. My mother had done the trick. She had inflated a dog, and all Babbington marveled at her talent for it. So did she. Every now and then, even at the most unlikely times, while she was cooking, say, or sorting the laundry, I would see a light come into her eyes, and her face would brighten, and I would know that she was relishing afresh the surprise arrival of someone she had always wanted to meet: Ella Piper Leroy, local tycoon, Babbington notable, somebody.

One day when I came home from school, she was sitting at the dining room table, talking to Betsy Gaskell, the columnist who wrote the profiles that appeared in the *Babbington Reporter* under the rubric "We Pay a Call" and the pseudonym Egbert Penman. As my mother spoke, dispensing advice on making one's "crazy dreams"—her term—come true, her eyes gleamed with self-satisfaction, and my little chest swelled with pride. What a woman. What a mom. I stopped inside the door, dumbstruck, immobilized, awed by this confirmation of her fame, until I regained my composure sufficiently to tiptoe through the kitchen and up the stairs to my room, leaving her to savor her celebrity without the distraction of a son or sidekick. At the top of the stairs, before I closed my door, I could just hear her saying, "To succeed in business, you've got to have the common touch—"

MY FATHER never ceased to believe that Elegant Excursions and the Lunch Launch had been Porky White's ventures. He thought that my mother had been only an employee, and even afterward he thought that she continued to play a part because Porky required it. My mother never tried to convince him otherwise. I'm sure she knew that she never could have convinced him otherwise. My father was a man of firm convictions, one of those men who think that it is a very fine thing to have what they like to call the courage of one's convictions, one of those men that the rest of us consider pigheaded.

The week that he had spent on the boat with us changed him in one wonderful way: it made him realize how much he enjoyed my mother's company, what a pleasure it could be to work together. He retired early. I think he had been sick of working at the garage for quite a long time. He became my mother's partner in her subsequent ventures, and I never saw him exhibit anything but admiration for her undertakings forever after.

PATTI and I saw each other almost every day at school, of course, and sometimes I walked her home, but Eliza had returned from Europe, Dudley's house was no longer available to us, and Patti and I both considered the experiment complete, my paternity determined, so she and I returned to being friends again, and only friends, and she went back to dating thugs.

Then she vanished from Babbington for a few months, and the rumor was that she had gone away to have a child. When she returned, she was subdued, and her attitude made me think that the rumor must have been true. I wondered, and when I got tired of wondering, I asked her.

"Yeah," she said, and she began to sniffle. "It's true. I gave him up, you know, for adoption."

"Oh," I said. I was so completely incapable of saying anything that might have been of any use to her that I said nothing else.

She sniffled a bit more, then wiped her eyes and said, "I've gotta go."

"Yeah," I said. "Me too."

We hugged, and parted, and I didn't see her again in person for forty years. For a while I entertained the notion—and entertained myself with the notion—that I might have been the father of Patti's child, that I might even have taken the big first step on the way to becoming the sort of profligate rogue who leaves a trail of bastards where'er he rambles, but it was just a game that I was playing with myself. The timing was all wrong, off by a couple of months.

Patti dropped out of school and embarked on a small career in music, first singing backup for doo-wop groups that never quite made it, not even at the one-hit-wonder level, and then as lead singer of her own group, Little Patti and the Sexpots, a group that didn't get much air play but enjoyed a certain underground popularity. Their records were treated as novelties, something passed from hand to hand under the table, like the blues songs of Dirty Red. Her cover of "I Want a Hot Dog for My Roll" was excellent, I thought, and I also liked "Madman's Dog," one of her own compositions. Her voice was not strong, but it was clear and sweet, and that made a curious contrast with the raunchy lyrics. She never got very far, but recently she has enjoyed a new popularity. I'd call it a comeback, but that would imply an earlier success. Albertine and I caught her late show at the Silver Hound, downtown, a couple of weeks ago. She was hot. Her voice has a bit of gravel in it now, and she sang a slow, wise, and wistful version of "When You Dance" that made my eyes as misty as Captain Mac's were when he told us that he really did have to sell *Arcinella*.

USING PARTS FROM WRECKED MOTORCYCLES, I built a single-seater airplane the following year, after completing a correspondence course in welding. I flew the plane to New Mexico, where I spent the summer studying the fossils of ancient mollusks. Not long after my return from New Mexico, I met Albertine Gaudet and fell in love. Albertine and I went off to college, separately, but found that we couldn't bear being apart. We married. We had two sons. I taught school for a while. Then I answered an ad and became the most recent in a series of pseudonymous authors of the Larry Peters series of adventure books for boys. With some of the spoils from the series, Albertine and I bought a tumbledown hotel,

Small's Hotel, on Small's Island in Bolotomy Bay, where we lived for many years.

I never quite stopped suspecting that Bert Leroy was not my father, but after a while I decided that it didn't really matter whether he was or not. I was my mother's son, and my own man.

56
The End

MY PARENTS SURPRISED EVERYONE when they abandoned Babbington for New Hampshire. They had often vacationed there, so the location wasn't surprising, but my mother's willingness to give up her status, her local fame as "Ella, who used to run Ella's Lunch Launch," was. She and my father were still years away from what was considered the usual retirement age, and my mother seemed to be at the top of her game, but away they went.

So it was from West Burke, New Hampshire, that my father called Small's Hotel on a winter's day fourteen years ago to tell me that my mother was dying of cancer.

"It's why we left," he said. "Why we left Babbington. Her secret. The cancer. She didn't want to tell anyone. And she didn't want everyone to remember her as 'Ella, who died of cancer.'"

"Of course," I said. "I understand."

Albertine and I left the hotel in the care of Suki, the chef, and drove to West Burke. It was a long snowy drive; along the way we played tapes of music from my mother's heyday, when swing was in flower and she was dating the Leroy boys.

We pulled into the hospital parking lot, tires crunching the dry snow, got out, doors resounding in the brittle air, and walked to the entrance.

The hospital was small, friendly, almost cozy. The whole staff seemed to know my mother, and they had been expecting Albertine and me. My mother was sleeping, and they were reluctant to wake her.

"I know you came a long way," said one of the nurses, "but I think it's best to let her wake on her own."

"Of course," I said. "That's fine. We'll wait."

"I'm sorry to make you wait, but it's just that she's apt to be a little disoriented when she wakes up, and I'd like to give her time to get her bearings before you go in."

"I understand," I said. "That's considerate of you. Thank you." Albertine gave my hand a squeeze.

Albertine and I sat in the waiting room with my father. None of us had anything to say—or, to be more accurate about it, none of us cared to say anything. The essential subject of anything we might have said, whether we had talked about the weather or the cosmos, would have been my mother's death, its approach, its inevitability, and none of us wanted to talk about that, so we said nearly nothing.

The nurses fussed over us, brought us tea and cookies; finally, one emerged from the ward, and after some whispering at the nurses' station, she came over to us and said, "You can see her now."

She was fettered by wires and tubes, bloated with accumulated fluids, barely able to speak, but she seemed to brighten when she saw us, and she wanted to say something to each of us. When my father bent over her to kiss her, she pulled at him and got him to bend lower and wheezed something in his ear that made him swallow and wipe his eyes and excuse himself to pull himself together.

I heard what she said to Albertine. She had to pause between the words, and she barely got them all out. It was, "Take good care of my baby."

When it was my turn, and I leaned over her, the thought blew into my mind that she might want to say something about my paternity. Maybe she was going to tell me that what Patti had guessed was right, that she had loved Buster first, more, and forever, that even though Bert was my biological father, she considered Buster my spiritual father. But she didn't say anything remotely like that. She gasped "*Arcinella.*" She struggled for breath, shaking her head and, despite the fact that she could barely breathe, managed to say, "It was—"

"—quite a ride," I finished for her.

She pulled me even closer, and in a rattle finished for herself, "—a real blow job!"

The effort exhausted her.

I held her hand, and when she seemed to doze, I squeezed it and told her that I would see her again the next day.

Back in the waiting room, one of the nurses sighed, seemed to consider whether it would be appropriate to say what she was about to say, and decided to say it: "I just wanted to tell you how much fun Ella is to have around."

"Fun?" I said.

"Oh, yes. She keeps us all laughing."

"But—she could barely speak."

"Oh—of course—but—I mean before—"

"Oh."

"She told us all those stories, those funny stories."

"Funny stories."

"About all the crazy things you did."

"Crazy things? What crazy things?"

"Oh, I don't know—"

Another suggested, "The way you ran around trying to get all those kittens to stay in your little red wagon."

"Oh," I said. "That. Huh. I was just a little kid—a toddler."

The first added, "How you were afraid of clams!"

There were about six of them now.

"Heh-heh-heh," I chuckled affably. "It wasn't quite that way. I wasn't actually afraid of them—and besides, I was a little boy."

"What about that trip up a river in a boat you made out of an old box?"

"In fact—it was quite an adventure—for a boy, a very young boy, which is what I was when I did that."

"That radio you built that never worked?"

"Well, actually my grandfather built it. I just helped."

"Helped make it not work?"

"Well, in a sense."

Hilarity reigned.

"The science project that you still haven't finished?"

"I'm working on it."

"The flying motorcycle that never got off the ground?"

"Oh, now, come on. I flew that thing all the way to New Mexico."

That claim brought groans and, of course, more laughter.

"Let me ask you this," I said. "Did she ever tell you about the Lunch Launch?"

"No—"

"She didn't?"

"She didn't tell us about that."

"She told you all those stories about me, and she never told you about *Arcinella*?"

Heads were shaken. Blank looks were displayed.

"How she bought a clam boat, painted it in tropical colors, and plied the bay selling sandwiches?"

"No."

"How I kept the boat afloat all summer even though it was sinking?"

"Nothing like that."

"The mishaps, the merriment, the close shaves?"

"No."

"Her success? Her fame? She didn't tell you any of that?"

"Nothing at all."

"Well," I said, "let me tell you," and I told them a briefer, simpler version of the story I have just told you, and while I was telling it, my mother, Ella, who for one unforgettable summer ran Ella's Lunch Launch, died.